喚醒你的英文語感！

Get a Feel for English !

用英文Show自己，博得好印象

About Me

我怎麼介紹我?

增篇加值版

作者 長尾和夫、Ted Richards　總編審 王復國

貝塔語言出版
Beta Multimedia Publishing

高點 美語系列

序

　　到了國外，就能深切感受到自己與其他非英語系國家的人相比，英文說得有多麼不好了。明明買了好多英語會話書、反覆練習了各種句型，卻仍苦於說不出流利的英語，這樣的學習者還真是不在少數。而造成這問題的主要原因之一，就是因為大家其實都盲目地記了一堆「與自己毫無關連的」句型和詞彙。

　　非英語母語人士學英語之所以覺得口說部分很困難，原因正是「無法談論與自己有關的話題」，畢竟大家以往幾乎沒有「整理與自身相關的話題，並加以輸出的機會」。而本書便是以這種徹底「整理與輸出」解決方案為重要課題來進行製作的。全書精選自我介紹時最常觸及的 100 個話題，詳列了 2000 個具體描述自己的好用詞彙，以「連續提問」的對話形式、「自問自答」練習，並提供「多種回應說法」等特色，和坊間同類書籍形成明顯區隔。

　　本書的第一個特色是：模擬出國時會遇到的各種情境，在內容規劃上設計成一個人也能充分練習的形式。在這方面，我們特別著重於協助讀者獨自培養「整理自己＋輸出（開口說出）整理後內容」的能力。請以書中豐富的提示內容為基礎，用自己的話將關於自己的所有事統整歸納成筆記。而在書裡，我們連筆記空間都替讀者準備好了。此外，本書附贈的 MP3 還會以道地的英語不斷向讀者提出「有關您自身的問題」。請各位假裝自己正在和來自英語系國家的外國友人對話，並務必於發問後 5 秒內回答完畢。

透過這樣的練習，讀者便能利用本書進行彷彿置身海外、臨場感十足又確實有效的英語會話練習。

另外，請記得先運用本書的各個單元，不斷反覆針對各類事項來「整理自己」。若少了這麼扎實的「事前準備」動作，就絕對無法在突發狀況下，將自己的話轉化為英語，並自然而然地脫口而出。

本書的第二特色則是：有別於以往的英語會話練習書，我們提供的是「能拓展會話內容」的練習方式。本書不採一問一答的演練形式，而是在讀者回答完一個問題後，由英語道地的外國朋友繼續不斷地丟出問題。只要反覆進行這樣兩階段的提問訓練，相信讀者的回應力，甚至是發問力，都會大幅躍進。若本書能提升讀者的英語應答力，還能進一步醞釀出您更積極、活躍的英語會話力，那就是編輯全體最大的快樂了。

最後，此書改版時，特別於書末加值彙整了一些在參加「研究所與求職面試」時，經常會出現的提問及其應對方式。相信對於在申請學校或工作時，需進行英文面試的讀者而言，這部分必能提供相當大的助益。

A+ Café 代表
長尾和夫

C○NTENTS

📖 本書使用說明

本書是透過不斷回答與「自己」相關的提問，來強化東方人最不擅長的英語口說能力。只要先整理好關於自己的大小事，你的會話能力便會有令人難以置信的大幅進步。

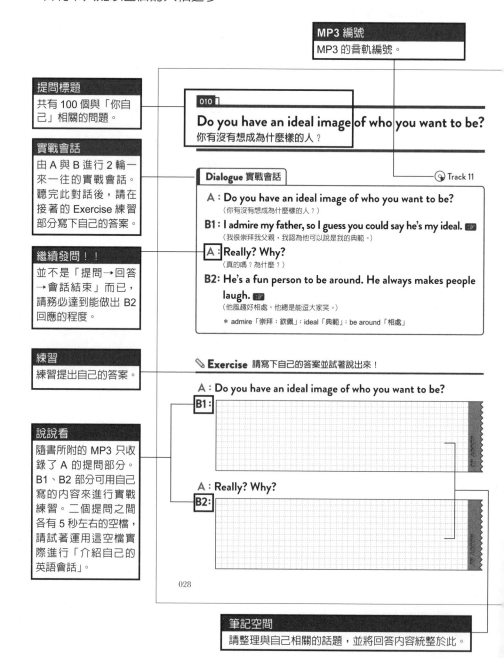

MP3 編號
MP3 的音軌編號。

提問標題
共有 100 個與「你自己」相關的問題。

實戰會話
由 A 與 B 進行 2 輪一來一往的實戰會話。聽完此對話後，請在接著的 Exercise 練習部分寫下自己的答案。

繼續發問！！
並不是「提問→回答→會話結束」而已，請務必達到能做出 B2 回應的程度。

練習
練習提出自己的答案。

說說看
隨書所附的 MP3 只收錄了 A 的提問部分。B1、B2 部分可用自己寫的內容來進行實戰練習。二個提問之間各有 5 秒左右的空檔，請試著運用這空檔實際進行「介紹自己的英語會話」。

010

Do you have an ideal image of who you want to be?
你有沒有想成為什麼樣的人？

Dialogue 實戰會話　　　　　　　　　　　　　🅰 Track 11

A： Do you have an ideal image of who you want to be?
（你有沒有想成為什麼樣的人？）

B1： I admire my father, so I guess you could say he's my ideal.
（我很崇拜我父親，我認為他可以說是我的典範。）

A： Really? Why?
（真的嗎？為什麼？）

B2： He's a fun person to be around. He always makes people laugh.
（他風趣好相處。他總是能逗大家笑。）

＊ admire「崇拜；欽佩」；ideal「典範」；be around「相處」

✎ Exercise 請寫下自己的答案並試著說出來！

A： Do you have an ideal image of who you want to be?

B1：

A： Really? Why?

B2：

028

筆記空間
請整理與自己相關的話題，並將回答內容統整於此。

實戰對話中 **B1**、**B2** 的其他回應說法

在 Exercise 部分寫下或練習講出自己
的答案時,便可參考此處說法。

不同的回應說法

Substitution 更多回應說法!

☞ **B1**

● **For me, my older sister has always been my role model.**
（對我來說,我姐姐一直都是我的榜樣。）
＊ role model「榜樣:可做為模範的人」

● **There's a woman at work that I really look up to.**
（在我工作的地方上有位女性真的讓我十分尊敬。）
＊ look up to「尊敬」

  TIPS 英語很少使用 senior「前輩」、junior「後輩」這類表達方式。

● **No, I don't have any particular ideal.**
（沒有,我並沒有特別尊崇的典範。）

TIPS
這裡統整了許多與會
話內容相關的注意事
項,及實用資訊。

☞ **B2**

● **I respect her because she speaks her mind and doesn't care about what other people think of her.**
（我很尊敬她,因為她有話直說,並不在意別人怎麼想她。）
＊ speak one's mind「有話直說:說出自己的意見」

● **She's good at her job, but she's also very warm and down-to-earth. I want to be like that.**
（她工作能力很強,但是非常溫和、樸實。我想成為像她那樣的人。）
＊ down-to-earth「樸實的:腳踏實地的」

● **I think it's better to accept who you are, instead of trying to be like someone else.**
（我覺得人最好能接受自己,而不要試圖模仿他人。）
＊ accept「接受」

例句重點字彙、片語
或句型解說

VOCABULARY 具體描述自己的好用字!

a person who is kind to everyone 對每個人都很親切的人 **/** compassionate 有同情心的 **/**
courageous 勇敢的 **/** popular 受人歡迎的 **/** understanding 善解人意的 **/** get along with everyone
與大家相處融洽 **/** take on challenges 接受挑戰 **/** a person with one's own way of doing things
依自己方式行事的人 **/** with great leadership skills 具有絕佳領導能力的 **/** with a rich imagination
具有豐富想像力的 **/** with guts 有膽量的 **/** with foresight 有遠見的

描述自己的好用詞彙
在 Exercise 處寫下自
己的回答時,便可參
考、活用這些詞彙與
說法。

Unit 1 自我介紹　029

⦿ MP3 使用說明

本書 MP3 內容是以「**標題提問 → Dialogue 實戰會話 → Exercise
→ Substitution 更多回應說法**」的順序收錄。而收錄內容只限英語
部分。

(((運用 MP3 練習方式)))

❶ Dialogue 實戰會話

請在聽完單元標題提問之後,繼續聆聽運用了該提問的對
話範例。

❷ Exercise

MP3 只收錄了「Dialogue 實戰對話」裡角色 A 的問題。
而在 A 提問之後,會有一段空檔(5 秒鐘無聲),請在
此空檔中以事前整理好的內容為基礎,嘗試用英語回答。
別擔心「要是講錯怎麼辦?」這種問題,即使句子不完
整也無所謂,最重要的其實是要看你能說出多少關於自
己的事情。請試著反覆練習,直到能脫口說出關於自己
的內容。

❸ Substitution 更多回應說法

聽取 B1、B2 的其他回應說法。

Unit 1

自我介紹
Self-introduction

首先，就從整理與自己相關的事情和經驗開始吧！

What's your name?
Where were you born?
Are you an outgoing person?
What's the most moving experience
you've ever had?
• • •

appearance

name

Taiwan culture

friends

work

dreams

interest

families

religion

experience

What's your name?

貴姓大名？

Dialogue 實戰會話　　　　　　　　　　　🅖 Track 02

A：**What's your name?**
（貴姓大名？）

B1：**I'm Meiya. My friends call me A-ya.** 🖝
（我叫美雅。朋友都叫我阿雅。）

A：**That's a nice name. What does it mean?**
（這名字真不錯。它代表什麼意思呢？）

B2：**It means "beautiful and graceful" in Chinese.** 🖝
（這在中文裡，是指「美麗優雅」之意。）

✎ **Exercise** 請寫下自己的答案並試著說出來！

A：**What's your name?**

B1：

A：**That's a nice name. What does it mean?**

B2：
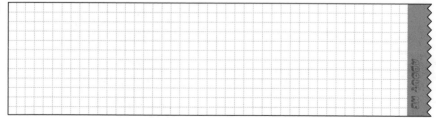

Substitution 更多回應說法！

☞ B1

- **My real name is Liyi. You can call me Victor.**

  （我真正的名字叫立一，你可以叫我維克特。）

  ＊ real「真正的」；call「叫」

- **My name is Ruyin, but everyone calls me Xiao Yin.**

  （我的名字是如音，不過大家都叫我小音。）

- **Amy Chen. Call me Amy.**

  （我叫陳艾美。請叫我艾美就好。）

  TIPS 被問到姓名時，不要只回答姓氏，請回答全名或名字（first name）。

☞ B2

- **It means "one," because I was the first child. Actually, I was named after my grandfather.**

  （那代表「一」之意，因為我是第一個小孩。事實上，我是以我祖父之名命名的。）

  ＊ actually「其實」；be named after...「以……命名」

- **The characters for my name mean "like music."**

  （我名字所用的字代表「像音樂一樣（動聽）」之意。）

  ＊ character「文字」

- **I'm not sure how you say it in English. It's a very common name in Taiwan.**

  （我不確定用英文該怎麼說。這在台灣是很常見的名字。）

  ＊ common「常見的；一般的」

Vocabulary 具體描述自己的好用字！

family name / surname 姓氏 / a common / popular name 常見的名字 / nickname 綽號 / maiden [ˋmedn] name 娘家姓；婚前姓 / middle name 中間名 / single-character given name 單名 / two-character family name 複姓 / take one character from someone's name 從某人的名字中取一個字

How old are you?
您多大年紀？

Dialogue 實戰會話　　　　　　　🎧 Track 03

A：How old are you?
（您多大年紀？）

B1：Actually, I just turned twenty-four last week. ☞
（事實上，我上週才剛滿 24 歲。）

A：When's your birthday?
（你什麼時候生日？）

B2：January 30. I'm an Aquarius. What's your sign? ☞
（1 月 30 日。我是水瓶座。你是什麼星座的？）

* sign「星座」

TIPS 和對方比較有交情時，才方便詢問年齡。另外，雖然 zodiac sign（星座）話題廣受歡迎，但 blood type（血型）則不然，因為不知道自己血型的人還挺多的。

✎ **Exercise** 請寫下自己的答案並試著說出來！

A：How old are you?
B1：
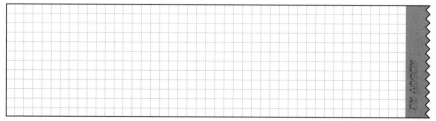

A：When's your birthday?
B2：
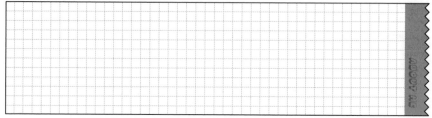

☞ **B1**

- **How old do I look? Actually, I'm twenty-six.**

  （我看起來像幾歲？其實我已經 26 歲了。）

- **I'm too old to tell.**

  （我已老得無法透露年齡了。）

  * too... to...「太……以致於無法……」

- **I'm younger than I look.**

  （我比外表看來年輕。）

  * than I look「比外觀還……；比外表更……」

☞ **B2**

- **I was born in May. That's how I got my name.**

  （我是 5 月生的。而那正是我名字的由來。）

  * That's how...「那正是……的方法」

- **My birthday is on December 25. I was my parents' Christmas present.**

  （我的生日是 12 月 25 日。我是我父母的聖誕禮物。）

- **Actually, I was born on the same day as Jeremy Lin.**

  （事實上，我和林書豪同一天生。）

  * be born「誕生」；the same day as...「和……同一天」

VOCABULARY 具體描述自己的好用字！

be older than I look 我比外表看起來老 / be born on December 8 12 月 8 日出生 / be born in summer 在夏天出生 / have a late birthday 晚生 / turned 20 two months ago 2 個月前剛滿 20 歲 / be almost 18 快 18 歲了 / will be 25 next year 明年就 25 歲 / be 25 years and 3 months old 25 歲又 3 個月 / **Aries** [ˋɛrɪz] 白羊座 / **Taurus** [ˋtɔrəs] 金牛座 / **Gemini** [ˋdʒɛməˏnaɪ] 雙子座 / **Cancer** [ˋkænsə] 巨蟹座 / **Leo** [ˋlio] 獅子座 / **Virgo** [ˋvɝgo] 處女座 / **Libra** [ˋlaɪbrə] 天秤座 / **Scorpio** [ˋskɔrpɪˏo] 天蠍座 / **Sagittarius** [ˏsædʒɪˋtɛrɪəs] 射手座 / **Capricorn** [ˋkæprɪˏkɔrn] 摩羯座 / **Aquarius** [əˋkwɛrɪəs] 水瓶座

Where were you born?
你在哪裡出生的？

Dialogue 實戰會話　　　　　　　　　　🎧 Track 04

A：**Where were you born?**
（你在哪裡出生的？）

B1：**I was born in Kenting, Taiwan.** ☞
（我出生於台灣的墾丁。）

A：**Really? What is Kenting famous for?**
（真的嗎？墾丁什麼很有名？）

B2：**Well, it has a beautiful National Park for one thing.** ☞
（嗯，首先，它有一座漂亮的國家公園。）

＊ be famous for... 「以……著稱」

✎ **Exercise** 請寫下自己的答案並試著說出來！

A：**Where were you born?**

B1：

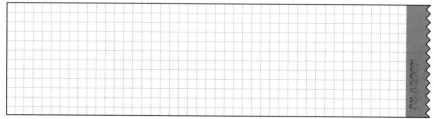

A：**Really? What is ＿＿＿ famous for?**

B2：

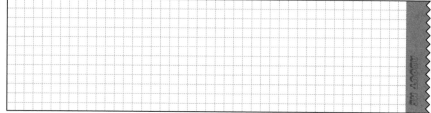

Substitution 更多回應說法！

☞ **B1**

- **I was born and raised in Tainan.**
  （我在台南出生、長大。）
  ＊ be born and raised in... 「在……出生、長大」

- **I'm from Beitou, a palce in the north of Taiwan.**
  （我來自北投，一個在台灣北部的地方。）
  ＊ in the north of... 「在……的北部」

- **I was born in Puli in Nantou County, but I grew up in Taichung.**
  （我出生於南投縣埔里，但是在台中長大。）
  ＊ county 「縣；郡」；grow up 「長大」

☞ **B2**

- **Many famous Taiwanese businesspeople are from Tainan.**
  （很多有名的台灣企業家都來自台南。）

- **My hometown is famous for its hot springs. Have you ever taken a bath in a hot spring?**
  （我的故鄉以溫泉著名。你有沒有泡過溫泉？）
  ＊ hot spring 「溫泉」；take a bath 「泡澡」

- **It's famous for its four W's: water, wine, women, and weather.**
  （它有四樣東西很有名：水、酒、美女和天氣。）

꧁ **𝒱𝒪𝒞𝒜𝐵𝒰𝐿𝒜𝒴** 具體描述自己的好用字！

be born in the middle of Taiwan 出生在中台灣 / **near...** 接近…… / **on the outskirts of...** 在……郊區 / **be famous as a tourist spot** 是有名的觀光勝地 / **a place with lots of holiday homes** 擁有很多度假別墅的地方 / **a dairy farm town** 一個酪農城鎮 / **be famous for pineapple cake** 以鳳梨酥聞名 / **its tasty vegetables** 其美味的蔬菜 / **its fireworks display** 其煙火表演 / **be notorious for its rude drivers** 因粗魯無禮的開車者而臭名昭彰 / **its high crime rate** 其高犯罪率 / **the second biggest city** 第二大都市 / **a city with a population of one million** 擁有 100 萬人口的都市 / **a town around one hour by train from Taipei** 距離台北約 1 小時火車車程的小鎮

How tall are you?
你身高多高？

Dialogue 實戰會話　　　　　　　　　　　　　🎧 Track 05

A：**How tall are you?**
（你身高多高？）

B1：**I'm about five-ten, I think.** ☞
（我想，大約是 5 尺 10 寸吧。）

A：**How much do you weigh?**
（你多重？）

B2：**About 75 kilograms or so. How much is that in pounds?** ☞
（大概 75 公斤左右。那應該是多少磅呢？）

* weigh「有……重」

TIPS 5 尺 10 寸正式說法為 Five feet, ten inches.，不過一般都會省略單位。而有時也說成 Five-foot ten.。

✏️ **Exercise** 請寫下自己的答案並試著說出來！

A：**How tall are you?**
B1：

A：**How much do you weigh?**
B2：

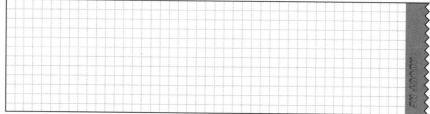

Substitution 更多回應說法！

☞ **B1**

- **I'm 165 centimeters tall. I don't know how tall that is in feet.**
  （我身高 165 公分。我不知那是多少英尺高。）
  * in feet「以英尺計算」
  TIPS 1 英尺等於 30.48 公分。

- **I'm a little over six feet. In Taiwan, I'm a giant.**
  （我身高 6 尺出頭。在台灣算是巨人了。）
  * a little over...「超過……一些」

- **I'm five-foot three. I'm shorter than I look.**
  （我身高 5 尺 3 寸。我比外表看起來矮一些。）

☞ **B2**

- **That's a secret. I'm actually a lot fatter than I look.**
  （那是個祕密。我比外表看起來要胖很多。）
  * fatter than...「比……更胖」

- **Last time I checked, I weighed 200 pounds. I need to go on a diet.**
  （上次量的時候，我大約 200 磅重。我該減肥了。）
  TIPS 將公斤換算成磅時，要乘以 2.2 倍。而 My weight is ___. 或 My height is ___. 這類說法雖然也能達意，但聽起來並不自然。

- **I'm not sure, but I've gained around five pounds since coming to the US.**
  （我也不很確定，不過到美國之後，我大約胖了 5 磅。）
  * gain「增加（體重）」

𝒱ＯＣＡＢＵＬＡＲＹ 具體描述自己的好用字！

height 身高 / weight 體重 / a healthy build 健康的體型 / metabolic syndrome [ˌmɛtəˋbɑlɪk ˋsɪnˌdrom] 新陳代謝症候群 / macho 陽剛的 / skinny 瘦巴巴的 / high / low body fat ratio 高 / 低體脂肪率 / lose / gain 3 kilograms 瘦 / 胖了 3 公斤 / lose / gain a lot of weight 瘦 / 胖了很多 / go on a diet 減肥；節食 / rebound 復胖 / be still growing 還在長（高）/ taller / shorter than average 比平均身高高 / 矮 / have a medical checkup / exam 接受健康檢查 / 體檢

Are you an outgoing person?
你是外向的人嗎？

Dialogue 實戰會話
🎧 Track 06

A : Are you an outgoing person?
（你是外向的人嗎？）

B1 : I'm kind of a loner. I like to do things on my own. 👉
（我有點孤僻。我喜歡自己做自己的事。）

A : What do you consider to be your strong point?
（你覺得自己的長處是什麼？）

B2 : I think I'm good at handling stress. I work well under pressure. 👉
（我想我很擅長處理壓力。我在壓力之下仍能表現良好。）

* strong point「長處」；outgoing「外向的」；be good at「擅長」

✏️ **Exercise** 請寫下自己的答案並試著說出來！

A : Are you an outgoing person?
B1 :

A : What do you consider to be your strong point?
B2 :

Substitution 更多回應說法！

☞ B1

- **I'm not exactly a social butterfly, but I enjoy meeting people.**
  （我不完全是交際花型的人，但是我喜歡與人接觸。）

  ＊ not exactly...「不完全是……」；social butterfly「交際花；善交際的人」

- **I probably come off as shy at first, but if you get to know me, I'm pretty talkative.**
  （我一開始可能表現得很害羞，不過認識我之後，就會知道我其實滿健談的。）

  ＊ come off as...「表現得……」；talkative「健談的」

- **I've always been a fairly introverted person. I get butterflies in my stomach when I have to speak to a group of people.**
  （我一直都是相當內向的人。當我必須在一群人面前發言時，就會很緊張。）

  ＊ introverted「內向的」；get butterflies in one's stomach「緊張」

☞ B2

- **I'm a good listener. My friends often come to me with their problems.**
  （我是個很好的傾聽者。我的朋友們有問題的時候常找我商量。）

  ＊ one's problem「某人的問題」

- **I think I'm a pretty easygoing person. It takes a lot to upset me.**
  （我認為我是很好相處的人。要激怒我並不容易。）

  ＊ easygoing「隨和的；好相處的」；upset「激怒；使心煩」

- **I'm pretty good with my hands. I like to make things.**
  （我的手很巧。我喜歡做東西。）

  ＊ be good with one's hands「手很靈巧」

ＶＯＣＡＢＵＬＡＲＹ 具體描述自己的好用字！

bad point 缺點 / **quiet** 文靜的 / **extravert** 個性外向的（人）/ **introvert** 個性內向的（人）/ **shy** 害羞的 / **optimist** 樂天派 / **pessimist** 悲觀主義者 / **gloomy** 陰沉；陰鬱的 / **cheerful** / **upbeat** 活潑的；樂觀的 / **cautious** 謹慎的；小心的 / **laid back** 閒散的；悠閒的 / **affectionate** 溫柔親切的 / **kind** 和藹的 / **short-tempered** 急性子的 / **clumsy** 笨拙的 / **calm and composed** 沉著冷靜的

What kind of build do you have?

你是什麼體型？

Dialogue 實戰會話　　　　　　　　　　🔊 Track 07

A：What kind of build do you have?
（你是什麼體型？）

B1：I'm quite petite, even by Taiwanese standards. ☞
（即使以台灣人的標準來看，我仍算是很嬌小的。）

A：What kind of features do you have?
（你的長相有何特徵？）

B2：My eyes are my most prominent feature. I have big, puppy-dog eyes. ☞
（我的眼睛最有特色。我有一雙小狗般的大眼睛。）

＊ build「體格；體型」; petite [pɛˋtit]「嬌小的」; even「即使是……」; feature「特徵；相貌」; prominent「凸出的；顯眼的」

✎ **Exercise** 請寫下自己的答案並試著說出來！

A：What kind of build do you have?

B1：

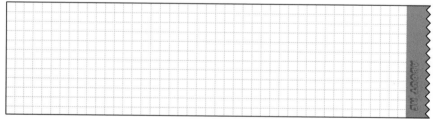

A：What kind of features do you have?

B2：

☞ **B1**

● **I'm heavy-set. People often ask me if I play rugby.**
（我體格魁梧。大家常常問我是不是有玩橄欖球。）
＊ heavy-set「體格魁梧的」【美】

● **I'm quite slim. Because of my job, I have to watch my figure.**
（我很苗條。因為工作的關係，我必須很注意身材。）
TIPS 注意，「身材」的英文應該用 figure 來表達才對。

● **I'm a little on the chubby side.**
（我是稍微偏圓潤型的。）
＊ chubby「圓潤；豐滿」；on the... side「偏……的」

☞ **B2**

● **I have a light complexion, and I have dimples when I smile.**
（我的膚色白皙，而且笑起來有酒窩。）
＊ complexion [kəm`plɛkʃən]「（臉的）膚色」；dimples [`dɪmplz]「酒窩」（複數）

● **People sometimes tell me that I look more Japnnese than Chinese.**
（有時有人會跟我說，我看起來比較像日本人，而不太像中國人。）
＊ look more... than...「看起來比較像……而不像……」

● **The celebrity I resemble the most is Jackie Chan.**
（我最像的名人是成龍。）
＊ celebrity [sɪ`lɛbrətɪ]「名人」；resemble「類似；像」

VOCABULARY 具體描述自己的好用字！

slender 苗條的；纖細的 / **slightly overweight** 稍稍過重 / **tall and lanky** 又高又瘦 / **delicate** 纖弱的；嬌貴的 / **light** / **dark-complexioned** 皮膚白 / 黑的 / **have freckles** 有雀斑 / **black** / **chestnut** / **blond** / **red hair** 黑 / 栗 / 金 / 紅髮 / **shoulder-length**（頭髮）及肩的 / **straight** / **curly** / **wavy hair** 直 / 捲 / 波浪捲髮 / **mustache** [`mʌstæʃ] / **beard** / **sideburns** [`saɪd,bɜnz] / **goatee** [go`ti] 小鬍子 / 鬍鬚 / 鬢角 / 山羊鬍 / **wear blue-rimmed glasses** 戴著藍框眼鏡 / **one's hair is dyed brown** 某人的頭髮染成了褐色

What's the most moving experience you've ever had?
至今為止最讓你感動的經驗是什麼事？

Dialogue 實戰會話	🔊 Track 08

A : What's the most moving experience you've ever had?
（至今為止最讓你感動的是什麼事？）

B1 : I'll never forget the time I saw an aurora. ☞
（我永遠都忘不了看到極光的那一刻。）

A : That must have been an amazing experience! What was it like?
（那一定是個很棒的經驗！感覺如何？）

B2 : I can't describe it. It was too beautiful for words! ☞
（我無法形容。它美得難以言喻！）

＊ aurora [ɔˋrɔrə]「極光」；describe「形容；描述」

✎ **Exercise** 請寫下自己的答案並試著說出來！

A : What's the most moving experience you've ever had?

B1 :

A : That must have been an amazing experience! What was it like?

B2 :

Substitution 更多回應說法！

☞ B1

- **The birth of my son was a real life-changing experience for me.**
  （我兒子的出生是改變了我一生的經驗。）
  * life-changing「改變一生的」
- **The first thing that comes to mind is my best friend's wedding.**
  （第一個浮現在我腦海中的是我最好朋友的婚禮。）
  * come to mind「浮現在腦海中」
- **My first trip abroad was an experience I'll never forget.**
  （第一次的海外旅遊是我永遠忘不了的經驗。）
  * trip abroad = trip overseas「海外旅遊」

☞ B2

- **It's the only time in my life that I cried tears of joy.**
  （那是我這輩子唯一一次流下喜悅眼淚的時候。）
  * tears of joy「喜悅的眼淚」
- **I don't normally cry much, but I was in tears the whole time.**
  （我通常不愛哭，但是當時卻一直哭個不停。）
  * normally「通常」；the whole time「一直」
- **It made me realize that the world is much bigger than I had ever imagined.**
  （這件事讓我領悟到，世界比我想像的還要大很多。）
  * realize「領悟到」；imagine「想像」

𝒱ᴏᴄᴀʙᴜʟᴀʀʏ 具體描述自己的好用字！

be moved by... 因……而感動 / be moved to tears by... 因……而流下感動的眼淚 / be (so moved that one is) left speechless（感動得）說不出話來 / shout with joy 開心地大叫 / get carried away 得意忘形 / make a big fuss 大驚小怪 / the happiest experience 最開心的經驗 / the most moving experience 最感動的經驗 / the biggest surprise 最大的驚喜 / the most fun 最大的快樂 / the greatest experience 最棒的經驗 / dream comes true 夢想成真 / the greatest memory 最棒的回憶 / the happiest moment 最快樂的時刻 / like something out of a dream 彷彿做夢一般 / once-in-a-lifetime 一生一次的

What's the saddest experience you've ever had?
至今為止讓你覺得最悲傷的是什麼事？

Dialogue 實戰會話 　　　　　　　　　　　🔊 Track 09

A： What's the saddest experience you've ever had?
（至今為止讓你覺得最悲傷的是什麼事？）

B1： I was crushed when our family dog died. ☞
（我們家的狗死掉時，我難過到不行。）

A： Oh, that's so sad! My saddest experience was being cheated on by my boyfriend.
（噢，那真的很令人傷心！我最悲傷的經驗是被男朋友劈腿。）

B2： Wow, that must have been terrible. ☞
（哇，那感覺一定很糟。）

＊ be crushed「受到極大打擊」；be cheated on「被劈腿」

✎ **Exercise** 請寫下自己的答案並試著說出來！

A： What's the saddest experience you've ever had?

B1：
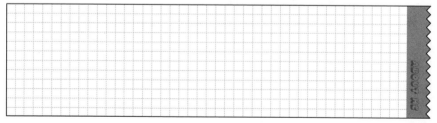

A： Oh, that's so sad! My saddest experience was being cheated on by my girlfriend.

B2：
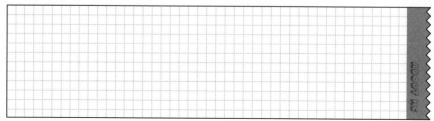

Substitution 更多回應說法！

☞ B1

- **I was really depressed when my best friend since elementary school moved away.**
  （當我從小學時代就認識的最好朋友搬走時，我非常難過。）
  ＊ be depressed「沮喪；難過」
- **I lost a friend when I was in college.**
  （大學時，我有個朋友過世了）
  ＊ lost 為 lose「失去」的過去式
- **Not getting into my first choice of university was a pretty crushing experience for me.**
  （沒能進入我大學的第一志願，對我來說是相當嚴重的打擊。）
  ＊ first choice「第一志願」；crushing「造成強烈打擊的」

☞ B2

- **Wow, what a jerk! How did you find out about it?**
  （哇，真是個混蛋！你是怎麼發現的？）
- **Wow, that must have been devastating. Did you have someone to talk to?**
  （哇，那一定很慘。你有找人談談嗎？）
  ＊ devastating [ˋdɛvəsˏtetɪŋ]「毀滅性的」
- **I've had my share of bad experiences with women, too.**
  （交女友我也曾有過不好的經驗。）
  ＊ have one's share of...「我也曾有過……的經驗」

VOCABULARY 具體描述自己的好用字！

a trying experience 一次令人難受的經驗 / a shocking event 一個令人震驚的事件 / heartbreaking 令人心碎的 / be shocked 受到打擊 / be completely devastated 被徹底打垮 / be unable to go on 無法繼續 / difficult 難熬的 / lonely 孤獨的 / hopeless 絕望的 / heartbroken 心碎的 / consult with... 和……談談 / confess to... / confide in... 向……坦承；向……吐露 / console 撫慰 / care for... 關懷…… / be kind to... 善待…… / touching 感人的 / pitiful 可憐的 / weep in sympathy 流下同情的眼淚

Do you have a dream?

你有夢想嗎？

Dialogue 實戰會話　　　　　　　　　　　🔘 Track 10

> **A：Do you have a dream?**
> （你有夢想嗎？）
>
> **B1：Yes, I do, but it's a secret. If I tell you, you'll laugh.** ☞
> （有啊，不過那是秘密。如果跟你說，你一定會笑我。）
>
> **A：Really? Why is that?**
> （真的嗎？為什麼？）
>
> **B2：Well, the chances of my dream coming true are very slim. But I want to keep trying.** ☞
> （嗯，因為我夢想實現的可能性微乎其微。不過我還是會持續努力。）
>
> * chances of... 「⋯⋯的可能性」；slim 「（可能性）低；渺茫」；keep trying 「持續努力」
> **TIPS** 「夢想」的英文不應說成 future dream / goal，請特別注意。

✎ **Exercise** 請寫下自己的答案並試著說出來！

A：Do you have a dream?

B1：

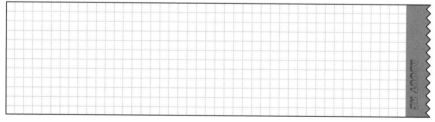

A：Really? Why is that?

B2：

Substitution 更多回應說法！

☞ B1

- **When I was little, I wanted to be an actress. But I gave up on that in high school.**
  （我小的時候，一心想成為女演員。不過到高中我就放棄了那個夢想。）
  * give up on... 「放棄……」

- **I've always dreamed of being a teacher.**
  （我一直都夢想著要成為老師。）
  * dream of... 「夢想著……」

- **I'm saving up money so that I can open up my own café.**
  （我正在存錢，好開一間屬於我自己的咖啡廳。）
  * save up (money) 「存錢」

☞ B2

- **I realized I'm not talented in that way. I think it's important to find a vocation you're suited for.**
  （我了解到自己並沒有那方面的才能。我認為找個適合自己的職業是很重要的。）
  * realize 「了解到」；vocation 「職業」

- **I guess it's because I like talking to people. I want to help people in some way.**
  （我想這是因為我喜歡和人交談。我想以某種方式幫助他人。）
  * in some way 「以某種方式」

- **Well, I think you're never too old to learn something new.**
  （嗯，我認為學新東西永遠不嫌晚。）
  * too... to... 「太……以致於不能……」

VOCABULARY 具體描述自己的好用字！

three-year goal 三年的目標 / difficult goal 困難的目標 / dream that I hope to realize 我想實現的夢想 / dream that is unlikely to come true 不太可能實現的夢想 / make a dream come true 使夢想實現 / lead a happy married life 過著幸福美滿的婚姻生活 / have lots of children 有許多小孩 / be a useful member of society 成為社會上有用的人 / become a translator 成為翻譯者 / fly all over the world 飛遍世界各地 / have a stable job 有個穩定的工作 / live peacefully in the country 在鄉下過恬靜的生活 / live a colorful life in the big city 在大都市過多采多姿的生活

Do you have an ideal image of who you want to be?
你有沒有想成為什麼樣的人？

Dialogue 實戰會話　　　　　　　　　　　🔊 Track 11

A：Do you have an ideal image of who you want to be?
（你有沒有想成為什麼樣的人？）

B1：I admire my father, so I guess you could say he's my ideal.
（我很崇拜我父親，我認為他可以說是我的典範。）

A：Really? Why?
（真的嗎？為什麼？）

B2：He's a fun person to be around. He always makes people laugh. ☞
（他風趣好相處。他總是能逗大家笑。）

* admire「崇拜；欽佩」; ideal「典範」; be around「相處」

✎ **Exercise** 請寫下自己的答案並試著說出來！

A：Do you have an ideal image of who you want to be?
B1：

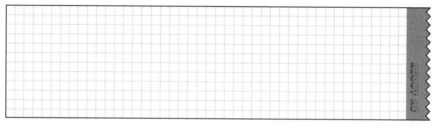

A：Really? Why?
B2：

Substitution 更多回應說法！

☞ B1

- **For me, my older sister has always been my role model.**
  （對我來說，我姐姐一直都是我的榜樣。）
  * role model「榜樣；可做為模範的人」
- **There's a woman at work that I really look up to.**
  （在我工作的地方上有位女性真的讓我十分尊敬。）
  * look up to「尊敬」
  TIPS 英語很少使用 senior「前輩」、junior「後輩」這類表達方式。
- **No, I don't have any particular ideal.**
  （沒有，我並沒有特別尊崇的典範。）

☞ B2

- **I respect her because she speaks her mind and doesn't care about what other people think of her.**
  （我很尊敬她，因為她有話直說，並不在意別人怎麼想她。）
  * speak one's mind「有話直說；說出自己的意見」
- **She's good at her job, but she's also very warm and down-to-earth. I want to be like that.**
  （她工作能力很強，但是非常溫和、樸實。我想成為像她那樣的人。）
  * down-to-earth「樸實的；腳踏實地的」
- **I think it's better to accept who you are, instead of trying to be like someone else.**
  （我覺得人最好能接受自己，而不要試圖模仿他人。）
  * accept「接受」

VOCABULARY 具體描述自己的好用字！

a person who is kind to everyone 對每個人都很親切的人 / compassionate 有同情心的 / courageous 勇敢的 / popular 受人歡迎的 / understanding 善解人意的 / get along with everyone 與大家相處融洽 / take on challenges 接受挑戰 / a person with one's own way of doing things 依自己方式行事的人 / with great leadership skills 具有絕佳領導能力的 / with a rich imagination 具有豐富想像力的 / with guts 有膽量的 / with foresight 有遠見的

Have you ever done any volunteer work?

你有沒有做過義工？

Dialogue 實戰會話　　　　　　　　　　　🎧 Track 12

A : Have you ever done any volunteer work?
（你有沒有做過義工？）

B1 : Last year I helped collect signatures for a petition.
（去年我有為一項請願幫忙收集連署簽名。）

A : What made you do that?
（是什麼原因讓你那麼做？）

B2 : We were trying to stop the construction of a high-rise condominium in our neighborhood.
（我們當時想阻止一棟高層公寓在我們鄰近區域建造。）

* signature「簽名」；petition [pə`tɪʃən]「請願；請願書」；high-rise「高樓的」；
condominium [ˏkɑndə`mɪnɪəm] 各戶有獨立產權的公寓（大廈）

✎ **Exercise** 請寫下自己的答案並試著說出來！

A : Have you ever done any volunteer work?

B1 :

A : What made you do that?

B2 :

Substitution 更多回應說法！

☞ B1

- **I do volunteer PTA work for my daughter's school. This year I'm a crossing guard.**
  （我在我女兒的學校擔任 PTA 導護志工。今年我負責交通導護工作。）
  * PTA「家長 - 教師聯誼會」；crossing guard「交通導護」

- **When I was studying abroad, I did some volunteer work teaching Chinese.**
  （我在國外留學的時候，做過一些教中文的義工工作。）
  * study abroad「出國留學」

- **I did some volunteer work with refugees in Cambodia after I graduated from college.**
  （大學畢業後，我曾做義工幫助柬埔寨難民。）
  * refugee「難民」；Cambodia [kæm`bodɪə]「柬埔寨」

☞ B2

- **I think it's important to be part of a community.**
  （我覺得融入社區成為其中一員是很重要的。）
  * community「社區」

- **It's supposed to be voluntary, but actually everyone has to do it.**
  （這件事本來應該是自願的，但是事實上每個人都必須做。）
  * be supposed to...「應該是……」

- **I wanted to get out and meet people. I needed a change.**
  （我想出去認識大家，我需要改變。）

VOCABULARY 具體描述自己的好用字！

sense of values change 價值觀改變 / be a good experience for me as well 對我自己來說也是很好的經驗 / contribute to the local community / society 對當地社區 / 社會有貢獻 / work without compensation 無報酬的工作 / pick up garbage around town 在市區撿垃圾 / help with fund-raising activities 幫忙募款活動 / help at the childcare center 在托兒中心幫忙 / visit a nursing home 訪問療養院 / work with the hearing-impaired 協助聽障人士 / look after a foreign exchange student 照顧一個國外來的交換學生 / be a foster parent for a child from a developing country 領養一個來自開發中國家的兒童 / help with the running of a marathon event 協助舉辦馬拉松活動

更多好用字彙：職業

accountant ▸ 會計師	**nursing care worker** ▸ 護理人員
tax accountant ▸ 稅務師	**pharmacist** ▸ 藥劑師
lawyer / attorney [əˋtɜnɪ] ▸ 律師	**veterinarian** [ˌvɛtərəˋnɛrɪən] ▸ 獸醫
judicial scrivener [dʒuˋdɪʃəl ˋskrɪvənə] ▸ 司法書記	**physical therapist** ▸ 物理治療師
administrative scrivener ▸ 行政代書	**journalist** ▸ 新聞工作者
architect ▸ 建築師	**reporter** ▸ 記者
banker ▸ 銀行家	**editor** ▸ 編輯
receptionist ▸ 接待員；櫃台服務人員	**carpenter** ▸ 木工
office clerk ▸ 辦公室職員	**electrician** ▸ 電工
sales clerk ▸ 銷售人員；業務員	**firefighter** ▸ 消防員
hair stylist ▸ 髮型設計師	**police detective** ▸ 刑警
childcare worker ▸ 保母	**police officer** ▸ 警官
surgeon ▸ 外科醫師	**professor** ▸ 教授
nurse ▸ 護士	**assistant professor** ▸ 助理教授

對話回應好用句 ①：贊成・同意

「是啊」

● **Yeah!**（是啊！）
▸ 為 Yes. 較不正式的說法。

● **Yup.**（是啊！）
▸ 為 Yes. 較不正式的說法。

● **Uh-huh.**（是啊。）
▸ 代表同意或贊成，用於對話答腔時。

- -

「我也一樣」

● **Me, too!**（我也是！）

● **So did I.**（我也一樣！）
▸ 聽取對方 "I thought..."「我以為……」之類的發言後，用來表示「我當時也如此。」的說法。

● **So do I.**（我也如此！）
▸ 表示「我也這麼覺得」。

● **You and me both.**（你我都是！）
▸ 表示「我也一樣！」的答腔說法。

Unit 2

家庭成員・人際關係
Families and Relationships

請整理你的家庭、小孩、親友及結婚等最貼身的人際關係資訊，並練習讓會話變得更豐富活潑。

Do you have any brothers or sisters?
Do you have any pets?
Do you have a best friend?
What kind of marriage is your ideal?
...

appearance

name

Taiwan culture

friends

work

dreams

interest

families

religion

experience

Do you have any brothers or sisters?
你有兄弟姊妹嗎？

Dialogue 實戰會話　　　　　　　　　　　　　🔊 Track 13

A：**Do you have any brothers or sisters?**
（你有兄弟姊妹嗎？）

B1：**Yeah, I have one brother and one sister.** ☞
（有，我有一個弟弟和一個妹妹。）

A：**Do you get along with your family?**
（你和家人處得好嗎？）

B2：**I'm very close to my sister, but my brother and I don't get along that well.** ☞
（我和妹妹感情很好，但是和弟弟就處得不是那麼好了。）

* that「那麼樣地」

✎ **Exercise** 請寫下自己的答案並試著說出來！

A：**Do you have any brothers or sisters?**
B1：

A：**Do you get along with your family?**
B2：

Substitution 更多回應說法！

B1

- **No, I'm an only child. That's probably why I like being alone.**
  （沒有，我是獨生子／女。這可能是我總喜歡獨處的原因。）
  * only child「獨生子」
- **I just have one older brother. I've always wanted a younger brother of my own, though.**
  （我只有一個哥哥。不過我總希望能有個弟弟。）
- **Yeah, I come from a big family. I have two brothers and two sisters.**
  （有，我來自大家庭。我有兩個兄弟和兩個姊妹。）
  * come from...「來自……」

B2

- **My sister and I do everything together. We're like best friends.**
  （我的姊姊不論做什麼都和我黏在一起。我們就像是最好的朋友。）
  * best friend「最好的朋友」
- **We get along OK, but now we're all too busy with our own lives to see each other.**
  （我們處得還不錯，但是現在我們各自的生活都過於忙碌，因而無法見面。）
  * see each other「與對方見面」
- **For a long time, my brother and I weren't on speaking terms, but recently we made up.**
  （我哥哥和我有很長一段時間彼此不講話，但是最近我們和好了。）
  * be on speaking terms「彼此說話的關係」；make up「和好」

- - - - - **VOCABULARY** 具體描述自己的好用字！ - - - - -

be on good / bad terms with... 和……關係良好／不好 / **older / elder brother /sister** 哥哥／姐姐 / **younger brother / sister** 弟弟／妹妹 / **nuclear family** 核心家庭；小家庭 / **large / extended family** 大家庭 / **fatherless / motherless family** 無父／無母家庭；單親家庭 / **son** 兒子 / **daughter** 女兒 / **eldest son** 長子 / **second son** 次子 / **third son** 三子 / **oldest** 最大（長）的 / **second-oldest** 第二大的 / **middle child** 排行中間的小孩 / **second-youngest** 第二小的 / **youngest** 最小的 / **uncle** 叔叔；伯伯 / **aunt** 姨媽；姑媽 / **cousin** 堂／表／兄弟姊妹 / **nephew** 姪子；外甥 / **niece** 姪女；外甥女

Unit 2 家庭成員・人際關係　**035**

What does your father do?
你父親從事什麼工作？

Dialogue 實戰會話	🔊 Track 14

A：What does your father do?
（你父親從事什麼工作？）

B1：He used to be a police officer, but he retired early, for health reasons. 📖
（他原本是個警官，但是後來因為健康因素提早退休了。）

A：Really? Does your mother work?
（真的啊？那你母親有在工作嗎？）

B2：No, she's been a homemaker for as long as I can remember. 📖
（沒有，我記憶中，我媽一直都是全職的家庭主婦。）

* retire「退休；退隱」；for health reasons「因健康因素」

TIPS 「家庭主婦」也可說成 housewife，但是最近流行以 homemaker 來稱呼，這樣比較不會有性別歧視問題。

✏️ **Exercise** 請寫下自己的答案並試著說出來！

A：What does your father do?

B1：

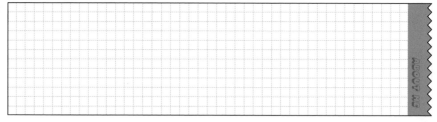

A：Does your mother work?

B2：

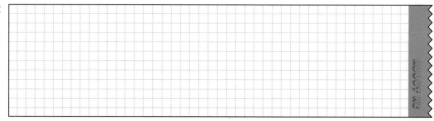

☞ B1

- **He's retired. Nowadays he keeps himself busy by tending (to) his garden.**

  （他退休了。現在都忙著照顧他的花園。）

  * tend (to)...「照顧……」

- **He works for a software company.**

  （他在軟體公司工作。）

  * software「軟體」

  TIPS 以上班族來說，英文通常會說明是在哪一類的公司工作，而幾乎不會採用 He's an ordinary office worker.（他是一般的上班族。）這種說法。

- **He works for the city. It's not the most glamorous job, but the life of a civil servant seems to suit him.**

  （他在市政府上班。那不是最光鮮亮麗的工作，但是公務員的生活似乎很適合他。）

  * glamorous「光鮮亮麗的」；suit「適合」

☞ B2

- **She teaches flower arrangement. She'd be happy to teach you, if you're interested.**

  （她教插花。如果你有興趣，她一定很樂意教你。）

  * flower arrangement「插花」

- **She works part-time as a secretary. She says her pension isn't enough to live on.**

  （她兼差做祕書。她說她的退休金不夠她過生活。）

  * secretary「祕書」

- **She runs a little antique shop. It's more of a hobby than a job, though.**

  （她經營一家小小的古董店。不過，與其說那是一份工作，其實更像是興趣。）

  * run「經營」；more of... than...「與其說是……其實更像是……」

𝓥𝓸𝓬𝓪𝓫𝓾𝓵𝓪𝓻𝔂 具體描述自己的好用字！

work at a big / medium-sized / small company 在大 / 中 / 小型企業裡工作 / put off one's retirement 延後退休 / be a branch manager at a trading company 在貿易公司分公司當經理 / be the manager of... 做……的經理 / do nothing since someone retired 退休後什麼也不做 / live off one's savings 靠存款度日 / national / employee pension 國民年金 / 退休金 / live off one's pension 靠退休金度日 / retirement allowance 退休津貼 / be a workaholic 是個工作狂

Do your grandparents live with you?
你和祖父母一起住嗎？

Dialogue 實戰會話　　　　　　　　　　　　　🔊 Track 15

A： Do your grandparents live with you?
（你和祖父母一起住嗎？）

B1： My grandmother lives with us. My grandpa passed away a few years ago. ☞
（我祖母和我們一起住。我祖父幾年前過世了。）

A： I'm sorry to hear that. Personally, I think the more people under one roof, the merrier.
（很遺憾你祖父過世了。我個人覺得，越多人同住在一個屋簷下就越快樂。）

B2： I agree. And I think children have a responsibility to look after their parents when they get older. ☞
（我同意。而且我認為當父母年老的時候小孩有責任要照顧他們。）

＊personally「就我個人而言」；responsibility「責任」；look after（＝ take care of）「照顧」

✎ **Exercise** 請寫下自己的答案並試著說出來！

A： Do your grandparents live with you?

B1：

A： Personally, I think the more people under one roof, the merrier.

B2：

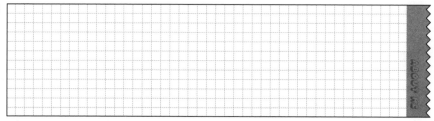

☞ **B1**

- **No, my grandmother lives with my older brother's family.**
  （沒有，我祖母和我哥哥一家人住在一起。）
  * live with... 「和……住在一起」

- **Eventually they'll move in with us. Now they're still healthy; they prefer to live on their own.**
  （他們終究會搬來和我們一起住。現在他們還很健康，喜歡自己住。）
  * eventually 「終究」；prefer to... 「偏好……」

- **No, we live separately. They live far away, in Pingtung, so we don't get to see them much.**
  （沒有，我們分開住。他們住在遙遠的屏東，所以我們很少見面。）
  * separately 「分別」；get to... 「有機會（做）……」

☞ **B2**

- **That's true. And it's good for the kids to have their grandparents around, too.**
  （那確實是。而且小孩有祖父母陪伴也是很好的。）
  * have... around 「有……陪伴」

- **I suppose, but I think living with her mother-in-law is stressful for my mother.**
  （我是這麼想，不過我覺得對我媽來說，跟婆婆同住是壓力很大的。）
  * mother-in-law 「岳母；婆婆」

- **I agree. My parents worry about our grandparents, too, but it's hard for them to move out of the place they've been living their whole lives.**
  （我同意。我爸媽也很擔心我的祖父母，但是要他們搬離住了一輩子的地方，實在很難。）

ＶＯＣＡＢＵＬＡＲＹ 具體描述自己的好用字！

grandpa 祖父 / grandma 祖母 / great-grandfather 曾祖父 / grand-grandmother 曾祖母 / grandchild 孫子／女 / father-in-law 岳父；公公 / daughter / son-in-law 媳婦／女婿 / nursing home 養老院；護理之家 / day care center 日間照護中心 / senile dementia [ˈsinaɪl dɪˈmɛnʃɪə] 老年痴呆症 / bedridden elderly person 長期臥病的老人 / have bad legs (= be unable to walk) 不良於行 / care for / cherish the elderly 關懷／愛護長者 / learn from the elderly 向老人學習

Do you have any pets?
你有養寵物嗎？

Dialogue 實戰會話　　　　　　　　　　　🎧 Track 16

A：Do you have any pets?
（你有養寵物嗎？）

B1：No, we're not allowed to have pets in our apartment building. ☞
（沒有，我們住的公寓大樓禁止飼養寵物。）

A：Really? I have a toy poodle. He is so adorable!
（真的嗎？我們家養了一隻玩具貴賓狗，牠超可愛的！）

B2：You're so lucky! I want a Chihuahua so bad! ☞
（你真幸福！我好想養隻吉娃娃！）

> **TIPS** 想表達「真羨慕你！」時，通常不說 I envy you!，而會採取 Lucky you!、Wow!、That's great!、I hate you! 等表達方式。

✏️ **Exercise** 請寫下自己的答案並試著說出來！

A：Do you have any pets?
B1：

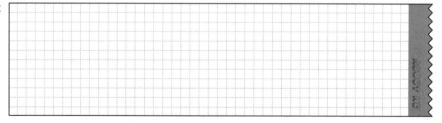

A：Really? I have a toy poodle. He is so adorable!
B2：

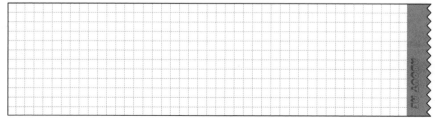

Substitution 更多回應說法！

☞ B1

- **We have a cat named Latte . He's like part of the family.**
  （我們養了隻叫拿鐵的貓。牠就像我們家的一份子。）
  * named... 「被命名為……；叫……」
- **I have a turtle that I won at a turtle-scooping game.**
  （我養了一隻在撈烏龜遊戲裡贏到的烏龜。）
  * scoop 「撈」
- **We used to have a dog, but we had to give him away.**
  （我們以前養了一隻狗，但是後來不得不送人。）
  * give away 「送給別人養」

☞ B2

- **I wish I had a dog! I hate coming home to an empty house.**
  （真希望我有一隻狗！我好討厭回到空蕩蕩的家。）
  * hate +V-ing 「討厭……」；empty 「空的」
- **Wow, toy poodles are so cute! What's his name? Do you have a picture of him?**
  （哇，玩具貴賓狗很可愛耶！牠叫什麼名字？你有牠的照片嗎？）
  * wow 「哇；哇賽」
- **Personally, I prefer cats. Cats are more independent.**
  （我個人比較喜歡貓，貓的個性比較獨立。）

········ **VOCABULARY** 具體描述自己的好用字！ ········

puppy 小狗 / **male dog** 公狗 / **female dog (= bitch)** 母狗 / **adult dog** 成犬 / **senior dog** 老狗 / **kitten** 小貓 / **male cat (= tomcat)** 公貓 / **female cat (= she-cat)** 母貓 / **adult cat** 成貓 / **senior cat** 老貓 / **mixed breed** 混種的 / **with a pedigree** [ˋpɛdə͵gri] 純種的；有血統證明的 / **ferret** [ˋfɛrɪt] 雪貂 / **guinea** [ˋgɪnɪ] **pig** 天竺鼠 / **parakeet** 鸚鵡 / **veterinarian (= vet)** 獸醫 / **take... to the vet** 帶……去給獸醫看 / **stray dog** / **cat** 流浪狗 / 貓 / **pick... up off the street** 從路上把……撿來 / **pet food** 寵物飼料 / **pet cage** 寵物籠 / **bird cage** 鳥籠 / **dog house** 狗屋 / **collar** 項圈 / **chain** 鍊子 / **leash** [liʃ] 皮帶 / **pet wear** 寵物服飾 / **feeder** 餵食器 / **water tray** 水盤 / **pooper scooper** 撿糞鏟 / **poop bag** 糞袋 / **pet tricks** 寵物才藝 / **do tricks** （由寵物）表演才藝 / **sit** 坐下 / **shake** 握手 / **walk in a circle** 轉圈圈 / **lie down** 趴下 / **play dead** 裝死

Do you see your parents much?

你常和你父母見面嗎？

Dialogue 實戰會話 ⏺ Track 17

A : Do you see your parents much?
（你常和你父母見面嗎？）

B1 : Nowadays I only see them around 2 or 3 times a year. I'm
so busy with work. ☞
（現在一年只見他們二、三次面。我工作實在很忙。）

A : What kinds of things do you do together?
（你們在一起都做什麼活動呢？）

B2: Oh, nothing special. We just hang out and talk.
Sometimes I take them shopping. ☞
（噢，沒什麼特別的。我們就聚聚聊聊天。有時我會帶他們去買東西。）

＊ hang out「消磨時間」

✎ **Exercise** 請寫下自己的答案並試著說出來！

A : Do you see your parents much?
B1 :

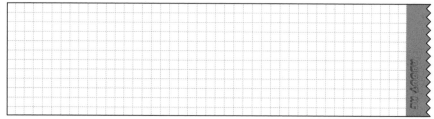

A : What kinds of things do you do together?
B2:

Substitution 更多回應說法！

☞ B1

● **Since they live far away, I only get to see them on New Year's.**
（因為他們住得很遠，所以我只在過年時有機會見到他們。）

● **I still live with my parents, so I see them every day.**
（我還跟父母住在一起，所以每天都會見到他們。）

● **They live in the same neighborhood, so we see each other quite often — maybe around 2 or 3 times a week.**
（他們就住在我家附近，所以我們很常見面——週大概 2、3 次左右。）

☞ B2

● **We go out to dinner together every week. Sunday is "family day" at our house.**
（我們每週都會一起出去吃一次晚餐。週日是我們家的「家庭日」。）
* go out... 「外出；出門」

● **My mother-in-law comes over to babysit nearly every day. I don't know what I'd do without her.**
（我婆婆幾乎每天都來幫忙帶小孩。我實在不知道如果沒有她我該怎麼辦。）
* baby sit 「照看小孩」；nearly 「幾乎；差不多」

● **Last summer I took them to Hawaii. It was their first trip overseas.**
（去年夏天我帶他們去夏威夷玩。那是他們第一次出國旅遊。）

VOCABULARY 具體描述自己的好用字！

live two stations away from us 住離我們 2 個車站的地方 / live in the same neighborhood 住在附近 / live about five hours away by train 住在火車車程約 5 小時的地方 / talk on the phone every week 每週通電話 / talk face-to-face on Skype 用 Skype 面對面說話 / exchange e-mails every day 每天互寄電子郵件 / go back to one's parents' home once a year 一年回老家一次 / visit us once a month 每個月來看我們一次 / do something nice for one's parents 對父母好（注意：由於英文裡並沒有相當於「孝順」的詞彙，故此說法才能表達類似意義）

Were your parents strict?
你的父母管教很嚴格嗎？

Dialogue 實戰會話　　　　　　　　　　🔊 Track 18

A：Were your parents strict when you were a child?
（你小的時候，父母管教很嚴格嗎？）

B1：My mother wasn't that strict, but my dad was scary.
（我媽沒那麼嚴格，不過我爸很可怕。）

A：Do you think you'll be strict with your own kids?
（你認為你會對自己的小孩很嚴格嗎？）

B2：No, I'll probably be a pushover. I don't know how to be
strict with kids. ☞
（不會，我可能會對小孩百依百順。我不知道該怎麼對小孩嚴格。）

* strict「嚴格管教的」；pushover「對人百依百順的；容易心軟的人」

✏ **Exercise** 請寫下自己的答案並試著說出來！

A：Were your parents strict when you were a child?
B1：

A：Do you think you'll be strict with your own kids?
B2：

Substitution 更多回應說法！

☞ B1

- **Compared to my friend's parents, my mom and dad were pretty lenient.**
  （和我朋友的父母相比，我媽和我爸算是相當寬容的。）
  * lenient [`linjənt]「管教溫和的；寬容的」

- **My father was a real disciplinarian. He would always say, "Spare the rod, spoil the child."**
  （我父親是非常嚴格的人。他總會說：「不打不成器」。）
  * disciplinarian [ˌdɪsəplɪˋnɛrɪən]「嚴格的人」；rod「棒；桿」；spoil「寵壞」

- **They used to punish me a lot, but I think I deserved it. I gave them a lot of trouble.**
  （他們以前常常處罰我，不過我覺得我罪有應得。我給他們帶來很多麻煩。）
  * deserve「應得」

☞ B2

- **I'm not as strict as my parents were. I want my kids to have more confidence in themselves.**
  （我不像我爸媽那麼嚴格。我希望我的小孩能更有自信些。）

- **I imagine I'll be pretty lenient. I don't want to spoil my kids, though.**
  （我想我應該會管教得很寬鬆。不過我也不想寵壞小孩。）

- **I try to be patient and loving, but sometimes they really push my buttons.**
  （我會試著多用一點耐心與愛心，但是有時他們真的會激怒我。）
  * push someone's buttons「激怒某人」

VOCABULARY 具體描述自己的好用字！

be spoiled 被寵壞的 / let me do whatever I want 讓我做我想做的 / corporal [`kɔrpərəl] punishment 體罰 / spanking 打屁股 / discipline 管教 / curfew [`kɝfju] 門禁 / punish 處罰 / scold someone constantly 不斷責罵某人 / problem child 問題兒童 / juvenile delinquent 不良少年 (少女) / perfect child 模範生 / mature 成熟的 / gifted 有天分的 / quiet 文靜的 / precocious 早熟的 / noisy 吵鬧的 / undisciplined 散漫的 / a child who listens to one's parents 聽父母話的小孩

What are your parents like?
你父母是怎樣的人？

A：What are your parents like?
（你父母是怎樣的人？）

B1：My mother's very active and social, but my father prefers to stay at home.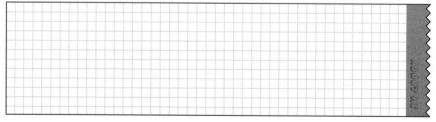
（我母親很活躍而且善於社交，但是我父親卻喜歡待在家裡。）

A：Are they still in good health?
（他們都還很健康嗎？）

B2：Fortunately, yes, but I worry about them. They're not getting any younger.
（很幸運地，是的，不過我很擔心他們，他們已不再年輕了。）

✎ **Exercise** 請寫下自己的答案並試著說出來！

A：What are your parents like?

B1：

A：Are they still in good health?

B2：

Substitution 更多回應說法！

☞ B1

● **My father is very bossy at home, but outside the home he's quite mild-mannered.**

（我父親在家相當跋扈，但是一出去就變得溫文儒雅。）

　＊ bossy「愛指揮別人的；跋扈的」；mild-mannered「溫文儒雅的；溫良恭謹的」

● **My mother is a lot like me, I think. She likes to go out and do things.**

（我覺得我母親跟我很像。她喜歡外出活動。）

● **They have a great relationship. When I get married, I want to be like them.**

（他們的關係很好。如果我結婚的話，我會想和他們一樣。）

　＊ relationship「關係」

☞ B2

● **Physically they're doing fine, but my father's getting a little senile.**

（就身體來說，他們倆都還很好，但是我父親開始有點老糊塗了。）

　＊ senile [`sinaɪl]「衰老；老態龍鍾的」

● **My father hasn't been doing very well. He has trouble walking.**

（我父親最近身體不太好。他不太能走路。）

　＊ have trouble walking「不太能走」

● **They're in great shape. I worry about what's going to happen when they get older, though.**

（他們很健康。不過我很擔心他們上了年紀以後的狀況。）

　＊ in great shape「身體很健康」

· · · · · ·　ⓋⓞⒸⒶⒷⓊⓁⒶⓇⓎ 具體描述自己的好用字！

are both doing fine 都還健在 / **both passed away** 都已經過世了 / **be still living** 還活著 / **have arthritis** [ɑr`θraɪtɪs] 有關節炎 / **have bad knees** 膝蓋不好 / **have a bad back** 腰背不好 / **be hard of hearing** 重聽 / **have a heart attack** 心臟病發作 / **have a stroke** 中風 / **have trouble seeing / hearing / speaking / eating / walking / getting around** 看／聽／說話／吃／走路／四處走動有問題 / **wander about** 漫步 / **be bedridden** 久病臥床 / **be 20 years younger than one's age** 比實際年齡年輕 20 歲 / **be still in good health** 依然很健康 / **be still healthy and walking around** 依然健康地四處走動 / **care for one's parents** 照料雙親 / **be exhausted from caring (for one's parents)** 因照顧（父母）而筋疲力竭

What's your boyfriend / girlfriend like?
你男朋友／女朋友是怎樣的人？

Dialogue 實戰會話　　　　　　　　　　　　🔊 Track 20

A : **What's your boyfriend like?**
（你男朋友是怎樣的人？）

B1: **He's the strong, silent type. He lets me do all the talking.** ☞
（他是那種強壯、沉默型的人。他都讓我負責講話。）

A : **I can see why you get along. What does he look like?**
（看得出來這就是你們合得來的原因了。他長得如何？）

B2: **He looks a little bit like Keanu Reeves.** ☞
（他長得有點像基努李維。）

* let someone do all the talking「讓（某人）負責講話」

✎ **Exercise** 請寫下自己的答案並試著說出來！

A : **What's your boyfriend like?**
B1:

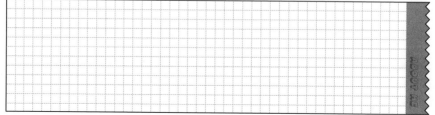

A : **I can see why you get along. What does he look like?**
B2:

☞ **B1**

- **She has a great sense of humor. That's what first attracted me to her.**
  (她很幽默。這正是她一開始吸引我的原因。)
  * attract「吸引」
- **He's a little shy, but once you get to know him, he's easy to talk to.**
  (他有點害羞，不過熟了以後，很容易跟他聊開。)
- **He's kind of a computer geek. But he's very kind and caring.**
  (他有點像電腦宅男。但是他非常體貼而且有愛心。)
  * kind and caring「體貼又有愛心」

☞ **B2**

- **She's gorgeous. It was actually her looks that I first fell for.**
  (她長得很漂亮。其實我一開始就是迷上了她的外表。)
  * fall for...「愛上……」
- **He's fairly good-looking, if you ignore his receding hairline.**
  (如果你忽略他不斷後退的髮線，那他長得還算滿好看的。)
  * ignore「忽略」；recede [rɪ`sid]「後退」
- **He's really into fashion, so he's a very sharp dresser. He's pretty average-looking, though.**
  (他很熱衷於時尚，所以很會穿衣服。不過他長得還滿普通的。)
  * be into...「熱衷於……」；sharp dresser「很會穿衣服的人」

VOCABULARY 具體描述自己的好用字！

be just dating 還在約會階段 / **a man / woman one is seeing / going out with** 正在交往的男性 / 女性 / **boyfriend** 男朋友 / **girlfriend** 女朋友 / **be boyfriend and girlfriend** 成為男女朋友 / **be going out** 開始交往 / **a committed relationship** 認真的交往 / **a keeper** 不想放過的對象 / **break up** 分手 / **dump someone** 甩了某人 / **be dumped** 被甩 / **really good-looking / beautiful** 真的很帥 / 美 / **ordinary-looking / average** 長相一般 / 普通 / **not very good-looking / beautiful** 長得不很帥 / 漂亮 / **unattractive-looking / ugly** 長得不吸引人 / 醜

Do you take after your parents?
你像不像你父母？

A：Do you take after your parents?
（你像不像你父母？）

B1：Everyone says I'm the spitting image of my mother when she was young. 👉
（大家都說，我長得跟我媽年輕時一模一樣。）

A：Really? Some people say daughters take after their fathers and sons take after their mothers.
（真的嗎？有人說女兒會像爸爸，而兒子會像媽媽。）

B2：That's not the case in my family. 👉
（我們家並非如此。）

* take after「像；與……相似」；spitting image「簡直一模一樣的人」（口語）

✎ **Exercise** 請寫下自己的答案並試著說出來！

A：Do you take after your parents?

B1：

A：Really? Some people say daughters take after their fathers and sons take after their mothers.

B2：

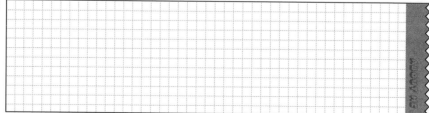

☞ **B1**

- **My mother and I are complete opposites.**
  （我媽和我完全相反。）
  * opposite「相反」（名詞）
- **People say I'm a lot like my father.**
  （大家都說我很像我爸。）
  * a lot like...「很像……」
- **I'm like my mother in some ways and like my father in others.**
  （我在某些方面很像我媽，在其他方面又像我爸。）
  * ... in some ways and... in others「在某些方面……，在其他方面……」

☞ **B2**

- **I suppose that's true to some extent. I have my father's eyes and nose.**
  （我想在某個程度上的確如此。我的眼睛和鼻子像爸爸。）
  * to some extent「在某個程度上」
- **I don't look like my father, but I inherited his stubbornness.**
  （我長得不像我爸，但是有遺傳到他的頑固性格。）
  * inherit「繼承；因遺傳而獲得」；stubbornness [`stʌbənnɪs]「頑固」
- **I look a lot like my father, but our personalities are completely different.**
  （我長得很像我爸，但是個性完全不同。）
  * personality「個性」

VOCABULARY 具體描述自己的好用字！

spitting image 一個模子刻出來的；長得一模一樣 / take after... 長得、舉止像…… / look like... 看起來像…… / have someone's face 臉長得很像…… / have someone's build 體型很像…… / have someone's personality 個性很像…… / look a lot like... 看來很像…… / look a bit like... 看來有點像…… / don't look much like... 看來不太像…… / look nothing like... 一點兒也不像……

Do you have a best friend?
你有沒有最要好的朋友？

Dialogue 實戰會話　　　　　　　　　　🔊 Track 22

A：**Do you have a best friend?**
（你有沒有最要好的朋友？）

B1：**I have one good friend who I like to hang out with.** ☞
（我有個好朋友，我很喜歡跟他混在一起。）

A：**How did you meet?**
（你們怎麼認識的？）

B2：**We were in the same club in college.** ☞
（我們大學時參加了同一個社團。）

✎ **Exercise** 請寫下自己的答案並試著說出來！

A：**Do you have a best friend?**
B1：

A：**How did you meet?**
B2：

☞ **B1**

- **My husband and I are like best friends. I can talk to him about anything.**
  （我先生和我就像最好的朋友。我什麼事都能跟他說。）

- **I'm still best friends with my friend from high school. Once we start talking, we can't stop.**
  （我和高中時代的朋友一直維持著最要好的朋友關係。我們一旦聊起來，就停不了。）
  * Once..., ...「一旦……，就……」

- **I've become good friends with a woman whose daughter goes to the same nursery school as mine.**
  （我和我女兒的托兒所同學的媽媽成了好朋友。）
  * nursery school「托兒所」

☞ **B2**

- **We joined our company at the same time. We were in the same training group.**
  （我們是同時進公司的。當時我們分在同一個培訓小組裡。）
  * training group「培訓小組」

- **We met through a mutual friend. My friend and his friend used to work together.**
  （我們是透過一個共同的朋友認識的。我的朋友和他的朋友以前曾共事過。）
  * mutual「共同的」；used to「過去曾」

- **We've known each other forever. We grew up in the same neighborhood and went to the same schools.**
  （我們彼此認識很久了。我們在同一個社區長大，唸同樣的學校。）
  * forever「一直都」

VOCABULARY 具體描述自己的好用字！

best friend of the same /opposite sex 同 / 異性好友 / male / female friend 男 / 女性朋友 / close friend 密友 / childhood buddies 童年死黨 / friend of a friend 朋友的朋友 / be in the same community on Facebook 在臉書上屬於同一個社群 / get to know (each other) through Twitter 透過推特認識 / meet at a drinking party 在一次喝酒的聚會中認識 / still meet someone often 現在仍經常與某人見面 / meet someone occasionally 偶爾與某人見面 / hardly ever meet someone 現在幾乎不太和某人見面

Do you think it's tough being a parent?

你覺得為人父母很辛苦嗎？

A：Do you think it's tough being a parent?
（你覺得為人父母很辛苦嗎？）

B1：It's not easy, but the joys make up for all the hardship.
（是不輕鬆，但是快樂可以補償所有的辛苦。）

A：I imagine you also learn a lot from your kids, too.
（我想你應該也從孩子的身上學到了不少。）

B2：That's so true. I can see myself in my daughter. It's quite humbling. ☞
（確實是如此。我可以從我女兒身上看到自己。真是挺讓人羞愧的。）

* make up for... 「補償……」；humbling「令人羞愧的」

✎ **Exercise** 請寫下自己的答案並試著說出來！

A：Do you think it's tough being a parent?
B1：
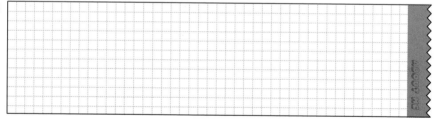

A：I imagine you also learn a lot from your kids, too.
B2：
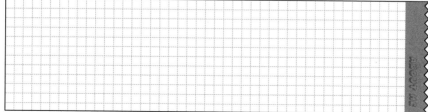

☞ **B1**

- **It's so much harder than I expected. I had no idea how exhausting raising a child would be!**

  （比我想像的困難多了。我原先根本不知道養小孩會有多麼累人。）

  * exhausting「令人精疲力竭的」；raise「養育」

- **Personally, I don't plan on having kids for the time being. I'm satisfied with my life the way it is.**

  （我個人目前沒計畫要生小孩。我對現在的生活狀況相當滿意。）

  * plan on...「計畫要……」；the way it is「現在的情況」

- **It's a lot of work. Fortunately, my husband is very cooperative.**

  （事情很多。幸好我先生非常配合。）

  * cooperative「合作的」

☞ **B2**

- **Oh, definitely. You learn to look at the world with different eyes.**

  （噢，那當然。你會學習用不同的眼光來看世界。）

  * learn to...「學習……」

- **Yes, I think being a parent really forces you to grow as a person. I used to be so selfish!**

  （是的，我覺得為人父母真的會迫使人成長。我以前好自私。）

  * force someone to...「強迫（某人）……」

- **I suppose that's true, but I don't know if I have what it takes to be a parent.**

  （我認為確實是如此。不過我不知道自己是否具備為人父母的條件。）

  * what it takes to...「成為……的必要條件」

VOCABULARY 具體描述自己的好用字！

childrearing 養育子女 / parenting（父母）撫養（子女）/ a 24-hour job 24 小時不休息的工作 / be a role model for one's child 成為小孩的榜樣 / pacify a child 安撫孩子 / get a child to go to sleep 哄孩子睡 / give a child milk 餵奶 / breast feed 哺餵母乳 / change a baby's diaper 替寶寶換尿布 / give a child a bath 幫小孩洗澡 / child cries at night 小孩晚上啼哭 / don't get enough sleep from looking after children 因照顧小孩而睡眠不足 / be worn out from looking after children 因照顧小孩而累垮 / ferry kids to and from daycare / school 接送小孩往返於托兒所 / 學校

Do you think you should push your kids to study?
你是否覺得應該要逼小孩念書？

Dialogue 實戰會話　　　　　　　　　　　　　　　🎧 Track 24

> **A：** Do you think you should push your kids to study?
> （你是否覺得應該要逼小孩念書？）
>
> **B1：** I try not to push my kids too hard. Fortunately, they're pretty good about doing their homework. ☞
> （我盡量不把孩子逼得太緊。幸運的是，他們功課都做得很好。）
>
> **A：** I'm not sure what's better. Should I push my kids to study, or should I let them play and have fun?
> （我不確定怎麼做比較好。我應該逼小孩念書，還是應該讓他們開心地玩？）
>
> **B2：** It's a tough call, but basically I think kids should grow at their own pace. ☞
> （這實在很難決定，不過基本上，我認為小孩應該按照自己的步調來成長。）
>
> ＊ push someone to...「逼迫（某人）做……」

✎ **Exercise** 請寫下自己的答案並試著說出來！

A： Do you think you should push your kids to study?

B1：

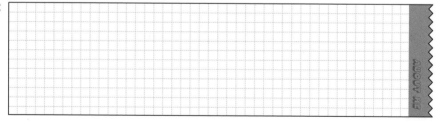

A： I'm not sure what's better. Should I push my kids to study, or should I let them play and have fun?

B2：

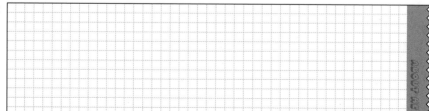

Substitution 更多回應說法！

☞ **B1**

- **I'm not that strict, but I give my kids a hard time if they come home with a bad test score.**
  （我並不很嚴格，但是如果他們考試考不好，回家還是會挨我的罵。）
  * give someone a hard time「讓（某人）不好過；責罵（某人）」

- **As long as they do their homework, I let my kids do what they want.**
  （只要他們有做功課，我就讓他們做自己想做的事。）
  * As long as...「只要……」

- **As an adult, I've come to understand the importance of studying hard, so I would probably make my kids study.**
  （身為大人，我已了解到努力讀書的重要性，所以我應該會要求小孩讀書。）
  * importance「重要性」

☞ **B2**

- **Personally, I think nothing good comes of giving kids lots of free time.**
  （我個人認為，給小孩太多自由時間是不會帶來什麼好處的。）
  * come of...「來自……」

- **I think it's important to instill good study habits from a young age.**
  （我認為，從小就開始灌輸良好的讀書習慣是很重要的。）
  * instill「（逐漸地）灌輸」

- **If we don't make them study, they're just going to spend all their time playing video games.**
  （如果我們不督促孩子念書，他們就會把所有的時間都花在打電動。）
  * video game「電動遊戲」

VOCABULARY 具體描述自己的好用字！

public school 公立學校 / **private school** 私立學校 / **cram school** 補習班 / **prep school** 大學先修班 / **take piano** / **swimming** / **ballet lessons** 學鋼琴 / 游泳 / 芭蕾 / **get good** / **bad grades** 獲得好 / 壞成績 / **get a good** / **bad score on a test** 考試考得好 / 差 / **child with excellent grades** / **average grades** / **bad grades** 成績優秀 / 成績普通 / 成績不好的小孩 / **grades get worse** / **have improved** 成績退步 / 有進步 / **be good** / **bad at math** 擅長 / 不擅長數學 / **Chinese** 國語 / **social studies** 社會 / **science** 自然科學 / **physical education (=P.E.)** 體育

024

How did you meet your husband / wife?
你是怎麼認識你先生 / 太太的？

Dialogue 實戰會話　　　　　　　　　　　🎧 Track 25

A：How did you meet your husband?
（你是怎麼認識你先生的？）

B1：We met at a dating party in college. ☞
（我們是在大學的聯誼會上認識的。）

A：How did you end up going out together?
（你們後來是怎麼開始交往的？）

B2：We hit it off right away. He asked me out on a date, and before we knew it, we were an item. ☞
（我們一拍即合。他開口約我，然後我們不知不覺就成了一對。）

* end up...「最後……」；hit it off「一拍即合」；be an item「在一起；成為情侶」

✎ **Exercise** 請寫下自己的答案並試著說出來！

A：How did you meet your husband?
B1：

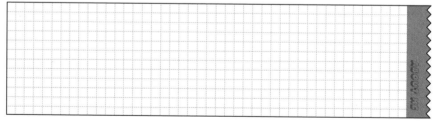

A：How did you end up going out together?
B2：

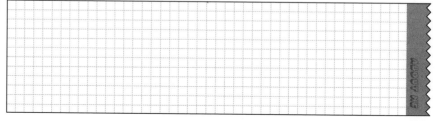

☞ B1

- **This is kind of embarrassing, but we actually met through an online matchmaking site.**
  （說來有點令人難為情，不過我們是透過相親網站認識的。）
  * embarrassing「令人難為情的」；matchmaking「相親；作媒」

- **We met through work. She was actually a client, so we had to keep our relationship a secret.**
  （我們是透過工作認識的。她其實是我的客戶，所以當時我們的關係必須保密。）
  * client「顧客」；keep sth. a secret「將某事保密」

- **We actually went to the same high school. I had always liked him, but I never had the nerve to talk to him.**
  （事實上我們唸的是同一所高中。我一直都很喜歡他，但是一直沒有勇氣跟他告白。）
  * have the nerve to...「有勇氣做……」

☞ B2

- **He asked me out to lunch one day, and one thing led to another.**
  （有天他約我出去吃午飯，然後事情就這麼進展下去了。）
  * one thing leads to another「事情一件接著一件發生」

- **I don't remember how it started, but we used to text each other constantly.**
  （我不記得事情到底是怎麼發生的，不過我們以前總是不斷傳簡訊給對方。）
  * constantly「不斷地」

- **We got to talking, and found we had a lot in common. He asked me out on a date, and the rest is history.**
  （我們開始聊天，然後發現我們有許多共通點。他約我出去，而接下來的你都已經知道了。）
  * the rest is history「接下來的你都知道了」

Vocabulary 具體描述自己的好用字！

meet at a class reunion 在同學會上認識 / meet through a matchmaking agency 透過相親公司認識 / meet someone on a trip 在旅遊時認識某人 / be my father's subordinate 是我父親的下屬 / be introduced by a friend 經由朋友介紹 / regular customers at the same shop / restaurant / café 同一間店 / 餐廳 / 咖啡廳的常客 / meet in a college club 在大學社團裡認識 / approach someone at a bar 在酒吧裡搭訕某人 / an arranged marriage 相親結婚

025

What's your idea of a good marriage?
你認為理想的婚姻是怎樣的？

Dialogue 實戰會話　　　　　　　　　　　🎧 Track 26

A : **What's your idea of a good marriage?**
（你認為理想的婚姻是怎樣的？）

B1 : **I want to marry someone who will encourage me to persue my own career.**
（我想和會鼓勵我繼續追尋事業的人結婚。）

A : **Really? I guess everyone's different. Do you want to have kids?**
（真的嗎？我想每個人的想法都不同。你想要小孩嗎？）

B2 : **Of course! I want to work and have kids, too. Is that asking too much?**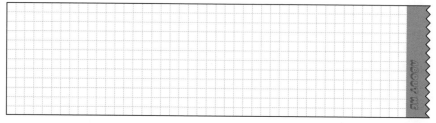
（當然想！我要工作也要小孩。這樣太貪心了嗎？）

＊ ask too much「要求太多」

✏ **Exercise** 請寫下自己的答案並試著說出來！

A : **What's your idea of a good marriage?**

B1 :

A : **Really? I guess everyone's different. Do you want to have kids?**

B2 :

☞ **B1**

- **Since job transfers are common in my line of work, I'd want my husband to come with me wherever I go.**

  （由於我這類工作經常會有職務調動的情形，所以我希望不論我調到哪裡先生都能配合我。）

  ＊ common「一般的」；line of...「某類的……」

- **Someday I'd like to get away from the city and lead a quiet life in the country.**

  （有朝一日，我想離開都市到鄉間過著寧靜的生活。）

  ＊ get away from...「離開……」

- **Everything has to be 50-50. I don't want a husband who thinks that a woman's place is in the home.**

  （一切都必須對等。我不想嫁一個認為女人就該待在家的老公。）

  ＊ 50-50「五五對分的」

☞ **B2**

- **Sure, but not right away. I'm not in any hurry to have kids.**

  （當然想，但是不是現在。我不急著生小孩。）

- **Eventually, but I want to see the world first. If I have kids, I won't be able to travel.**

  （終究會，但是我想先看看這個世界。如果生了小孩，我就沒辦法旅行了。）

- **Not really. I don't think I'm cut out for raising kids.**

  （不很想有。我不覺得我適合養育小孩。）

  ＊ be cut out for...「天生適合……」

⋯⋯⋯⋯ **VOCABULARY** 具體描述自己的好用字！ ⋯⋯⋯⋯

find Mr. / Miss Right 找到理想的對象 / **be ready to tie the knot** [nɑt] 準備結婚安定下來 / **have a big family** 擁有大家族 / **someone with the same values as me** 和自己價值觀相同的人 / **support someone financially** 在經濟上支持某人 / **feel comfortable with** 和……在一起時覺得舒適自在 / **take the initiative** 採取主動 / **understand one's way of thinking** 了解一個人的想法 / **someone whose interests are compatible with mine** 與我興趣相符的人

026

What are your kids doing?
你的小孩在做什麼？

Dialogue 實戰會話　　　　　　　　　　　🎧 Track 27

A：**What are your kids doing?**
（你的小孩在做什麼？）

B1：**My children are both in high school. The older one is
studying for his college entrance exams.** ☞
（我的兩個孩子都在唸高中。老大正在準備大學入學考。）

A：**Do you worry about their future?**
（你會擔心他們的將來嗎。）

B2：**As a parent, I can't help but worry. I try as much as
possible not to interfere, though.** ☞
（為人父母，我忍不住會擔心。但是我盡量不干涉就是了。）

＊ can't help but... 「忍不住……」；interfere 「干涉」

✎ **Exercise** 請寫下自己的答案並試著說出來！

A：**What are your kids doing?**

B1：

A：**Do you worry about their future?**

B2：
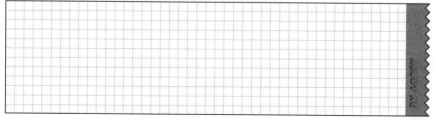

Substitution 更多回應說法！

☞ B1

- **They've both graduated from college, but my younger one can't seem to hold down a job.**
  （他們兩個都大學畢業了，但是小的那個似乎總是無法好好保有一份工作。）
  * hold down a job「保有一份工作」
  TIPS can't hold down a job 也可說成 go from one job to another「不斷換工作」。

- **My daughter is studying abroad, and my son is in medical school.**
  （我女兒在國外留學，而我兒子正在唸醫學院。）

- **They've all flown the nest. The last one left for college last September.**
  （他們都已經離家獨立。最小的在九月份念大學去了。）

☞ B2

- **They're adults now, so they have to live their own life. Their future is their responsibility.**
  （他們都是大人了，所以必須自立。他們的未來是自己的責任。）

- **It's hard to be optimistic nowadays, but my kids are pretty sharp. I'm sure they'll do fine.**
  （當今這時代，實在很難讓人樂觀，不過我的小孩都很聰明。我相信他們都會過得很好。）
  * sharp「敏銳的；聰明的」

- **When they first left for college, I worried about them constantly, but now I'm OK.**
  （當他們剛離家念大學時，我總是擔心個不停，不過現在我已經好多了。）

VOCABULARY 具體描述自己的好用字！

little child 幼兒 / nursery school 托兒所 / kindergarten 幼稚園 / a second grader 小學二年級生 / be in one's third year of junior high 國中三年級 / a high school freshman / sophomore / junior 高一／二／三 / a college freshman / sophomore / junior / senior 大一／二／三／四 / take a year off to study for entrance exams 花一年念書重考聯考 / graduate from high school / college 高中／大學畢業 / go to grad / graduate school 念研究所 / work in the finance / IT industry 在金融業／資訊業工作 / be still sponging on one's parents 還在倚賴父母 / get married and leave home 結婚並離家 / be living overseas on business 因工作而旅居海外

active ▸ 活躍的	**trusting** ▸ 輕易信任別人的
discreet ▸ 謹慎的	**delicate** ▸ 嬌弱的
punctual ▸ 守時的	**open-minded** ▸ 心胸寬闊的
generous / broad-minded ▸ 慷慨的；度量大的	**flashy** ▸ 俗麗的
persevering ▸ 堅忍的	**persistent** ▸ 堅持不懈的
reserved ▸ 含蓄的；沉默寡言的	**impatient** ▸ 沒耐性的
reckless ▸ 魯莽的	**obliging** ▸ 殷勤的
slovenly ▸ 邋遢的	**pushy** ▸ 強勢的
sensitive ▸ 敏感的	**sissy** ▸ 娘娘腔的
outspoken ▸ 坦率的	**polite** ▸ 有禮貌的（⟷ rude 粗魯的）
hasty ▸ 輕率的	**energetic** ▸ 精力充沛的
meddlesome ▸ 愛管閒事的	**modest** ▸ 謙虛的 （⟷ conceited [kən`sitɪd] 自負的）
stingy / cheap ▸ 小氣的；吝嗇的	**macho** ▸ 有男子氣概的；陽剛的 （⟷ wimp 軟弱的）
indecisive ▸ 優柔寡斷的	**perky** ▸ 生氣勃勃的
obedient ▸ 順從的	

對話回應好用句 ② ：贊成・同意

「沒錯！」

● **No doubt!**（毫無疑問！）
▸ 表達「沒錯」之意，屬於較輕鬆隨興的回應方式。

● **No doubt about that.**（那毫無疑問！）
▸ 表示「一點都沒錯」。about that 就是「關於那點」之意。

● **Without a doubt!**（毫無疑問！）
▸ 和 No doubt! 的說法類似。

● **For sure.**（肯定如此！）
▸ 用來表達強烈同意之意。

● **No question.**（毫無問題！）
▸ 即「沒錯；就是這樣」之意。

Unit 3

生活型態
Life Style

盡量整理關於自己生活型態的資訊，並融入對話內容。
努力成為一個話題豐富的談天對象吧！

What do you usually do on the weekends?
Do you do social networking?
What are you into lately?
Do you have any habits that you want to change?
...

appearance

name

Taiwan culture

friends

work

dreams

interest

families

religion

experience

027

What time do you get up every day?
你每天幾點起床？

Dialogue 實戰會話　　　　　　　　　　🎧 Track 28

> **A：What time do you get up every day?**
> （你每天幾點起床？）
>
> **B1：When I have to work, I usually get up at 5 a.m.**
> （要上班的日子，我通常早上 5 點起床。）
>
> **A：What time do you go to sleep? Personally, I need at least 8 hours of sleep every day.**
> （你幾點睡呢？我個人每天至少需要 8 小時的睡眠。）
>
> **B2：I'm usually in bed by midnight. If I don't get 6 hours of sleep, I can't concentrate on my work.** 👉
> （我通常會在半夜 12 點前就寢。如果睡不到 6 小時，我就會無法專心工作。）
>
> * midnight「半夜 12 點」；concentrate on...「專心……；全神貫注於……」

✎ **Exercise** 請寫下自己的答案並試著說出來！

A：What time do you get up every day?

B1：

A：What time do you go to sleep? Personally, I need at least 8 hours of sleep every day.

B2：

Substitution 更多回應說法！

☞ B1

● **If I don't have to work, I'm usually in bed until 8 o'clock.**
（如果不用上班，我通常都會睡到 8 點。）

● **It varies. During the week I get up at around 6:30, but on weekends I like to sleep in.**
（要看情況。平日我大約 6:30 起床，但是週末我喜歡賴床。）
* vary「有變化」；sleep in「賴床」

● **I'm up at the crack of dawn every morning. When I leave the house, it's still half-dark.**
（我每天清晨時分就起床。出門時天都還沒完全亮。）
* at the crack of dawn「清晨；黎明」

☞ B2

● **I try to go to bed by midnight, but when I go out drinking I'm up until 2 or 3 a.m.**
（我盡量在半夜 12 點前就寢，但是如果我出門喝酒，就會熬到凌晨 2、3 點。）

● **During the week, I go to sleep at around 11, but on weekends I tend to stay up late.**
（平日我通常 11 點左右就寢，但是週末我往往會熬夜到很晚。）
* tend to...「傾向於……」；stay up「熬夜」

● **I'm usually up until 3 in the morning surfing the Net. I only need around 5 hours of sleep.**
（我通常會一直上網到凌晨 3 點左右。我只需要約 5 小時的睡眠。）
* surf [sɜf]「上網」

VOCABULARY 具體描述自己的好用字！

stay up until the wee hours of the morning 熬夜至凌晨（一、二點鐘）/ burn the midnight oil 挑燈夜戰；徹夜苦讀（或工作）/ dawn 黎明 / sunrise 日出 / day break 破曉 / wake up 醒來；起床 / wake someone up 叫醒某人 / alarm clock 鬧鐘 / alarm clock with a snooze [snuz] function 有貪睡功能的鬧鐘 / suffer from lack of sleep 苦於睡眠不足 / can sleep well 能睡得好 / can't sleep much 睡不久 / have insomnia [ɪnˈsɔmnɪə] 失眠 / take a sleeping pill 吃安眠藥 / wake up in the middle of the night 半夜醒來

028

What do you usually do on the weekends?
你週末通常都做些什麼事？

Dialogue 實戰會話 🎧 Track 29

> A：**What do you usually do on the weekends?**
> （你週末通常都做些什麼事？）
>
> B1：**I like to stay at home and catch up on sleep on the weekends.** ☞
> （我週末都喜歡待在家裡補眠。）
>
> A：**Really? It's always tough to go back to work on Monday, isn't it?**
> （真的呀？週一要回去上班總是讓人很痛苦，不是嗎？）
>
> B2：**Yeah, the weekend passes so quickly. I wish every weekend were a three-day weekend.** ☞
> （是啊，週末總是過得好快。我真希望每個週末都連放三天。）
>
> * catch up on... 「彌補……」；three-day weekend 「連放三天的長週末」

✎ **Exercise** 請寫下自己的答案並試著說出來！

A：**What do you usually do on the weekends?**

B1：

A：**Really? It's always tough to go back to work on Monday, isn't it?**

B2：

Substitution 更多回應說法！

B1

- I usually meet my boyfriend on the weekend. We're both too busy to meet during the week.
（我週末通常都會和男朋友見面。我們平日都忙得沒空相見。）
- My husband and I usually take the kids somewhere, like the park or the zoo.
（我先生和我通常都會帶著孩子出去走走，比如去公園或動物園之類的。）
- I like to hang out with my friends. We often go to the movies together.
（我喜歡和朋友混在一起。我們經常一起去看電影。）

B2

- Actually, after two days with my kids, I'm ready to go back to work.
（事實上，跟小孩相處 2 天之後，我已經準備好要回去上班了。）
＊ be ready to...「準備好要⋯⋯」
- Tell me about it. I really have to drag myself out of bed on Monday morning.
（就是說嘛！週一早上真的很難起得來。）
＊ drag oneself out of bed「勉強自己起床」
- Yeah, you should see me on Monday morning. I'm such a zombie.
（是呀，你應該看看我週一早上的樣子。簡直就像個殭屍。）
＊ zombie [ˋzɑmbɪ]「殭屍；行屍走肉的人」

VOCABULARY 具體描述自己的好用字！

hate Sunday nights 討厭週日晚上 / **TGIF (Thank God It's Friday)** 感謝老天，今天是星期五 / **go out** 外出 / **get out of the house** 出門去 / **go for a drive** 開車兜風去 / **go on a date** 去約會 / **go to the park** 去公園 / **walk one's dog** 遛狗 / **play with one's pet** 和寵物玩 / **take a short trip** 做個短程旅遊 / **eat out at nice restaurants** 去好餐廳吃一頓 / **go clothes shopping** 去逛街買衣服 / **do exercise** 做運動 / **leisurely surf the Net** 悠閒地上網 / **take it easy** 放輕鬆 / **have friends over** 請朋友到家裡來玩 / **throw a party** 辦宴會；開派對 / **see a baseball / soccer game** 看棒球 / 足球賽 / **play video games** 打電動 / **get a massage** 去按摩 / **get a haircut** 去理髮 / **go to the beauty salon** 上美容院

029

What do you do when you have a vacation?
放長假時你都做些什麼事？

Track 30

Dialogue 實戰會話

A：**What do you do when you have a vacation?**
（放長假時你都做些什麼事？）

B1：**I like to travel. If I can get at least one week off, I go overseas.**
（我喜歡旅行。如果能休至少一星期的假，我就會出國。）

A：**What's your idea of a perfect holiday?**
（你心目中的完美假期是怎樣的？）

B2：**If I can do nothing but lie around on a beach for a few days, that's a perfect holiday.**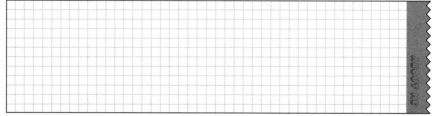
（如果什麼都不做，只躺在沙灘上過個幾天，就算是完美的假期了。）

* lie around「懶散地躺著」

✎ **Exercise** 請寫下自己的答案並試著說出來！

A：**What do you do when you have a vacation?**
B1：

A：**What's your idea of a perfect holiday?**
B2：

Substitution 更多回應說法！

☞ B1

- **I usually go to my parents' home in Hualien, and meet up with old friends.**
  （我通常都會回花蓮的老家，並見見老朋友。）
  * parents' home「老家」

- **When I go traveling, I like to experience the local culture, instead of just sightseeing.**
  （我去旅行的時候，喜歡體驗當地文化，而不只是遊覽。）
  * local culture「當地文化」；sightseeing「觀光；遊覽」

- **I like to go to beach resorts. My favorite place is Hawaii.**
  （我喜歡去海灘勝地。我最愛的地方是夏威夷。）

☞ B2

- **For me, there's nothing better than relaxing at a hot spring resort.**
  （對我來說，沒有什麼比去溫泉勝地放鬆一下更棒的了。）
  * hot spring「溫泉」

- **If possible, I'd like to spend a month or two backpacking around Asia.**
  （如果可能的話，我會想花一到兩個月在亞洲各地進行背包客旅行。）
  * backpack「背包客旅行」

- **My idea of a great vacation is fine wine, delicious food, and a nice hotel overlooking the sea.**
  （我心目中最棒的假期要有美酒、美食，和一間可眺望海景的好旅館。）
  * overlook「眺望」

VOCABULARY 具體描述自己的好用字！

can't take long vacations 無法休長假 / can't take more than one week off 無法休超過一星期的假 / take a 3-week vacation 度 3 週的長假 / be usually busy with club activities 通常忙於社團活動 / want to help with the parenting 幫忙育兒工作 / take it easy in the country with one's family 在鄉下與家人一起並放鬆身心 / try writing a novel 嘗試寫小說 / take a college course for adults 修習為成人開設的大學課程 / study to get a qualification 為了取得資格（證照）而唸書 / play online games to one's heart's content 盡情地玩線上遊戲 / take a bus trip across America 進行橫越美國的巴士之旅 / travel around Japan visiting secluded hot springs 進行日本各地的秘湯之旅 / travel around Europe by rail 坐火車遊遍歐洲

030

Are you a morning person or a night person?
你是早起的人，還是晚睡的人？

Dialogue 實戰會話　　　　　　　　　　　　 Track 31

A：Are you a morning person or a night person?
（你是早起的人，還是晚睡的人？）

B1：I'm an early bird. I usually get up at 5. ☞
（我是早起的鳥兒。我通常 5 點就起床了。）

A：Do you think it's better to get up early in the morning?
（你覺得早起比較好嗎？）

B2：Definitely. I can beat the morning rush hour and get some work done before my coworkers arrive. ☞
（當然囉。可以搶在交通尖峰期之前到，並且在同事來之前就完成一些工作。）

＊ beat「搶在……之前」

✎ **Exercise** 請寫下自己的答案並試著說出來！

A：Are you a morning person or a night person?
B1：

A：Do you think it's better to get up early in the morning?
B2：

Substitution 更多回應說法！

☞ B1

● I'm a night owl. I'm up until 2 or 3 a.m. every night.

（我是夜貓子。我每晚都熬夜到凌晨 2、3 點。）

＊ night owl「夜貓子」

● I wouldn't call myself a morning person, but I have to get up at 6 every morning to make my family's breakfast.

（我不算是早起的人，不過我每天都必須 6 點起床幫家人做早餐。）

● It's hard to say. I don't stay up late, but I don't like to get up early, either.

（很難說。我不熬夜，但是也不喜歡早起。）

＊ hard to say「很難說」

☞ B2

● Yes, I do. I'd get up earlier if I could, but some things are easier said than done.

（是的，我的確這麼認為。我會盡量早起，但是有些事總是說起來容易做起來難。）

＊ easier said than done「說起來容易做起來難」

● Yeah, I find that I'm able to get things done more quickly and efficiently in the morning.

（是啊，我發現我早上比較能又快又有效率地把事情辦妥。）

＊ get things done「把事情辦妥」

● It's probably healthier to get up early, but I find it easier to work late at night, when it's nice and quiet.

（早起可能比較健康，但是我覺得深夜工作比較舒適，因為晚上挺安靜的。）

＊ nice and...「挺……」

VOCABULARY 具體描述自己的好用字！

The early bird catches the worm. 早起的鳥兒有蟲吃。 / Early to bed and early to rise makes a man healthy, wealthy, and wise. 早睡早起能讓人健康、富足又聰明。 / early riser 早起的人 / late riser 晚起的人 / go to sleep early 早睡 / stay up late 熬夜 / wake up late 起得晚 / sleep all morning 睡到中午 / have an early-morning job 早班工作 / work starts at noon 從中午開始工作 / have a night job 夜班（晚班）工作 / often have to work the night shift 經常要值夜班 / one's working hours are flexible 某人的工作時間是有彈性的 / like the quiet of the late night hours 喜歡深夜時分的寧靜 / like the invigorating feel of the early morning hours 喜歡清晨時分精神振作的感覺 / go for an early-morning walk 晨間散步 / go running at night 夜間慢跑

031

Do you do social networking?
你玩不玩社群網路？

A： Do you do social networking?
（你玩不玩社群網路？）

B1： I don't do Facebook, but I have a Plurk account. ☞
（我不玩臉書，但是我有噗浪帳號。）

A： Really? Why is that?
（真的啊？為什麼？）

B2： Most of my coworkers do Plurk. It's really popular in Taiwan. ☞
（我大部分的同事都玩噗浪。在台灣還滿流行的。）

✎ **Exercise** 請寫下自己的答案並試著說出來！

A： Do you do social networking?

B1：

A： Really? Why is that?

B2：

Substitution 更多回應說法！

☞ B1

● **No, but I have a blog. I haven't been very good about updating it, though.**
(沒有，但是我有部落格。不過我一直不善於更新內容。)
* update「更新」

● **I did Facebook for a while, but I got tired of it. Recently, I started Twitter.**
(我玩過一陣子臉書，但是玩膩了。我最近開始玩推特。)
* get tired of...「對……感到膩了」

● **I'm into Twitter. It's quite addictive. Have you tried it?**
(我很迷推特。它真的會令人上癮。你有沒有試過？)
* addictive「使人上癮的」

☞ B2

● **I don't feel comfortable about posting personal information on the Internet.**
(我不習慣將個人資訊張貼到網路上。)
* post「(將資訊等) 張貼 (到網上)」

● **To be honest, I don't understand what the big deal is with social networking sites.**
(老實說，我實在不懂社群網站有什麼大不了的。)
* big deal「至關重大的事」

● **Twitter is great because I can see what famous people are thinking and doing.**
(推特很棒，因為我可以知道名人在想什麼、做什麼。)

𝒱𝒪𝒞𝒜𝘽𝒰𝐿𝒜ℛ𝒴 具體描述自己的好用字！

sign up for... 登錄…… / username 使用者名稱 / password 密碼 / log in 登入 / log out 登出 / post a comment / photo / video 張貼留言 / 照片 / 影片 / receive a friend request 收到朋友邀請 / friend / unfriend someone (在社群網站上) 加入 / 取消朋友 / follow / unfollow someone (在 IG 上) 追蹤 / 取消追蹤某人 / follow someone back 回頭追蹤某人 / send a direct message 傳送直接訊息 / add to one's favorites 加到我的最愛 / post a comment to a specific person with @ 以 @ (符號) 針對特定人物張貼留言 / respond 回覆 / retweet 轉推 (轉貼他人文章) / block someone (在社群網站上) 封鎖某人 / post a link to a site 張貼連往某網站的連結 / write pictographs [ˋpɪktəˌgræfs] 使用表情符號

What are you into lately?
你最近在迷什麼？

Dialogue 實戰會話　　　　　　　　　　　　🔘 Track 33

A：**What are you into lately?**
（你最近在迷什麼？）

B1：**I took up running recently. I go running every morning.** 🔝
（我最近開始跑步。我每天早上都去跑。）

A：**Wow, really? Why?**
（哇，真的嗎？為什麼？）

B2：**My life was in a rut, and I needed a change.** 🔝
（我的生活一成不變，我需要一點變化。）

* in a rut「一成不變」

✏️ **Exercise** 請寫下自己的答案並試著說出來！

A：**What are you into lately?**

B1：
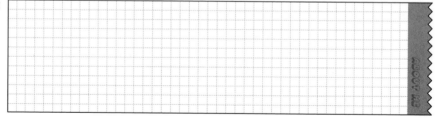

A：**Wow, really? Why?**

B2：

Substitution 更多回應說法！

☞ B1

- **Recently I'm really into reggae. I can't stop listening to it!**
  （我最近很迷雷鬼音樂。我忍不住要一直聽！）
  * reggae [ˋrɛge]「雷鬼」；can't stop + V-ing「忍不住做……」
- **I've been taking a yoga class recently. It's great!**
  （我最近都在上瑜珈課。很不錯！）
  * recently「最近」
- **My friend got me hooked on FarmTown. I want to quit, though.**
  （我朋友害我迷上農場小鎮遊戲。不過我想戒掉了。）
  * FarmTown「農場小鎮」（線上遊戲的名稱）

☞ B2

- **Listening to reggae music really gets me going.**
  （聽雷鬼音樂真能讓我振奮。）
  * get someone going「振奮某人」
- **I was getting fat, and I felt like I needed to do something to get in shape.**
  （我越來越胖了，所以覺得需要做些什麼來改善體態。）
  * get in shape「達成健康體態」
- **It takes up too much of my time. It's really addictive.**
  （這件事花我太多時間。真的會令人上癮。）
  * addictive「使人上癮的」

VOCABULARY 具體描述自己的好用字！

be addicted to... 沉迷於……；對……上癮 / be crazy about... 瘋迷…… / be nuts over... 瘋迷…… / be obsessed with... 迷戀…… / can't stop playing / doing something 忍不住一直玩 / 做…… / I'm a big fan of... 我是……的頭號粉絲（愛好者）/ I want to try... 想想嘗試…… / ... was boring at first ……一開始很無趣 / get tired of... 對……感到厭煩 / lose interest in... 對……失去興趣 / be not at all interested in... 對……一點興趣也沒有 / couldn't care less about... 對……毫不在意 / can't stand... 無法忍受…… / I started playing golf last year. 我去年開始打高爾夫球。/ I've been into snowboarding for the past 5 years. 過去 5 年我一直很迷滑雪板。/ I've been obsessed with tennis for many years. 多年來我一直很迷網球。/ I've been into Japanese movies for the past few years. 這幾年來我一直很迷日本電影。

Are you an indoor or outdoor type of person?
你是居家型的人，還是戶外型的人？

Dialogue 實戰會話　　　　　　　　　　　🎧 Track 34

A： Are you an indoor or outdoor type of person?
（你是居家型的人，還是戶外型的人？）

B1： Well, I like to go fishing, so I guess you could say I'm an outdoor type.
（嗯，我喜歡釣魚，所以我想我算是戶外型的人。）

A： I'm not sure which one I am. Which do you think is better?
（我不確定我算哪一型。你覺得哪一型比較好呢？）

B2： I think it's good to know how to live off the land. People are spoiled by city life.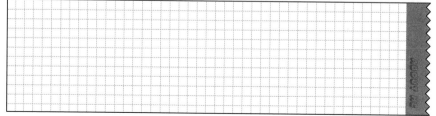
（我覺得懂得如何務農蠻好的。現代人都被都市生活給慣壞了。）

* be spoiled「被慣壞；被寵壞」

✎ **Exercise** 請寫下自己的答案並試著說出來！

A： Are you an indoor or outdoor type of person?

B1：

A： I'm not sure which one I am. Which do you think is better?

B2：

☞ **B1**

- **I don't know. I'm not the stay-at-home type, but I'm not into outdoor sports, either.**

  （我不知道。我不是那種宅在家裡的人，但是也不特別喜歡戶外運動。）

  * stay-at-home「宅在家裡」

- **I'm definitely not the outdoor type. My idea of roughing it is staying at a motel.**

  （我絕對不是戶外型的人。對我來說住汽車旅館就算是原始生活了。）

  * rough it「過原始生活」

- **I like to go camping and fishing, but I wouldn't want to live in the woods.**

  （我喜歡露營和釣魚，但是我並不想住在樹林中。）

☞ **B2**

- **People say it's greener to fish and hunt for yourself, but I'm skeptical.**

  （大家都說自己釣魚、狩獵是比較環保的，但是我對這點抱持懷疑態度。）

  * greener「比較環保的」；skeptical「懷疑的」

- **I think it's best to be a little bit of both. There's no need to be one or the other.**

  （我想最好兩種都有一點。沒有必要非此即彼。）

  * one or the other「非此即彼；非黑即白；二選一的」

- **If you don't know, you're probably not the outdoor type.**

  （如果你搞不清楚，那你大概就不是戶外型的。）

VOCABULARY 具體描述自己的好用字！

kayaking 玩小划艇 / canoeing 玩獨木舟 / rock climbing 攀岩 / skydiving 高空跳傘 / hang gliding 滑翔翼 / hiking 健行 / mountain climbing 登山 / take it easy at home 在家放鬆 / lie around at home 在家懶散地躺著 / relax on a sofa 懶洋洋地坐在沙發上 / recluse 隱士 / anime geek 日本動畫迷 / bookworm 書呆子 / book lover 愛書人 / do nothing but watch YouTube 什麼都不做只看 YouTube / make figurines [ˌfɪgjəˋrinz] 做模型玩偶（公仔）/ can't live without rental DVDs 少了出租 DVD 就活不下去 / surf the Net for hours on end 連續幾小時一直上網 / be addicted to online games 沉迷於線上遊戲 / tweet all day long 整天都在玩推特 / constantly update one's blog 不斷更新某人的部落格 / write a novel 寫小說 / draw pictures 畫畫

034

Are you taking lessons?
你有沒有在上什麼課？

Dialogue 實戰會話　　　　　　　　　　🔊 Track 35

A：**Are you taking lessons?**
（你有沒有在上什麼課？）

B1：**I started studying French recently.** ☞
（我最近開始在學法文。）

A：**That's great. What made you decide to do that?**
（真棒。你為什麼決定要學法文？）

B2：**I'm a big fan of French movies. I want to be able to watch them without subtitles.** ☞
（我是法國電影的頭號粉絲，我想不靠字幕就能看懂內容。）

* subtitles「字幕」

✏️ **Exercise** 請寫下自己的答案並試著說出來！

A：**Are you taking lessons?**

B1：

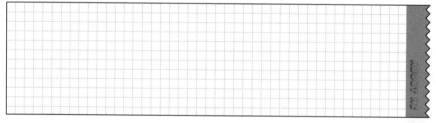

A：**That's great. What made you decide to do that?**

B2：

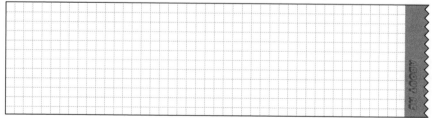

Substitution 更多回應說法！

☞ B1

- **I've been taking yoga classes at the local culture center.**
  （我一直在本地的文化中心上瑜珈課。）

- **Recently I've been studying the stock market on my own.**
  （我最近一直在自己研究股票市場。）
  ＊ stock market「股票市場」

- **I'm taking an online course on asset management.**
  （我正在上資產管理的線上課程。）
  ＊ online course「線上課程」

☞ B2

- **I like to maintain a wide variety of interests. It makes life more interesting.**
  （我喜歡維持廣泛的興趣，這樣生活會更有意思。）
  ＊ maintain「維持」

- **My friend was taking lessons, and recommended it to me.**
  （我朋友有在上課，而且很推薦我去。）
  ＊ recommend「推薦」

- **I want to have some skill to fall back on if I ever change jobs.**
  （如果我哪天要換工作，我希望能有個第二專長做為依靠。）
  ＊ fall back on「備案；（無其他辦法時）作為依靠」；ever「任何時候」

VOCABULARY 具體描述自己的好用字！

study to be an accountant 為了成為會計師而唸書 / study to get a qualification 為了取得資格（證照）而唸書 / study for self-improvement 為了提升自我而學習 / study in order to succeed in business 為了能事業有成而學習 / study in preparation for working life 為了準備就業而學習 / study in preparation for married life 為了準備結婚而學習 / take lessons for making friends 為了交朋友而去上課 / take kimono-dressing classes 上穿和服的課程 / pottery 陶藝 / nail art 美甲藝術 / photography 攝影 / piano 鋼琴 / tea ceremony 茶道 / flower arrangement 插花 / judo 柔道 / aikido 合氣道 / karate 空手道 / taichi 太極拳 / knitting 編織 / sewing 裁縫 / cooking 烹飪 / take night classes 上夜間課程 / take early-morning classes 上晨間課程 / take classes on one's days off 在假日上課 / study online 在線上學習 / e-learning 數位學習 / correspondence course 函授課程

035

What's your goal?
你的目標是什麼？

Dialogue 實戰會話　　　　　　　　　　　🔊 Track 36

A：What's your goal?
（你的目標是什麼？）

B1：If possible, I'd like to turn my hobby into a side business. ☞
（如果有可能，我希望能將興趣轉為副業。）

A：Are you doing something now to achieve that goal?
（為了達成該目標，你現在有在做什麼努力嗎？）

B2：Well, I'm working on a website now. ☞
（嗯，我現在正在做一個網站。）

* side business「副業」; website「網站」
TIPS Homepage（首頁）是指網站的主頁（第一頁）。

✎ **Exercise** 請寫下自己的答案並試著說出來！

A：What's your goal?
B1：

A：Are you doing something now to achieve that goal?
B2：

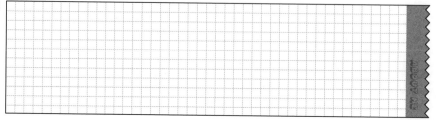

Substitution 更多回應說法！

☞ B1

- **I've always wanted to make a living as an artist.**

  （我一直很想以藝術家的身分來謀生。）

  * as an artist「以藝術家的身分」

- **I want to quit my job and start my own business.**

  （我想辭職，然後自行創業。）

  * start one's own business「創業」

- **Someday I hope to get promoted to branch manager.**

  （我希望有一天能晉升為分公司經理。）

  * get promoted to...「晉升為……」；branch「分公司」

☞ B2

- **I've been doing a lot of networking. In the art world, it's important to have connections.**

  （我已建立不少人脈。在藝術界，關係是很重要的。）

  * networking「人際網絡；人脈」

- **I've been saving up a little bit every month. I can't start a business without capital.**

  （一直以來我每個月都有存一點錢。沒有資金是無法創業的。）

  * capital「資金」

- **I'm planning to go back to school to get a business degree.**

  （我打算回學校去拿一個商學學位。）

Vocabulary 具體描述自己的好用字！

work one's butt off 拚了命工作 / **get one's business off the ground** 自行創立事業 / **make a lot of money** 賺大錢 / **find a job that is more satisfying** 找個更令人滿意的工作 / **get an MBA degree** 取得 MBA 學位 / **get a perfect score on the TOEIC** 拿到多益測驗滿分 / **get certified to become a CPA (Certified Public Accountant)** 拿到合格會計師證照 / **tax accountant** 稅務師 / **medium and small business consultant** 中小型企業顧問 / **get used to a job** 習慣某個工作 / **get ahead at work** 在工作上出人頭地 / **improve one's business skills** 提升某人的業務能力 / **create a successful online business** 網路創業成功 / **run a restaurant** 經營餐廳 / **get married by the age of...** 在……歲前結婚 / **save up NT$20 million by the age of...** 在……歲之前存到新台幣 2 千萬元 / **buy a house / condominium** 買一棟房子／一戶公寓 / **have an ordinary but happy family** 擁有平凡但幸福的家庭

036

What do you want to do after you retire?
退休後你想做什麼？

Dialogue 實戰會話　　　　　　　　　　　　🔊 Track 37

A：What do you want to do after you retire?
（退休後你想做什麼？）

B1：I want to sell my house and move to the country. ☞
（我想把房子賣了，然後搬到鄉下去。）

A：Really? That sounds like a nice way to spend your retirement.
（真的嗎？聽起來像是很不錯的退休生活方式。）

B2：You think so? I wish my wife felt that way. She's dead set against it. ☞
（你也這麼覺得嗎？真希望我太太也這麼想。她誓死反對這主意。）

* be dead set against... 「誓死反對………」

🖊 **Exercise** 請寫下自己的答案並試著說出來！

A：What do you want to do after you retire?

B1：

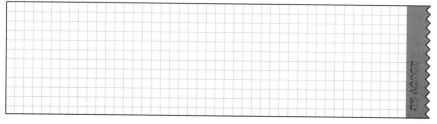

A：Really? That sounds like a nice way to spend your retirement.

B2：

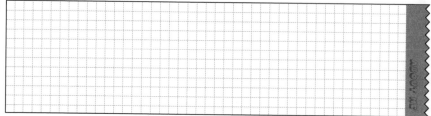

Substitution 更多回應說法！

☞ B1

- **My dream is to have a house in Hawaii, and travel all over the world.**
  （我的夢想是在夏威夷擁有一棟房子，然後去環遊世界。）
  ＊ all over the world「世界各地」

- **I want to be close to my kids, so I think I'll move to the city.**
  （我希望能靠近我的孩子，所以我想我會搬去都市住。）

- **I want to get away from the rat race, and live quietly in the mountains.**
  （我想遠離商界競爭，到山裡過著寧靜的生活。）
  ＊ rat race「商場的競爭」

☞ B2

- **Yeah, but it's probably not very realistic. I heard it's very expensive to live there.**
  （是啊，但是那可能不很切實際。我聽說住在那裡是非常貴的。）
  ＊ realistic「實際的」

- **I'm still in the planning stage. I haven't really thought it through yet.**
  （我還在計畫中。我還沒仔細考慮過。）
  ＊ think through「仔細考慮」

- **I need to save up some money. My pension won't be enough to live on.**
  （我必須存一些錢。我的退休金是不夠過日子的。）

𝒱ᴏᴄᴀʙᴜʟᴀʀʏ 具體描述自己的好用字！

retirement allowance 退休津貼 / pay off one's mortgage 付清房貸 / look after one's grandchildren 照顧孫子 / move in with one's children 搬去和孩子同住 / be near one's family 在家人附近 / live a healthy life 過著健康的生活 / be helpful to one's community 對社區有所貢獻 / throw oneself into volunteer work 投入義工活動 / have lots of time for one's hobbies 有很多時間可花在自己的嗜好上 / live in Vietnam after one's retire 退休後要住在越南 / travel around Taiwan by motor home 開著露營車遊遍台灣各地 / maintain one's current lifestyle 維持目前的生活型態 / appreciate one's wife / husband more 更珍惜太太 / 先生 / cherish the time one spends with one's wife / husband 珍惜和太太 / 先生在一起的時光 / don't want to be a burden on one's children 不想成為孩子的負擔

037

What do you usually do during the week?
你平日通常都在做些什麼？

Dialogue 實戰會話　　　　　　　　　　　　🎧 Track 38

A： What do you usually do during the week?
（你平日通常都在做些什麼？）

B1： I'm usually at the office all day long, and I don't get home until 9 or 10. 📝
（我通常整天都待在辦公室，9 或 10 點才回到家。）

A： Really? Maybe you need to manage your time better.
（真的嗎？也許你該做好時間管理。）

B2： You're right. Lately I hardly have any time to pursue my own interests. 📝
（你說的對。最近我幾乎都沒時間追求自己的興趣。）

* pursue「從事；進行」

✏️ **Exercise** 請寫下自己的答案並試著說出來！

A： What do you usually do during the week?
B1：

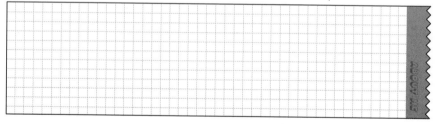

A： Really? Maybe you need to manage your time better.
B2：

☞ B1

- I joined the gym near my office, but I haven't been going much recently.
  （我加入了辦公室附近的健身房，但是最近幾乎都沒去。）
  * join「加入」

- I go drinking with my coworkers once in a while, but usually I'm too tired to do anything.
  （我偶爾會跟同事去喝一杯，不過通常我都是累到什麼事也做不了。）
  * coworker「同事」

- I'm too busy looking after my kids and doing the housework to do much of anything.
  （我忙著照顧小孩和做家事，沒辦法做什麼其他事情。）
  * too... to...「太……以至於無法……」

☞ B2

- Actually, I think the real problem is motivation. I have time, but I don't have the will.
  （事實上，我覺得真正的問題在於是否有動機。我有時間，但是沒有意願。）
  * motivation「動機」; will「意願」

- Yeah, there just isn't enough time in the day to do everything I want to do.
  （是啊，一天的時間總是不夠讓我做完所有想做的事。）

- You think so? I've never thought of it that way. What do you think I should do?
  （你這麼覺得嗎？我從來沒那樣想過。你覺得我該怎麼辦好？）
  * think of... that way「從那個角度想……」

VOCABULARY 具體描述自己的好用字！

be busy working on one's thesis 忙著寫論文 / be busy with job-hunting 忙著找工作 / cram for exams 為了考試而臨時抱佛腳 / have classes every day 每天都有課要上 / work overtime 加班 / get home late 晚歸 / be always pressed for time 總是被時間追著跑 / work from early morning to late at night 從清晨工作到深夜 / leave work at the scheduled time 準時下班 / go to night school 去上夜校 / stress builds up 壓力累積 / have no stress 沒有壓力 / blow off steam (=to relieve stress) 紓解壓力 / make a clear distinction between work and play 明確區分工作與玩樂 / make a to-do list 列出代辦事項清單 / use time effectively 有效利用時間 / have no time for anything besides work 沒時間做工作以外的任何事

038

What do you usually have for breakfast?

你早餐通常都吃些什麼？

Dialogue 實戰會話   Track 39

> **A：What do you usually have for breakfast?**
> （你早餐通常都吃些什麼？）
>
> **B1：I usually just have toast and a cup of coffee.** 📖
> （我通常只吃吐司和一杯咖啡。）
>
> **A：Do you do much cooking?**
> （你常做菜嗎？）
>
> **B2：My wife and I take turns cooking dinner. We often end up eating out, though.** 📖
> （我太太和我會輪流做晚餐。不過結果通常都是出去吃。）
>
> * take turns「輪流」

✎ **Exercise** 請寫下自己的答案並試著說出來！

A：What do you usually have for breakfast?

B1：

A：Do you do much cooking?

B2：

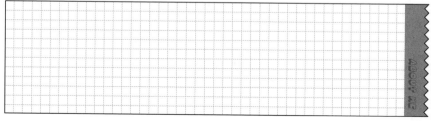

Substitution 更多回應說法！

☞ B1

- **My typical chinese breakfast—rice porridge, pickled vegetables, and dried shredded pork.**
  （我典型的中式早餐－稀飯、醬菜和肉鬆。）
  ＊ typical「典型的」

- **I often skip breakfast and just have a glass of vegetable juice instead.**
  （我常常不吃早餐，只以一杯蔬菜汁替代。）
  ＊ skip「省略；跳過」；instead「替代」

- **It varies, but I always have a cup of coffee. I need coffee to get me going in the morning.**
  （各式各樣的都有，不過我總會喝一杯咖啡。我早上需要咖啡來提神。）

☞ B2

- **No, I'm a lousy cook. I let my husband do most of the cooking.**
  （不，我很不會做菜。大部分烹飪的事都交由我先生處理。）
  ＊ lousy「糟糕的；差勁的」

- **I try to, but unfortunately, I'm too busy to do much cooking during the week.**
  （我試著做，但是不幸的是，我平日太忙了，實在沒辦法常常做菜。）

- **Yeah, I love to cook. I especially enjoy coming up with new dishes of my own.**
  （是啊，我很喜歡做菜。我特別喜歡自己發明新菜色。）
  come up with...「想出……」

VOCABULARY 具體描述自己的好用字！

pack a lunch 包個午餐便當 / eat out 出去吃；外食 / eat at home 在家吃 / have pizza delivered 叫披薩外送 / order some pizza / sushi 訂比薩／壽司 / order something to go 點菜外帶 / cook every day 每天做菜 / almost never cook 幾乎從不做菜 / only cook when I feel like it 想做菜時才做 / hot green tea 熱的綠茶 / rice porridge 稀飯 / pickled vegetables 醬菜 / dried shredded pork 肉鬆 / soy milk 豆漿 / deep fried breadsticks 油條 / steamed bun 饅頭 / rice ball 飯團 / sesame flatbread with eggs 燒餅夾蛋 / egg fried sunny-side up 單面煎荷包蛋 / home-cooked box lunch 家常便當 / box lunch with food in the shape of cartoon characters 把菜做成卡通人物造型的便當

039

Do you have a car?
你有車嗎？

Dialogue 實戰會話　　　　　　　　　　　⊙ Track 40

A：Do you have a car?
（你有車嗎？）

B1：No, I don't really need a car in Taipei. ☞
（沒有，在台北我不太需要有車。）

A：Do you like to drive?
（你喜歡開車嗎？）

B2：Not really. I have a license, but I'm too scared to drive. ☞
（不很喜歡。我有駕照，但是實在很害怕所以不敢開。）

* scared「害怕的」

TIPS 要表達「我有駕照但是不會開車」，正確的英文是 I'm only a driver on paper.，而不要說成 paper driver。

✎ **Exercise** 請寫下自己的答案並試著說出來！

A：Do you have a car?

B1：

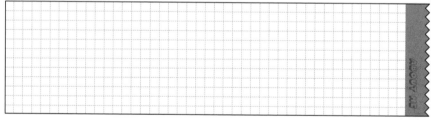

A：Do you like to drive?

B2：

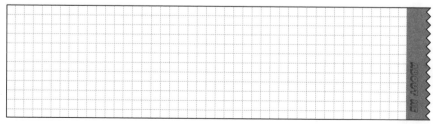

Substitution 更多回應說法！

☞ **B1**

- **Yeah, I just bought a new minivan last month.**
  （有啊，我上個月才剛新買了一台迷你廂型車。）
  * minivan「迷你箱型車」

- **I have an old Honda, but it's in the shop now.**
  （我有一台老 Honda，不過送修了。）
  * in the shop「送修」

- **No, but I really want one. Where I live, I need a car to get around.**
  （沒有，不過我真的很想買一台。我住的地方需要有車才方便移動。）
  * get around「到處跑」

☞ **B2**

- **I like to drive fast. Someday, I want to have a sports car.**
  （我喜歡開快車。我希望有朝一日能擁有一台跑車。）
  * sports car「跑車」

- **I'm not that crazy about driving myself, but I like to go for drives with my boyfriend.**
  （我並不熱衷於自己開車，但是我喜歡和男朋友去兜風。）
  * be crazy about...「熱衷於……」

- **Actually, I haven't gotten my driver's license yet.**
  （事實上，我還沒拿到駕照。）
  * driver's license「駕照」

Vocabulary 具體描述自己的好用字！

highway 高速公路 / traffic jam 塞車 / sign 標誌 / traffic light 紅綠燈；交通號誌 / traffic is heavy / light 車流量大 / 小 / new car 新車 / used car 中古車；二手車 / jalopy [dʒə`lɑpɪ] 老爺車 / subcompact car 輕型小汽車 / compact car 小汽車 / large-sized vehicle 大型車 / dump truck 傾卸車 / motorcycle 摩托車 / moped 電動腳踏車 / hybrid car 油電混合車 / rental car 租用車 / driving school 駕訓班 / convertible 敞篷車 / station wagon 旅行車 / sedan 轎車 / SUV (Sport Utility Vehicle) 休旅車 / automatic 自排 / manual / stick shift 手排 / rent a car 租車 / buy a new car 買一輛新車 / scrap a vehicle 報廢一輛車 / rent a parking space for NT$5,000 a month 以每月 5 千台幣租一個車位 / official vehicle inspection 正式車輛檢驗 / legal inspection 法定檢驗 / licence tax 牌照稅 / motor vehicle tax 汽車稅 / liability insurance 責任險 / voluntary insurance 自願險

040

Are you happy with your life now?
你滿不滿意現在的生活？

Dialogue 實戰會話　　　　　　　　　　　🔊 Track 41

A：**Are you happy with your life now?**
（你滿不滿意現在的生活？）

B1：**For the most part. I wish I had more money, though.** ☞
（大部分都滿意。不過我希望我有更多錢。）

A：**Why do you say that?**
（為何這麼說？）

B2：**I'd like to move to a bigger place. My apartment is a little cramped.** ☞
（我想搬進較大的房子住。我現在住的公寓太小了點。）

＊ for the most part「大致上；大部分」；cramped「狹窄的」

✎ **Exercise** 請寫下自己的答案並試著說出來！

A：**Are you happy with your life now?**
B1：

A：**Why do you say that?**
B2：

Substitution 更多回應說法！

☞ B1

- **More or less. I think I'm a very lucky person.**
  （大致滿意。我想我是個很幸運的人。）
  * more or less「大致；差不多」

- **I'm never quite satisfied, but I think that's a good thing.**
  （我從沒完全滿足過，不過我覺得這是件好事。）
  * quite「完全地」

- **To be honest, I'm not happy with my job.**
  （老實說，我對我的工作並不滿意。）
  * to be honest「老實說」

☞ B2

- **Well, I'm blessed with a loving husband and two beautiful kids.**
  （嗯，我很幸運地擁有一位鍾愛我的老公，還有兩個漂亮的孩子。）
  * be blessed with...「有幸擁有…」

- **I don't want to become complacent. I think it's important to keep taking on new challenges.**
  （我不想得意自滿。我認為不斷接受新的挑戰是很重要的。）
  * complacent「得意的；自滿的」

- **I don't feel like I'm living up to my potential. I want to do something more challenging.**
  （我覺得我還沒發揮所有的潛力。我想做些更有挑戰性的事。）
  * live up to...「實踐……」

Vocabulary 具體描述自己的好用字！

lead a fulfilling life 過著充實的生活 / work is satisfying 工作很令人滿意 / feel like something is missing from one's life 感覺人生好像少了些什麼 / one's love life leaves something to be desired 愛情生活有些不足 / be satisfied / dissatisfied with home 對家庭很滿意 / 不滿意 / romance 愛情 / income 收入 / private life 私生活 / want to live in a bigger house 想住大一點的房子 / make more money 多賺點錢 / eat more delicious food 多吃點美食 / indulge more 多享受一些 / spend more time with one's kids 多花點時間陪孩子 / be in a better romantic relationship 愛情更得意 / travel more 多去旅行 / have more time for one's interests 有更多時間做有興趣的事 / want more time / money 想要更多時間 / 金錢 / a more interesting job 更有趣的工作

041

Do you have any habits that you want to change?
有沒有什麼習慣是你想改掉的？

Dialogue 實戰會話　　　　　　　　🎧 Track 42

A：**Do you have any habits that you want to change?**
（有沒有什麼習慣是你想改掉的？）

B1：**Yeah, I have a bad habit of judging people.** ☞
（有啊，我有批評他人的壞習慣。）

A：**Really? Is there a person that you model yourself after?**
（真的嗎？有沒有誰是你仿效的對象？）

B2：**I wish I were more like my mother. She never has a bad word for anyone.** ☞
（我希望自己能更像我母親。她從來不說別人的壞話。）

* judge「批評」；model after...「以……為模範；以……為榜樣」；
  have a bad word for someone「說某人的壞話」

✎ **Exercise** 請寫下自己的答案並試著說出來！

A：**Do you have any habits that you want to change?**
B1：
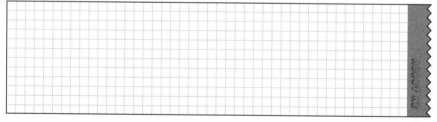

A：**Really? Is there a person that you model yourself after?**
B2：
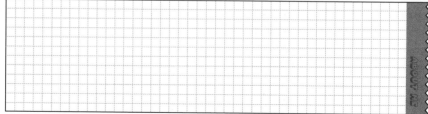

☞ **B1**

- **I wish I were better at expressing myself.**
  （我希望更善於表達自己。）
  * good at + V-ing「擅長……」

- **I have a bad habit of putting things off until the last minute.**
  （我有把事情拖到最後一分鐘才做的壞習慣。）
  * put off「延後；拖延」

- **I don't have a long attention span. I tend to get distracted easily.**
  （我無法長時間集中注意力。我常常很容易就分心了。）
  * attention span「注意力的持續時間」；get distracted「分心」

☞ **B2**

- **I wouldn't call him my role model, but my husband tends to be more open with his feelings.**
  （我不至於把他稱為榜樣，但是我先生比較能坦然表達他的感覺。）
  * be open with...「不隱藏……」

- **My wife never procrastinates. I wish I were more like her in that way.**
  （我太太從不拖延。我希望我這方面能更像她一點。）
  * procrastinate [proˋkræstə͵net]「拖延；耽擱」

- **My boss is very focused. I admire that about him.**
  （我的老闆非常專注。我很欽佩他這點。）
  * focused「專注的」

VOCABULARY 具體描述自己的好用字！

bad /good habit 壞 / 好習慣 / have a tendency to... 有……的傾向 / can't stop... 忍不住…… / break a habit 戒掉某個習慣 / try to change one's habits 試著改變個人的習慣 / give up smoking 戒菸 / don't get enough exercise 運動量不夠 / oversleep 睡過頭 / stay up late 熬夜 / eat too much 吃太多 / drink too much 喝太多（酒）/ tend to eat and drink to excess 容易暴飲暴食 / be short-tempered 脾氣暴躁 / too insensitive 太遲鈍 / oversensitive 過度敏感 / get nervous easily 容易緊張 / talk too much 話太多 / be too laid back 太散漫 / be too much on the go 過度活躍、忙碌 / get carried away easily 容易得意忘形 / be shy around strangers 怕生 / be too trusting of people 過於信任他人 / be too suspicious of people 過度猜忌他人 / a control freak 控制狂

turn over in bed ▶ 在床上翻身	**women-only car** ▶ 女性專用車廂
make the bed ▶ 鋪床	**sleep past one's station** ▶ 睡過站
brush one's teeth ▶ 刷牙	**air out** ▶ 通風
rinse one's mouth ▶ 漱口	**do the laundry** ▶ 洗衣服
smooth down one's messy hair ▶ 整理亂髮	**have a big / heavy lunch** ▶ 吃豐盛的午餐
do one's hair ▶ 做頭髮	**have a chat on the Internet** ▶ 在網上聊天
put in one's contact lenses ▶ 戴隱形眼鏡	**spend the day doing nothing** ▶ 一整天無所事事
put on makeup ▶ 化妝	**have a well-balanced diet** ▶ 飲食均衡
check one's fortune on... ▶ 在……上確認運勢	**have a drink with one's dinner** ▶ 晚飯時小酌一杯
feed the dog ▶ 餵狗	**take off one's makeup** ▶ 卸妝
give someone a ride to... ▶ 載（某人）到……	**read a book in the bathtub** ▶ 邊泡澡邊看書
doze off on the train ▶ 在火車上打瞌睡	**apply a facial mask** ▶ 敷面膜
skim through the newspaper ▶ 瀏覽報紙	**grind one's teeth** ▶ 磨牙
give up one's seat to... ▶ 讓座給……	**talk in one's sleep** ▶ 說夢話

對話回應好用句 ③：贊成·同意

「確實如此」

● **That's true.**（確實如此。）
  ▶ 聽了對方的話後，表示「的確如此、是啊、沒錯」等同意對方之意。

● **True.**（正是如此。）
  ▶ 和 That's true. 一樣，表示認同對方說法。

● **Right.**（沒錯。）
  ※ 和「正是如此」的意義相同，但較為輕鬆隨興。

● **You got that right.**（你說得一點都沒錯。）
  ▶ 此回應表達的就是「正是如此」之意。get that right 是「正確掌握了重點」的意思。

● **Sad but true.**（雖然很悲哀，但是確實是這樣。）
  ▶ 對於不想接受的事實，表示「很可惜，但是又不得不承認」的感覺。

Unit 4

興趣・嗜好
Interests and hobbies

　　跟興趣或嗜好有關的話題總是能讓對話更熱絡。
為了製造話題，一定要先妥善整理好和自身相關的資訊才行。
如果還能進一步主動以英語發問，就能激盪出更好的互動。

What kind of books do you like?
Do you collect anything?
Do you have any interests?
Do you have a special skill?
What kind of trips do you like to take?
• • •

appearance

name

Taiwan culture

friends

work

dreams

interest

families

religion

experience

042

What's your favorite sport?
你最喜歡什麼運動?

Dialogue 實戰會話　　　　　　　　　　　🎧 Track 43

A：What's your favorite sport?
（你最喜歡什麼運動?）

B1：I like to watch baseball, but I don't actually play any sports. ☞
（我喜歡看棒球,但是我事實上不做任何運動。）

A：Really? Personally, I think I need to get some more exercise.
（真的嗎?我個人覺得自己該多做點運動才好。）

B2：Yeah, me too. I'm thinking of joining a health club. Do you know a good place? ☞
（是啊,我也這麼覺得。我正在考慮是否要加入健身俱樂部,你知道哪家比較好嗎?）

✎ **Exercise** 請寫下自己的答案並試著說出來!

A：What's your favorite sport?
B1：

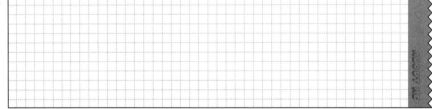

A：Really? Personally, I think I need to get some more exercise.
B2：

Substitution 更多回應說法！

☞ B1

- I'm not really into sports, but if I have a player to cheer for, I enjoy watching it.

  （我對運動沒什麼興趣，不過如果我有想支持的運動員，就會看得很開心。）

  ＊ cheer for... 「替……加油；支持……」

- I like all kinds of sports. I'm a very competitive person.

  （我喜歡各種運動，我是個競爭心很強的人。）

  ＊ competitive 「競爭的；競爭心很強的」

- I'm not very good at sports. I like to go skiing in the winter, though.

  （我不是很擅長運動。不過我很喜歡冬天去滑雪。）

  ＊ be good at... 「擅長……」；though 「不過」

☞ B2

- You think so? You seem to be in pretty good shape to me.

  （你這麼覺得嗎？對我來說你的身體狀況已經相當好了。）

  ＊ be in good shape 「維持良好體態」

- I recommend running. It's easy to do, and it's free! Since I started running, I feel great.

  （我推薦跑步，既簡單又不必花錢！自從我開始跑步後，感覺好極了。）

  ＊ recommend 「推薦」

- I play futsal every Saturday. You're welcome to join us.

  （我每週六都會去踢五人制足球，歡迎你一起加入。）

  ＊ futsal [ˈfuˌsæl] 「五人制足球」

VOCABULARY 具體描述自己的好用字！

team sport 團隊運動 / individual sport 個人運動 / spectator sport 觀賞性的運動 / be a big fan of the New Yorker Knicks 是紐約尼克隊的忠實球迷 / play on a team 在球隊中打球 / watch sports on TV / at the stadium 看電視播放 / 在體育館看運動比賽 / learn martial arts 學習武術 / judo 柔道 / karate [kəˈrɑtɪ] 空手道 / do yoga every day 每天做瑜珈 / work out at the gym 去健身房健身 / go jogging / walking 去慢跑 / 散步 / be in the rhythmic gymnastics club 加入韻律體操社 / participate in a bike road race 參加自行車公路賽 / win an archery [ˈɑrtʃərɪ] championship 贏得射箭比賽冠軍 / have been playing soccer since someone was in junior high 從國中就開始踢足球

043

What kind of TV shows do you like?
你喜歡哪種電視節目？

Dialogue 實戰會話　　　　　　　　　　　　🎙 Track 44

A：What kind of TV shows do you like?
（你喜歡哪種電視節目？）

B1：I like infotainment-type programs, like quiz shows. ☞
（我喜歡寓教於樂的節目，例如益智問答節目。）

A：Do you watch DVDs?
（你看 DVD 嗎？）

B2：Not that much. I prefer to watch movies on the big screen. ☞
（不太看。我比較喜歡在大螢幕上看電影。）

TIPS infotainment 為「寓教於樂；資訊娛樂化」的意思，由 information 和 entertainment 組合而成。

✎ **Exercise** 請寫下自己的答案並試著說出來！

A：What kind of TV shows do you like?

B1：

A：Do you watch DVDs?

B2：

Substitution 更多回應說法！

☞ B1

● **I don't watch TV much these days. I can't stand all the commercials.**
（我最近不太看電視。我受不了那一大堆的廣告。）
* stand「忍受」

● **Recently, I've gotten hooked on Korean dramas. They have lots of foreign dramas on satellite TV.**
（我最近迷上了韓劇。衛星電視播好多的外國戲劇。）
* get hooked on...「沉迷於……」；satellite TV「衛星電視」

● **I like anything, but I tend to watch comedy and variety programs.**
（我什麼都愛，不過我比較常看喜劇和綜藝節目。）

☞ B2

● **Yeah, I rent two or three DVDs a week. It's so much cheaper than going to the movies.**
（看啊，我一週會借個 兩、三片 DVD。這比去電影院看要便宜多了。）

● **Actually, I have a huge DVD collection. I can lend you some DVDs, if you like.**
（事實上我收藏了一大堆的 DVD。如果你想看，我可以借你一些。）
* collection「收集；收藏」

● **No, I prefer to watch videos online. I think DVDs will be obsolete in a few years.**
（不了，我喜歡上網看影片。我覺得 DVD 再幾年就會被淘汰了。）
* obsolete [`absə͵lit]「過時的」

VOCABULARY 具體描述自己的好用字！

digital terrestrial TV broadcasting 地面數位電視廣播 / commercial network 商業電視台（廣播電台）/ public TV 公共電視 / bilingual broadcast 雙語播放 / broadcast with subtitles 字幕播放 / tabloid TV news show 八卦電視新聞節目 / late night TV 深夜電視節目 / shopping program 購物節目 / sports live show 運動實況轉播節目 / documentary 紀錄片 / music program 音樂節目 / educational program 教育性節目 / miniseries 迷你影集 / cartoon 卡通片 / soap opera 肥皂劇 / news program 新聞節目 / weather forecast 天氣預報 / emergency earthquake warning 緊急地震警報 / tsunami warning 海嘯警報 / the 10th episode of the 5th season of *Lost*《Lost 檔案》第 5 季第 10 集（美國影集）

What kind of movies do you like?
你喜歡哪種電影？

Dialogue 實戰會話　　　　　　　　　🎧 Track 45

> **A：What kind of movies do you like?**
> （你喜歡哪種電影？）
>
> **B1：I like fantasy movies. I've seen all the *Harry Potter* movies.** ☞
> （我喜歡奇幻類電影。《哈利波特》的每一集我都看過了。）
>
> **A：Really? What's your favorite movie of all time?**
> （真的嗎？那你一直最愛哪一部電影？）
>
> **B2：Maybe *The Lord of the Rings*. I've seen it seven times!** ☞
> （可能是《魔戒》吧。我看了 7 遍！）
>
> ＊ *The Lord of the Rings* 中文片名為《魔戒》，以 J·R·R·托爾金 (Tolkien) 的同名小說《魔戒》三部曲改編而成，為奇幻史詩電影中的經典之作。

✎ **Exercise** 請寫下自己的答案並試著說出來！

A：What kind of movies do you like?

B1：

A：Really? What's your favorite movie of all time?

B2：

Substitution 更多回應說法！

☞ B1

- I prefer Japanese movies to foreign movies. Especially Japanese anime.

  （我比較喜歡日本電影，尤其是日本動畫，比較不喜歡外國電影。）

- I don't watch movies that much, but I tend to like romantic comedies.

  （我不常看電影，不過我偏好浪漫喜劇。）

  ＊ romantic comedy「浪漫喜劇」

- I'm not into big Hollywood blockbuster-type movies. I prefer down-to-earth movies.

  （我不怎麼喜歡好萊塢的那種賣座鉅片。我比較喜歡樸實的電影。）

  ＊ blockbuster-type「賣座鉅片型的」；down-to-earth「實際的；樸實的」

☞ B2

- It's a toss-up between *Memento* and *Inception*. I love Christopher Nolan's movies.

  （《記憶拼圖》和《全面啟動》我都喜歡，好難抉擇。我很喜歡克理斯多佛・諾藍拍的片。）

  ＊ be a toss-up between A and B「很難決定是 A 還是 B」

- I'm not sure, but the best movie I saw this year was *500 Days of Summer*.

  （我不確定，不過我今年看過最棒的電影是《戀夏 500 日》。）

- That would have to be *Star Wars*. I never get tired of watching it.

  （那一定就是《星際大戰》了。我怎麼都看不膩。）

ⓋⓄⒸⒶⒷⓊⓁⒶⓇⓎ 具體描述自己的好用字！

sci-fi (= science-fiction) 科幻 / mystery 懸疑 / musical 音樂劇 / horror 恐怖 / anime 動畫 / romance 浪漫愛情 / comedy 喜劇 / tragedy 悲劇 / adventure 冒險 / war 戰爭 / director 導演 / screenplay 電影腳本；劇本 / original work 原著 / starring role 主角 / leading actor 男主角 / supporting actress 女配角 / coming to theaters in March 2020 2020 年 3 月上映 / movie theater 電影院 / cinema complex 複合式電影院 / a box office smash 一部賣座強片 / number one at the box office 賣座第一 / a piece of crap movie 一部爛片 / a terrible movie 一部很糟的電影 / be based on the novel by... 改編自……小說 / win an Oscar for best screenplay 贏得奧斯卡最佳劇本獎

045

What kind of music do you listen to?

你都聽哪種音樂？

Dialogue 實戰會話　　　　　　　　　　　　Track 46

A：**What kind of music do you listen to?**
（你都聽哪種音樂？）

B1：**I like all kinds of music, but mostly I listen to pop music.** ☞
（我各種音樂都喜歡，不過我大部分時候是聽流行音樂。）

A：**Really? Who's your favorite singer?**
（真的嗎？那你最喜歡哪位歌手？）

B2：**I'm kind of embarrassed to say it, but I'm crazy about Michael Jackson.** ☞
（我有點不好意思說，不過我很迷麥可傑克森。）

＊ be embarrassed to...「不好意思……」

✎ **Exercise** 請寫下自己的答案並試著說出來！

A：**What kind of music do you listen to?**

B1：

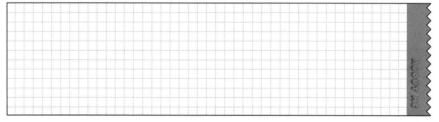

A：**Really? Who's your favorite singer?**

B2：

Substitution 更多回應說法！

☞ B1

- **I used to listen to nothing but rock music, but as I get older, I listen to classical music more.**
  （我以前只聽搖滾樂，不過隨著年紀漸長，我開始聽比較多古典樂。）
  * nothing but...「僅只……」

- **I can listen to almost anything except rap music.**
  （除了饒舌歌之外，我幾乎什麼都聽。）
  * except...「除了……之外」

- **I like soul music, but I listen mostly to old school stuff.**
  （我喜歡靈魂樂，不過我聽的多半是舊派的東西。）
  * old school stuff「舊派的東西」

☞ B2

- **I don't have one particular favorite, but I've always liked Madonna's music.**
  （我沒有特別喜歡哪一位，不過我一直都很喜歡瑪丹娜的音樂。）
  * particular favorite「特別喜愛的人、事、物」

- **You've probably never heard of her. She's not that popular even in Taiwan.**
  （你可能沒聽過這個人。即使是在台灣她也不太紅。）
  * even「即使……」

- **I like the lead singer of Coldplay. His voice gives me goosebumps.**
  （我喜歡酷玩樂團的主唱。他的聲音能讓我起雞皮疙瘩。）
  * give someone goosebumps「讓（某人）起雞皮疙瘩」

ＶＯＣＡＢＵＬＡＲＹ 具體描述自己的好用字！

jazz 爵士 / **fusion** 融合 / **heavy metal** 重金屬 / **rock** 搖滾 / **punk rock** 龐克搖滾 / **soul** 靈魂 / **R&B** 節奏藍調 (= Rhythm and Blues) / **easy listening** 輕音樂 / **hip hop** 嘻哈 / **rap** 饒舌 / **alternative** 另類 / **house music** 浩室音樂（一種電子舞曲）/ **trance** 出神（一種電子音樂）/ **60's rock** 六〇年代搖滾 / **early jazz** 早期爵士 / **Japanese teen idol music** 日本偶像團體的歌曲 / **listen to music on one's portable music player / MP3 player / iPod / headphones / earphones** 用可攜式音樂播放器 / MP3 播放器 / iPod / 頭戴式耳機 / 耳機聽音樂 / **types of music I like / I dislike / I'm not interested in** 我喜歡 / 討厭 / 沒興趣的音樂類型 / **can't live without music** 沒有音樂就活不下去 / **what's popular now** 現在流行的（音樂）

046

What kind of books do you like?
你喜歡哪種書？

Dialogue 實戰會話　　　　　　　　　　　　🔾 Track 47

> **A**：**What kind of books do you like?**
> （你喜歡哪種書？）
>
> **B1**：**I read anything, but I particularly like mysteries.** ☞
> （我什麼書都看，不過特別喜歡推理小說。）
>
> **A**：**Really? Who's your favorite writer?**
> （真的嗎？你最喜歡哪位作家？）
>
> **B2**：**My favorite is Kanae Minato. Unfortunately, I don't think her books have been translated into English.** ☞
> （我最喜歡湊佳苗。很可惜，我想她的書並沒有被翻成英文。）
>
> ＊ be translated into... 「被翻譯成……」
>
> **TIPS** 湊佳苗為日本當代推理小說家，作品曾獲多項文學獎。著有《告白》、《贖罪》、《為了 N》等書。

✏️ **Exercise** 請寫下自己的答案並試著說出來！

A：**What kind of books do you like?**

B1：
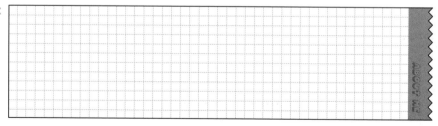

A：**Really? Who's your favorite writer?**

B2：
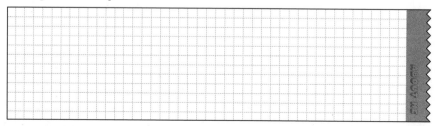

Substitution 更多回應說法！

☞ **B1**

- **I like to read autobiographies of famous people.**
  （我喜歡讀名人的自傳。）
  * autobiography「自傳」

- **I'm not much of a bookworm. I like to read comics, though.**
  （我沒那麼愛看書。不過我很愛看漫畫。）
  * bookworm「書呆子；（愛看書的）書蟲」

- **I'm a voracious reader of sci-fi novels. These days I download books to save money and space.**
  （我看很多科幻小說。最近我還會上網下載電子書，省錢又省空間。）
  * voracious [voˋreʃəs]「貪婪的」

☞ **B2**

- **I like Stephen King. Someday I want to be able to read his novels in English.**
  （我喜歡史蒂芬金。我希望有一天能讀懂他的英文小說。）

- **I don't have a particular favorite. Can you recommend someone who is easy to read?**
  （我沒有特別喜歡哪一位。你可以推薦一位作品較容易閱讀的作家嗎？）
  * easy to read「容易閱讀」

- **There are lots of good manga writers, but Osamu Tezuka is the greatest hands-down.**
  （好的漫畫家很多，但是手塚治虫毫無疑問是最棒的。）
  * hands-down「毫無疑問地；容易地」

- - - - - - - **VOCABULARY** 具體描述自己的好用字！ - - - - - - -

novel 小說 / **manga** [ˋmænɡɑ] 漫畫（尤指以成人主題為主的日本漫畫）/ **detective novel** 偵探小說 / **science fiction** 科幻小說 / **fantasy** 奇幻小說 / **romance** 愛情小說 / **horror** 恐怖小說 / **biography** 傳記 / **general fiction** 一般小說 / **non-fiction** 非小說類 / **self-help** 自我啓發類書籍 / **short stories** 短篇故事 / **poetry** 詩集 / **cell phone novel** 手機小說 / **work of literature** 文學作品 / **popular novel** 通俗小說 / **weekly** 週刊 / **monthly** 月刊 / **quarterly magazine** 季刊 / **buy a book on Amazon** 在 Amazon 網站買書 / **read a book on one's iPad / Reader / Kindle / smart phone** 用 iPad／閱讀器／ Kindle ／智慧型手機看書 / **install a book reader app** 安裝電子書閱讀器程式 / **download a book** 下載電子書

047

Can you play an instrument?
你會演奏樂器嗎？

Dialogue 實戰會話　　　　　　　　　　🔊 Track 48

> A：Can you play an instrument?
> （你會演奏樂器嗎？）
>
> B1：I took piano lessons when I was little, but I completely forgot how to play.
> （我小時候有學過鋼琴，但是現在完全忘了怎麼彈。）
>
> A：Seriously? Is there an instrument that you wish you could play?
> （真的假的？有沒有什麼樂器是你很想學會的？）
>
> B2：Someday I want to go back and learn the piano again.
> （我希望有一天能重新學會彈鋼琴。）
>
> ＊ go back「回去；追溯」

✎ **Exercise** 請寫下自己的答案並試著說出來！

A：Can you play an instrument?

B1：

A：Seriously? Is there an instrument that you wish you could play?

B2：

108

☞ **B1**

- I used to play the guitar when I was in college. I was in a band, actually.

  （念大學時我曾彈吉他。事實上，我當時參加了一個樂團。）

- No. I took violin lessons when I was in high school, but I was a bad student.

  （不會。高中時我學過小提琴，但是我學得並不好。）

  * bad student「程度不好的學生；成績不好的學生」

- Does the recorder count? I learned how to play the recorder in elementary school.

  （直笛也算嗎？我在小學時學過吹直笛。）

  * recorder「直笛」

☞ **B2**

- If I had longer fingers, I would study the piano.

  （如果我有修長的手指，我會學鋼琴。）

- I really want to learn how to play the guitar. Would you happen to know a good teacher?

  （我真的很想學吉他，你會不會剛好有認識好老師？）

  * happen to...「剛好……；碰巧……」

- I don't have the patience to learn how to play.

  （我沒耐性，無法學會演奏樂器。）

VOCABULARY 具體描述自己的好用字！

have perfect pitch 擁有絕對音感 / have no ear for music 沒音感 / have a tin ear 音痴 / be musically talented 有音樂天分 / have a gift for music 有音樂天賦 / be able to read music 看得懂樂譜 / play flute in a junior high orchestra club 在國中管弦樂團裡吹長笛 / play drums / play backup guitar / play bass / sing in a high school light music club 在高中的輕音樂社團裡打鼓 / 吉他伴奏 / 彈貝斯 / 主唱 / be in the local chorus [kɔrəs] 參加本地的合唱團 / be an orchestra conductor 擔任管弦樂隊的指揮 / play professionally in an orchestra 在管弦樂團內擔任專業演奏 / play the cello 彈奏大提琴 / can't hold down the chords on a guitar 無法按住吉他和弦 / can't make a noise on a clarinet [klærɪˋnɛt] 單簧管（黑管）吹不出聲音

048

Do you collect anything?
你有收集任何東西嗎？

Dialogue 實戰會話   🎧 Track 49

A：Do you collect anything?
（你有收集任何東西嗎？）

B1：I'm a coin collector. I collect coins from all over the world. ☞
（我收集硬幣。我收集世界各地的硬幣。）

A：That's interesting. What's the attraction?
（真有意思。硬幣的魅力何在？）

B2：Well, I like to travel, and looking at coins reminds me of all the places I've visited—and want to visit. ☞
（嗯，我喜歡旅行，而看見硬幣就能讓我回想起所有我曾去過的以及想去的地方。）

* remind someone of... 「使（某人）回想起……」

✎ **Exercise** 請寫下自己的答案並試著說出來！

A：Do you collect anything?

B1：
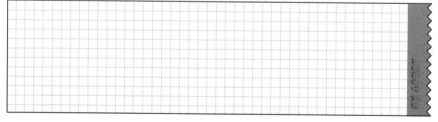

A：That's interesting. What's the attraction?

B2：
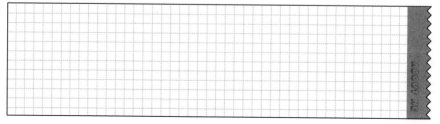

Substitution 更多回應說法！

☞ **B1**

- **I'm not exactly a collector, but I like bags. I have dozens of bags.**
  （我不算是收藏家，但是我很喜歡包包。我有幾十個包包。）
  * dozens of...「幾十個……；好幾打的……」

- **It's kind of a geeky thing to do, but I collect figurines.**
  （我的興趣有點古怪，我收集公仔。）
  * geeky「古怪的」；figurine「公仔；小玩偶」

- **I don't collect them as a hobby, but I have a vast collection of CDs.**
  （我不是為了興趣而收集，但是我收藏了大量的 CD。）
  * vast collection「大量的收藏」

☞ **B2**

- **I don't know, but I've been told that people who like bags are narcissists.**
  （我不知道耶，不過我曾聽別人說過，喜歡包包的人都是自戀狂。）
  * narcissist [nɑrˋsɪsɪt]「自戀狂」

- **I suppose it's a way of expressing my individuality.**
  （我想這是一種表達自我的方式吧。）
  * suppose「猜想」；individuality [ˏɪndəˏvɪdʒʊˋælətɪ] n. 個性；個人特徵

- **They're so fascinating! I think people who don't understand the appeal are really missing out.**
  （它們超迷人的！我覺得不懂其魅力的人真是虧大了。）
  * fascinating「迷人的」；miss out「錯失」

ＶＯＣＡＢＵＬＡＲＹ 具體描述自己的好用字！

stuffed doll 填充玩偶 / **ceramic** [səˋræmɪk] 陶器 / **limited edition cosmetic** 限量版化妝品 / **stationery** 文具 / **stamp** 郵票 / **baseball card** 棒球卡 / **antique** 古董 / **marble** 彈珠 / **anime DVD** 動畫 DVD / **character goods** 動漫角色商品 / **video game software** 電視遊戲軟體 / **various beer cans** 各種啤酒罐 / **game cards** 遊戲卡 / **comics for boys** 少年漫畫 / **Apple products** 蘋果公司的產品 / **autographs of one's idols** 偶像的親筆簽名 / **John Lennon CDs** 約翰藍儂的 CD / **all of the Gundam models** 所有鋼彈模型 / **railway paraphernalia** [ˏpærəfəˋnelɪə] 有關鐵路（火車）的各種東西 / **have a big collection of...** 擁有大量的……收藏 / **throw out one's collection of...** 將某人的……收藏扔掉 / **have a thing for...** 著迷於……

049

Do you like to go shopping, or do you prefer to use the Internet?
你喜歡親自去購物，還是上網買東西？

Dialogue 實戰會話　　　　　　　　　　　🎧 Track 50

A： Do you like to go shopping, or do you prefer to use the Internet?
（你喜歡親自去購物，還是上網買東西？）

B1： I like to shop, but nowadays I do most of my shopping online. ☞
（我喜歡親自去購物，但是最近我幾乎都是上網買。）

A： Why is that?
（為何會這樣？）

B2： It's so convenient! And when you consider the money you spend on transportation, it's also cheaper. ☞
（很方便啊！而且如果把交通費考慮進去，網購也比較便宜。）

* convenient「方便的」; transportation「交通運輸」

✏️ **Exercise** 請寫下自己的答案並試著說出來！

A： Do you like to go shopping, or do you prefer to use the Internet?

B1：

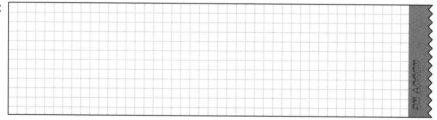

A： Why is that?

B2：

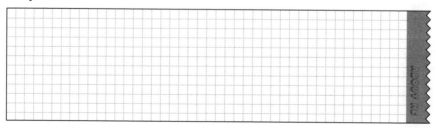

Substitution 更多回應說法！

☞ B1

- **I sometimes buy things online, but I prefer to shop at bricks-and-mortar stores.**
  （我有時候會上網購物，不過我比較喜歡在實體店面買東西。）
  * buy online「上網購物」；bricks-and-mortar「傳統的；有實體的」

- **I use both. It depends on what I'm buying.**
  （兩種都會。這要看我想買的是什麼。）
  * depend on...「依據⋯⋯；取決於⋯⋯」

- **I sometimes use auction sites, but mostly I shop at real stores.**
  （我有時會利用拍賣網站，不過通常都在實體商店購物。）
  * auction site「拍賣網站」

☞ B2

- **Everyone says it's safe, but I still worry about giving away my credit card information.**
  （大家都說網購很安全，但是我對於必須交出自己的信用卡資訊這件事還是很不放心。）
  * give away「交出；洩露」

- **With some things, it's important to see the actual product. Like shoes, for example.**
  （有些東西看到實際商品很重要。例如鞋子之類的。）

- **Call me old-fashioned, but I like to be able to talk to the salesclerks.**
  （就當我是老古板吧，但是我喜歡能和店員對話。）
  * old-fashioned「老派的；過時的」

Ⓥ𝕠𝕔𝕒𝕓𝕦𝕝𝕒𝕣𝕪 具體描述自己的好用字！

do window shopping 逛街 / often use online stores 經常利用網路商店 / items sold exclusively online 只限網路販售之商品 / browse through online shops 瀏覽網路商店 / bid 出價 / put up for auction 上架拍賣 / buy a book on Amazon 在亞馬遜書店買書 / pay by credit card 以信用卡付款 / buy a product together online 網路團購 / shop at an online supermarket 在網路超市購物 / put something in one's shopping cart 把某物放入購物車 / be delivered on the following day 隔日出貨 / free shipping for orders of NT$ 1,000 or more 台幣 1,000 元以上免運費 / pay COD 貨到付款（宅配代收）（**COD = cash on delivery**，在美國並不常見，他們通常採用信用卡付款）

050

What's your type?
你喜歡哪一類型的人？

Dialogue 實戰會話　　　　　　　　　　　🔊 Track 51

A：**What's your type?**
（你喜歡哪一類型的人？）

B1：**I tend to go for the athletic type.** ☞
（我偏好運動型的。）

A：**What do you consider most important?**
（你覺得最重要的是什麼？）

B2：**I think generosity is important. I can't stand cheapskates.** ☞
（我覺得慷慨最重要。我無法忍受小氣鬼。）

＊ go for... 「追求……；喜歡……」；generosity 「慷慨」；cheapskate 「小氣鬼」

TIPS 第一個問題也可說成：What's your type of guy / woman?（你喜歡哪種類型的男生 / 女生？）。

✎ **Exercise** 請寫下自己的答案並試著說出來！

A：**What's your type?**

B1：

A：**What do you consider most important?**

B2：

Substitution 更多回應說法！

☞ B1

- **I don't have a specific type, but artistic guys turn me off.**

  （我沒有特別喜歡的類型，但是藝術型的男生會讓我倒胃口。）

  * turn someone off「讓某人倒胃口」

- **I like women who have a mind of their own.**

  （我喜歡有自己想法的女生。）

  * have a mind of one's own「有自己的想法」

- **There's something about foreign men that attracts me.**

  （外國男人有某些特質很吸引我。）

  * attract「吸引」

☞ B2

- **A sense of humor is important. I want to be with someone who is fun to talk to.**

  （幽默感很重要，我想和聊起來有趣的人在一起。）

  * sense of humor「幽默感」

- **He has to be a confident person. I'm tired of going out with needy men.**

  （他必須是個有自信的人。對於和很需要愛的男人交往我已經感到厭煩了。）

  * needy「對愛情飢渴的」

- **The most important thing is that we have similar values.**

  （最重要的是我們要有相似的價值觀。）

  * have similar values「有相似的價值觀」

VOCABULARY 具體描述自己的好用字！

a romantic 浪漫的人 / a jock [jɑk] 運動健將 / a free spirit 無拘無束的人 / witty 機智的 / be good with children 和孩子處得很好 / be a good / bad dresser 很會 / 不會穿衣服的人 / kind 善良的 / geeky 古怪的 / intellectual 知識份子 / artistic 有藝術氣息的 / (very) beautiful（非常）漂亮的 / (very) good-looking（非常）好看的 / (very) ordinary（非常）普通的 / (very) unattractive-looking 長得（非常）沒有魅力的 / homely（人或容貌）不好看的（美式）/ independent 獨立的 / feminine 女性化的 / graceful 優雅的 / charming 迷人的 / someone with a cute smile 笑起來很可愛的人 / a strong-spirited woman 意志堅強的女性 / masculine [ˋmæskjəlɪn] 有男子氣概的 / effeminate [əˋfɛmənɪt] 沒男子氣概的 / dependable 可靠的 / generous 大方的；慷慨的 / considerate 體貼的 / tall 高的 / rich 有錢的 / sharp 精明的

051

Do you have any interests?
你有沒有什麼興趣嗜好？

Dialogue 實戰會話　　　　　　　　　　🔊 Track 52

A：Do you have any interests?
（你有沒有什麼興趣嗜好？）

B1：I'm interested in personal development. ☞
（我對自我開發很有興趣。）

A：Really? Is there something that you'd like to do in the future?
（真的嗎？你將來有想做些什麼事嗎？）

B2：I meditate a little bit every day, but I want to take it up more seriously. ☞
（我每天都做一點冥想，但是我想更認真地做這件事。）

* meditate「冥想；沉思」；take up「開始從事」

✎ **Exercise** 請寫下自己的答案並試著說出來！

A：Do you have any interests?
B1：

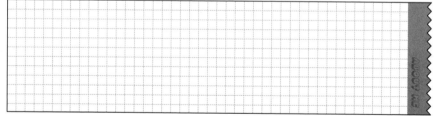

A：Really? Is there something that you'd like to do in the future?
B2：

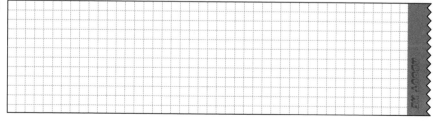

116

Substitution 更多回應說法！

☞ B1

- **I like reading, listening to music, watching movies, and cooking.**
  （我喜歡閱讀、聽音樂、看電影和烹飪。）

- **I like handicrafts—beadmaking, pottery, crocheting — you name it.**
  （我喜歡做手工藝——串珠、陶藝、勾針編織－你說得出來的我都喜歡。）

  * crocheting [kro`ʃetɪŋ]「編織」；you name it「任何你說得出來的」

- **Actually, I don't have any real hobbies, unless you call going drinking with friends a hobby.**
  （事實上，我沒有任何真正的嗜好，除非跟朋友喝酒也算是一種嗜好。）

  * unless...「除非……」

☞ B2

- **I'm thinking of starting a reading group.**
  （我正考慮要組個讀書會。）

  * reading group「讀書會」

- **If possible, I'd like to make things not just for myself, but for others, too.**
  （如果有可能的話，我不只想替自己，也想替別人做一些東西。）

  * if possible「如果有可能」

- **I don't know what I want to do, but I feel like I need a change. A new hobby would do me good.**
  （我不知道自己想做什麼，不過我覺得我需要改變。新的嗜好對我可能有好處。）

  * do someone good「對某人有益」

VOCABULARY 具體描述自己的好用字！

gardening 園藝 / sewing 裁縫 / knitting 編織 / making illustrated postcards 製作繪圖明信片 / artificial flower making 人造花製作 / wood carving 木雕 / sculpture 雕刻 / fishing 釣魚 / listening to music 聽音樂 / motorcycling 騎摩托車 / making jewelry 製作珠寶 / social dance 社交舞 / yoga 瑜珈 / cycling 騎自行車 / camping 露營 / home improvement 居家修繕 / creative cuisine 創意料理 / keeping the house tidy and in order 整理、打掃屋子 / video games 電動遊戲 / hiking 健行 / swimming 游泳 / traveling 旅行 / muscle training 鍛鍊肌肉 / marathon running 跑馬拉松 / going for drives 開車兜風 / snowboarding 玩滑雪板 / walking one's dog 遛狗 / photography 攝影 / be a DIY buff 是個 DIY 迷

052

Do you have a special skill?

你有沒有特殊技能？

Dialogue 實戰會話   🔘 Track 53

A : **Do you have a special skill?**
（你有沒有特殊技能？）

B1: **I'm very flexible, probably because I do ballet.** ☞
（我身體很柔軟，可能是因為我跳芭蕾舞。）

A : **Wow! How long have you been doing that?**
（哇！你跳多久了？）

B2: **I started taking lessons when I was five.** ☞
（我 5 歲就開始學了。）

* flexible「柔軟的」

✎ **Exercise** 請寫下自己的答案並試著說出來！

A : **Do you have a special skill?**

B1:
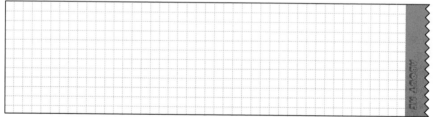

A : **Wow! How long have you been doing that?**

B2:

Substitution 更多回應說法！

☞ B1

- **I don't have any special talents, but I can belly dance.**
  （我沒有任何特殊才能，但是我會跳肚皮舞。）
  * talent「才能」

- **I write poetry. Some of my work has appeared in magazines.**
  （我會寫詩。我有一些作品曾經登在雜誌上。）
  * poetry「詩」；appear「出現」

- **I can juggle. It comes in handy at parties.**
  （我會雜耍。這在派對上很有用。）
  * juggle [ˋdʒʌgl̩]「雜耍；變戲法」；come in handy「派上用場；有用的」

☞ B2

- **I've been taking lessons for around three years.**
  （我學了大約 3 年。）

- **I've been writing for as long as I can remember.**
  （從我有記憶以來就一直在寫。）
  * as long as I can remember「從我有記憶以來」

- **It's something I picked up when I worked as a caterer in high school.**
  （那是我在高中校園提供團膳服務時學會的。）
  * caterer「外燴服務業者；團膳業者」

VOCABULARY 具體描述自己的好用字！

have a gift for music / languages 有音樂 / 語言天分 / be good with languages 語言能力好 / have a way with words 很會說話 / be good at impersonating people 很會模仿人 / do a good imitation of Mickey Mouse 很會模仿米老鼠 / have a qualification to teach flower arrangement / tea ceremony 擁有花道 / 茶道的教師資格 / have a gift for calligraphy 擁有書法天分 / drawing and painting 繪畫 / drawing illustrations 畫插畫 / writing 寫作 / composing music 作曲 / singing 唱歌 / karaoke 卡拉 OK / playing instruments 彈奏樂器 / photography 攝影 / making software 製作軟體 / cooking 烹飪 / be creative 有創造力 / well-liked 有人緣的；受歡迎的 / magnanimous [mægˋnænəməs] 有雅量的 / steady and sincere 穩定又誠懇的 / persevering 堅忍的 / competitive 好競爭的；好勝的 / have leadership ability 有領導力 / be good at making people laugh 擅長逗人笑

053

What's your favorite saying?

你最喜歡哪句俗諺？

Dialogue 實戰會話　　　　　　　　　🔊 Track 54

> **A**：What's your favorite saying?
> （你最喜歡哪句俗諺？）
>
> **B1**：My mother always used to say, "If you have nothing good to say, don't say it." ☞
> （我母親以前常說：「如果你沒什麼好話說，就別說了。」）
>
> **A**：Why do you like that?
> （你為什麼喜歡這句？）
>
> **B2**：If I'm not careful, I tend to get critical of others. ☞
> （因為我一不小心就容易批評別人。）
>
> ＊ get critical of... 「批評⋯⋯；挑剔⋯⋯」

✎ **Exercise** 請寫下自己的答案並試著說出來！

A：What's your favorite saying?
B1：
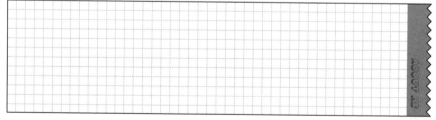

A：Why do you like that?
B2：
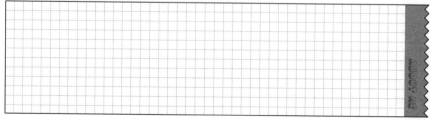

☞ **B1**

- **I like the Latin expression, "Carpe diem." It means " Seize the day."**
  （我很喜歡那句拉丁話，「Carpe diem.」。意思是「及時行樂、把握今天」。）

- **My favorite saying is "Don't look back."**
  （我最愛的一句話是「好馬不吃回頭草」。）
  * look back「回頭」

- **There's a popular Japanese saying that means "Treasure every meeting."**
  （有句日本俗諺非常有名，意思是「珍惜每次相遇」。）
  * treasure every meeting「珍惜每次相遇」（日文原文為：**一期一会**）

☞ **B2**

- **I think people are too wasteful. We need to take care of things more.**
  （我覺得人們太浪費了。我們必須更珍惜東西才行。）
  * wasteful「浪費的」

- **I think it's important to keep moving forward.**
  （我覺得持續向前邁進是很重要的。）
  * move forward「向前邁進」

- **I believe it's important to treat every person you meet with kindness and respect.**
  （我相信以善意和尊重的態度對待你所遇見的每一個人，是很重要的。）
  * treat「對待；看待」；respect「尊敬」

VOCABULARY 具體描述自己的好用字！

Carpe diem. 及時行樂。/ Seize the day. 把握今朝。/ You only live once. 人生只有一次。/ Money doesn't grow on trees. 錢財得來不易。/ Genius is one-percent inspiration, ninety-nine percent perspiration. 天才是一分的靈感加上九十九分的努力。/ The best things in life are free. 生命中最美好的東西是不用花錢的。/ Don't bite the hand that feeds you. 不可恩將仇報。/ Don't burn your bridges. 千萬別自斷後路。/ Time is money. 時間就是金錢。/ You can't take it with you. 生不帶來死不帶去。/ Waste not, want not. 不虛擲者無匱乏。/ Don't dwell on the past. 別沉湎於過去。/ You're never too old to learn. 活到老學到老。

Do you have a favorite town or place?
你是否有最喜愛的城市或地方？

Dialogue 實戰會話　　　　　　　　　　🔊 Track 55

A：Do you have a favorite town or place?
（你是否有最喜愛的城市或地方？）

B1：Tokyo is my favorite city in the world. ☞
（全世界我最愛東京。）

A：Why is that?
（為什麼？）

B2：It has something for everyone. ☞
（對每個人來說它都有某種魅力。）

✎ **Exercise** 請寫下自己的答案並試著說出來！

A：Do you have a favorite town or place?

B1：

A：Why is that?

B2：

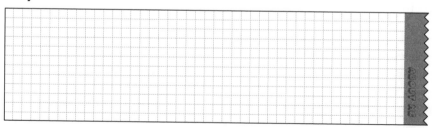

Substitution 更多回應說法！

B1

- **The more I get to know this town, the more I like it.**
（我越熟悉這個城鎮，就越喜歡它。）
＊ the more..., the more....「越……就越……」

- **I didn't like New York that much before, but it grows on you.**
（我以前並沒有那麼喜歡紐約，但是後來漸漸開始喜歡。）
＊ ... grow on someone「某人漸漸喜歡……」

- **Ginza is my favorite place to hang out.**
（我最喜歡去銀座閒逛。）
＊ hang out「閒逛」

B2

- **I guess I like the people. Everyone is so friendly and laid-back.**
（我想我喜歡那裡的人。每個人都很友善而且很悠閒。）
＊ laid-back「悠閒的；懶散的」

- **It attracts an interesting mix of people. As a foreigner, I don't feel out of place.**
（那裡吸引了形形色色的人。身為一個外國人，我並不會覺得格格不入。）
＊ mix of people「形形色色的人」; out of place「格格不入；不相稱的」

- **It's a very upscale and sophisticated place. When I go there, I feel like I'm in a movie.**
（那是個非常高檔又精緻的地方。我去那裡時，感覺就像置身在電影裡一般。）
＊ upscale「高檔的」

VOCABULARY 具體描述自己的好用字！

have a little bit of everything（市鎮等）麻雀雖小五臟俱全 / **cityscape** 都市景觀 / **shopping street** 商店街 / **bustling** 熙來攘往的；熱鬧的 / **urban** 都會的 / **rural** 鄉村的 / **quiet** 安靜的 / **exciting** 刺激的 / **beautiful scenery** 美麗的景緻 / **a quiet café** 一家寧靜的咖啡廳 / **a sophisticated street** 一條時髦的街道 / **splendid cityscape** 燦爛的都會風光 / **quiet upscale residential area** 閑靜的高級住宅區 / **the hustle and bustle of the city** 城市的喧囂 / **a million-dollar night view** 百萬夜景 / **a mature and sophisticated area** 一個成熟且高度發展的區域 / **skyscrapers in the urban subcenter** 在城市副都心的摩天大樓 / **a park with a great night view** 一座有美麗夜景的公園 / **a park with a view of the harbor** 一座有海港景色的公園 / **vast horizon** 寬闊的地平線 / **rich in nature** 自然生態豐富 / **the atmosphere of the city** 都市的氣氛

055

Is there a person you respect or admire?
你是否有尊敬或崇拜的人？

Dialogue 實戰會話 　　　　　　　　　　　🎙 Track 56

A： Is there a person you respect or admire?
（你是否有尊敬或崇拜的人？）

B1： My hero is Wang Yung-ching, an influential entrepreneur who founded a large business empire in Taiwan. 📖
（我心目中的英雄是王永慶，一位在台灣建立龐大企業帝國、很有影響力的創業家。）

A： Why do you admire him?
（你為什麼崇拜他呢？）

B2： He was a great leader and visionary. He's the kind of person that Taiwan needs now. 📖
（他是個很棒的領導者，也是有遠見的人。他正是台灣現在很需要的那種人。）

* admire「崇拜」；visionary「有遠見的人」

✎ **Exercise** 請寫下自己的答案並試著說出來！

A： Is there a person you respect or admire?
B1：

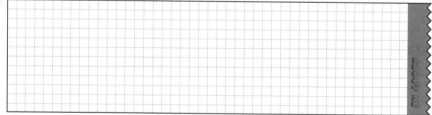

A： Why do you admire him?
B2：

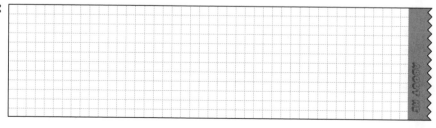

Substitution 更多回應說法！

☞ **B1**

- **My role model is Audrey Hepburn. I've seen almost all her movies.**
  (我的榜樣是奧黛麗赫本。我幾乎看過她所有的電影。)
  * role model「模範；榜樣」

- **I admire my grandfather. He was an amazing person.**
  (我很崇拜我的祖父。他是個了不起的人。)

- **I have a great deal of respect for Barack Obama.**
  (我非常尊敬巴拉克・歐巴馬。)
  * a great deal of...「極多的……」

☞ **B2**

- **She was so graceful and beautiful, and she also did a lot of humanitarian work.**
  (她是那麼地優雅又美麗，還做了許多人道主義的工作。)
  * graceful「優雅的」；humanitarian [hjuˌmænəˋtɛrɪən]「人道主義的；博愛的」

- **He went through so much adversity, and yet he was still the most loving and gentle person.**
  (他克服了許許多多的逆境，卻依舊是一位最有愛心又溫和的人。)
  * adversity「逆境」

- **He deserves a lot of credit for doing his best to tackle problems that he didn't create.**
  (他盡全力處理別人製造出來的問題，非常有功勞。)
  * deserve「應該；該得」credit「功勞；讚揚；信譽」；tackle「著手處理；對付」

VOCABULARY 具體描述自己的好用字！

be an inspiration to everyone 能啟發每個人 / have been through a lot 經歷了很多事情 / teach someone the meaning of responsibility 教導某人責任的意義 / a person who inspires hope 一個激發希望的人 / inspire courage 賦予勇氣 / be full of love 充滿愛 / teach someone the important things in life 教導某人人生中重要的事 / treat everyone alike 平等待人 / be kind to everyone 對人和善 / understand how the less fortunate feel 理解不幸者的感受 / a fair person 一個公平的人 / a pure and just person 一個清白而且正直的人 / a person who does not lie 一個不說謊的人 / with a strong sense of right and wrong 很有正義感；黑白分明 / be awkward but kind 笨拙但和善 / a compassionate person 一個有同情心的人 / a well-mannered person 一個有禮貌的人 / stick to one's principles 堅持原則

056

What kind of trips do you like to take?
你喜歡哪種旅行？

Dialogue 實戰會話 🎧 Track 57

A : What kind of trips do you like to take?
（你喜歡哪種旅行？）

B1 : Since I don't have time to plan trips on my own, I usually go on package tours. ☞
（由於我沒時間自己規劃旅程，所以我通常都參加套裝行程。）

A : Where do you want to go on your next trip?
（你下一次旅行想去哪裡？）

B2 : If I can take a long vacation, I'd like to travel around Europe by train. ☞
（如果能休長假，我想坐火車遊覽歐洲各地。）

✎ **Exercise** 請寫下自己的答案並試著說出來！

A : What kind of trips do you like to take?
B1 :

A : Where do you want to go on your next trip?
B2 :

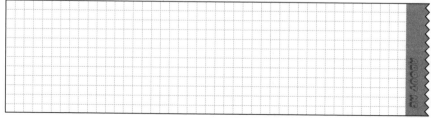

☞ **B1**

- **Since I started my own business, I often take working vacations.**
  （由於我已自行創業，所以通常都一邊工作一邊度假。）
  * working vacation「邊工作邊度假；度假打工」
- **Recently, I've become interested in ecotourism.**
  （最近，我開始對生態旅遊產生興趣。）
  * ecotourism [ˌiko`tʊrɪzəm]「生態旅遊」
- **I like to get away from the crowds and enjoy nature, all by myself.**
  （我喜歡自己一個人遠離人群並享受自然。）
  * get away from...「遠離……」

☞ **B2**

- **I want to go gambling in Las Vegas.**
  （我想去拉斯維加斯賭博。）
  * go gambling「去賭博」
- **I want to visit some of Europe's World Heritage Sites.**
  （我想去參觀歐洲的一些世界遺產。）
  * World Heritage Sites「世界遺產」
- **I want to go backpacking in Southeast Asia.**
  （我想到東南亞去做背包客旅行。）
  * go backpacking「進行背包客旅行」

VOCABULARY 具體描述自己的好用字！

casino 賭場 / adventure 冒險 / scuba diving 水肺潛水 / enjoy shopping and night life 享受購物與夜生活 / vacationing with kids 親子假期旅遊 / domestic / overseas trip 國內／國外旅遊 / go on a trip with... 和……一起旅行 / package tour 套裝（團體）旅遊 / travel alone 單獨旅行 / a 4-day, 3-night trip 四天三夜的旅行 / around-the-world trip 環遊世界 / bus tour 巴士旅遊 / train trip 火車旅遊 / restaurant tour 美食之旅 / trip to enjoy the natural scenery 享受自然風光的旅行 / sightseeing tour 觀光旅遊 / World Heritage Sites tour 世界遺產之旅

confectionery making ▸ 製作糖果糕點	**jigsaw puzzle** ▸ 拼圖
bread making ▸ 做麵包	**outdoor amusement** ▸ 戶外娛樂
handmade soba noodles ▸ 手工蕎麥麵	**mixed martial arts** ▸ 綜合武術
	windsurfing ▸ 風帆衝浪
watercolor painting ▸ 水彩畫	**hula** ▸ 草裙舞
oil painting ▸ 油畫	**ballroom dance** ▸ 社交舞
ink painting ▸ 水墨畫	**squash** ▸ 壁球
block print ▸ 版畫	**horse riding** ▸ 騎馬
music appreciation ▸ 音樂欣賞	**horseback racing** ▸ 賽馬
songwriting ▸ 詞曲創作	**sign language** ▸ 手語
star watching ▸ 觀星	**braille** ▸ 點字
magic trick ▸ 魔術	**foliage plant** ▸ 觀葉植物
aromatherapy ▸ 芳香療法	**home vegetable garden** ▸ 家庭菜園
palm reading ▸ 手相	**gardening** ▸ 園藝
	tropical fish ▸ 熱帶魚

對話回應好用句 ④：猶豫‧反對

「嗯，是這樣嗎？」

● **Hmm...**（嗯……）
  ▸ 表示正在思考的聲音。

● **Well...**（這個嘛……）
  ▸ 可用來表達類似「嗯……」這樣含糊其詞的感覺。

● **Not really...**（不盡然……）
  ▸ Not really. 相當於「不盡然」這樣的否定之意。主要用於無法完全接受對方說法的情況。

「我不這麼覺得耶」

● **I doubt that.**（這點我懷疑。）
  ▸ 用來表示「我不這麼覺得」的語氣。

● **I don't think so.**（我不這麼認為。）
  ▸ 為否定對方發言的說法。

● **I wouldn't say that.**（我不會這麼說。）
  ▸ 這句也表示「我不這麼覺得」。

Unit 5

職業・學業
Work and School

有關公司或學生時代的事情，要用英語談論往往出乎意料地困難。
請事先整理準備，真正對話時才會順暢愉快。

What do you do for a living?
Do you get along with your boss?
When do you feel most fulfilled at work?
What was your major in college?
Are you in any clubs?
...

appearance

name

Taiwan culture

friends

work

dreams

interest

families

religion

experience

057

What time do you start and finish work?
你的工作從幾點開始到幾點結束？

Dialogue 實戰會話　　　　　　　　　　　Track 58

A：**What time do you start and finish work?**
（你的工作從幾點開始到幾點結束？）

B1：**I usually work from 9 to 5, except when it's busy.** ☞
（除了繁忙時外，我通常從 9 點工作到 5 點。）

A：**Do you have to work a lot of overtime?**
（你必須常加班嗎？）

＊ overtime「加班」（名詞）；超過時間的（形容詞）；超過地（副詞）

B2：**Sometimes. It tends to get busy at the end of the month.** ☞
（偶爾。月底往往會很忙。）

✎ **Exercise** 請寫下自己的答案並試著說出來！

A：What time do you start and finish work?
B1：

A：Do you have to work a lot of overtime?
B2：

Substitution 更多回應說法！

☞ **B1**

- **If I'm working the early shift, I start at 7 and finish at 3.**
  （如果是值早班，我從 7 點開始做到 3 點結束。）
  * early shift「早班」

- **We have flextime at our office, but most of the full-time employees work from 10 to 6 or 7.**
  （我們公司採彈性工時制，不過大部分正職員工都從 10 點工作到 6、7 點。）
  * flextime「彈性工作時間」; full-time employee「正職員工」

- **Unless I'm filling in for someone else, I work from 10 to 3.**
  （除非是替別人代班，要不然我都從 10 點工作到 3 點。）
  * fill in for someone「替某人代班」

☞ **B2**

- **When it's busy, I have to put in around 20-30 hours of overtime a month.**
  （忙的時候，我一個月必須加班大約 20 到 30 小時。）
  * put in... hour「加班工作……小時」

- **Actually, we're not allowed to work overtime.**
  （事實上，我們是不被允許加班的。）
  * be allowed to...「被允許……」

- **Only at the end of each fiscal quarter.**
  （只有每個會計季度末會加班。）
  * fiscal quarter「會計季度」

VOCABULARY 具體描述自己的好用字！

early morning shift 早班 / night shift 晚班 / graveyard shift 大夜班 / have a flexible schedule 彈性工時制 / work irregular hours 工作時間不定 / unpaid overtime 無給加班 / work part-time 打工；兼職 / work full-time 做全職工作 / can set one's own working hours 可自行決定自己的工作時間 / overtime allowance 加班費 / work too much 工作過度 / die from overwork 過勞死 / order a subordinate to work overtime 命令屬下加班 / be forced to work overtime by one's boss 被主管強迫加班 / refuse to work overtime 拒絕加班 / be late 遲到 / leave early 早退 / leave the office at the scheduled time 準時下班 / have 2 days off a week 週休二日 / work only 3 days a week 一週只工作 3 天 / only have Wednesdays off 只有週三休假 / have almost no days off 幾乎沒有休假

058

What industry are you in?
你是做哪一行的？

Dialogue 實戰會話   ⊙ Track 59

A： **What industry are you in?**
（你是做哪一行的？）

B1： **I'm an accountant, but I work in the retail industry.** ☞
（我是會計師，不過我在零售業工作。）

A： **Really? What kind of company do you work for?**
（真的啊？你是為怎樣的公司工作？）

B2： **It's a big department store chain called Sogo.** ☞
（是一家叫崇光的大型連鎖百貨。）

✎ **Exercise** 請寫下自己的答案並試著說出來！

A：What industry are you in?

B1：

A：Really? What kind of company do you work for?

B2：

Substitution 更多回應說法！

☞ **B1**

- **I guess you could say I work in the IT industry.**
  （我想你可以說我是在資訊業工作。）
  * IT industry「資訊業」(IT=information technology)
- **I'm loosely involved in the medical industry.**
  （我做的算是醫療相關行業。）
  * loosely「不準確地」; be involved in...「與……相關；與……有關聯」
- **I work in the financial industry, but my own job doesn't have anything to do with finance.**
  （我在金融業工作，但是我本身的工作內容和金融無關。）
  * financial「財政的；金融的」

☞ **B2**

- **My company is a consultant for software companies.**
  （我們公司做的是軟體公司的諮詢顧問。）
  * consultant「顧問」
- **I work in the sales division of a company that makes medical equipment.**
  （我在醫療器材製作公司的業務部門工作。）
- **It's a securities company, but I'm in HR.**
  （是一間證券公司，但是我在人事部。）
  * securities company「證券公司」; HR「人事部；人力資源部」(=human resources)

VOCABULARY 具體描述自己的好用字！

the food service industry 餐飲業 / publishing 出版 / finance 金融 / healthcare 醫療保健 / entertainment 娛樂 / real estate 不動產 / construction 建築 / tourist 觀光 / aviation 航空 / printing 印刷 / advertising 廣告 / auto industry 汽車業 / life insurance 壽險 / materials 原物料 / fiber 纖維 / chemical 化學製品 / agriculture, forestry and fisheries 農林漁業 / trading company 貿易公司 / work for a department store 在百貨公司工作 / work for a clothing company 在服飾公司工作 / work freelance as a web designer 做自由接案的網頁設計師 / work as a home helper 做家務助理；幫傭 / work as a temp in a software company 在軟體公司當臨時雇員

059

What kinds of things do you do in your company?
你在公司裡都做怎樣的工作？

Dialogue 實戰會話　　　　　　　　　　Track 60

A: **What kinds of things do you do in your company?**
（你在公司裡都做怎樣的工作？）

B1: **Actually, I spend most of my days going around visiting other companies.** ☞
（事實上，我大部分時間都在四處拜訪其他公司。）

A: **What department do you belong to?**
（你隸屬於什麼部門？）

B2: **I'm in the client service department. Our job is to make sure our clients are happy.** ☞
（我在客服部。我們的工作就是要確保客戶滿意。）

✎ **Exercise** 請寫下自己的答案並試著說出來！

A: **What kinds of things do you do in your company?**

B1:

A: **What department do you belong to?**

B2:

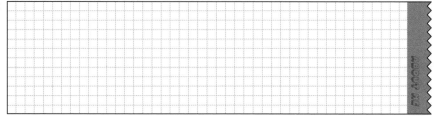

Substitution 更多回應說法！

B1

- **I'm in charge of training our new recruits.**
（我負責訓練新進員工。）
＊ be in charge of...「負責……」；recruit「新手；新進員工」
- **I mostly sit at my computer and do data entry all day long.**
（我大部分時候都整天坐在電腦前輸入資料。）
＊ all day long「一整天」
- **Anything they ask me to do — take phone calls, check e-mail, type documents, etc.**
（他們叫我做什麼我就做什麼——接電話、查看電子郵件和輸入文件資料等等。）
＊ document「文件」

B2

- **I'm the head of the personnel division.**
（我是人事部經理。）
＊ personnel [ˌpɜsn̩`ɛl] division「人事部」
- **I'm in accounting. I'm still a temp, though.**
（我在會計部。不過我還只是個臨時雇員。）
＊ accounting「會計」；temp「臨時雇員」（口語）
- **I work in management as an administrative assistant.**
（我在管理部做行政助理。）
＊ management「管理」；administrative [əd`mɪnəˌstretɪv] 行政的

VOCABULARY 具體描述自己的好用字！

general affairs department 總務部 / **research & development (R&D) team** 研究開發團隊 / **logistics** 物流 / **IT department** 資訊部門 / **management** 經營管理 / **export and import department** 進出口部門 / **purchasing department** 採購部門 / **public relations (PR) department** 公關部門 / **marketing department** 行銷部門 / **accounting department** 會計部 / **sales department** 業務部 / **production department** 生產部門 / **editing department** 編輯部 / **manufacturing department** 製造部門 / **planning department** 企劃部

060

What do you do for a living?
你從事什麼工作？

Dialogue 實戰會話　　　　　　　　　　　　　🔊 Track 61

A： **What do you do for a living?**
（你從事什麼工作？）

B1：**I work in the sales department of an electronics firm.** ☞
（我在電子公司的業務部工作。）

A： **Really? Is that an interesting job?**
（真的啊？那是個有趣的工作嗎？）

B2：**Yeah, it's nice because I get to meet a lot of different**
people. ☞
（是啊，這工作很不錯，因為我可以認識很多不同的人。）

✎ **Exercise** 請寫下自己的答案並試著說出來！

A：What do you do for a living?

B1：

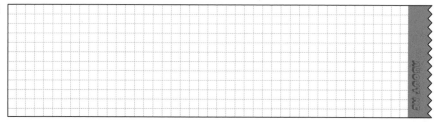

A：Really? Is that an interesting job?

B2：

☞ **B1**

- **I work part-time at a restaurant.**
  （我在一家餐廳打工。）
  * work part-time「兼職；打工」
  TIPS 中文的「兼職」和「打工」在英文裡並無不同，都用 work part-time「打工」來表示。

- **I'm working in a bank as a temp.**
  （我在銀行做臨時雇員。）

- **I'm between jobs right now, but my area of expertise is web design.**
  （我現在待業中，不過我的專業是網頁設計。）
  * be between jobs「待業中」；area of expertise [ˌɛkspɝ`tiz]「專業領域」

☞ **B2**

- **I'm still getting used to it, but the work itself is very rewarding.**
  （我還在適應，不過這工作本身讓我獲益良多。）
  * rewarding「有意義的、值得的」

- **It can be stressful at times, but I enjoy it.**
  （這工作有時壓力很大，但是我樂在其中。）
  * stressful「壓力大的」

- **Actually, I'm thinking of changing jobs. I have to work overtime almost every day.**
  （事實上，我正考慮要換工作。我幾乎每天都必須加班。）
  * change jobs「換工作」；work overtime「加班」

VOCABULARY 具體描述自己的好用字！

trading company 貿易公司 / electronics manufacturer 電子產品製造商 / travel agency 旅行社 / ad agency 廣告代理商 / government office 政府機關 / salesperson 業務員 / secretary 秘書 / receptionist 接待員；櫃台服務人員 / manager 經理 / executive 高層主管 / civil servant 公務員 / work on one's day off 在假日工作 / run a store / a private business 經營商店 / 個人事業 / do music-related work 做與音樂相關的工作 / work in a trading company 在貿易公司工作 / the pay is good / bad 薪水很好 / 差 / have to work overtime a lot 必須常常加班 / don't have to work overtime a lot / much 不須常常加班

061

Do you get along with your boss?
你和上司處得好不好？

Dialogue 實戰會話　　　　　　　　　　　🎧 Track 62

A: **Do you get along with your boss?**
（你和上司處得好不好？）

B1: **Yeah, I have a great relationship with my boss.** ☞
（很好，我和我老闆關係超好。）

A: **How about your coworkers?**
（那同事呢？）

B2: **They're a nice bunch, but mostly we just do our own thing.** ☞
（他們人都很好，但是我們通常都各做各的。）

* bunch「群；伙；幫」（口語）；do our own thing「各做各的事」

✎ **Exercise** 請寫下自己的答案並試著說出來！

A：**Do you get along with your boss?**

B1：

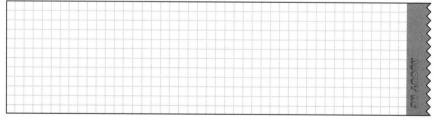

A：**How about your coworkers?**

B2：

Substitution 更多回應說法！

☞ B1

- **We don't see eye-to-eye on some things, but we manage to get along OK.**
  (對於某些事我們會意見不合，但是我們還是能夠和平相處。)
  * see eye-to-eye「意見一致」

- **He's very easy to talk to. If any problem comes up, he's ready to listen.**
  (和他說話非常輕鬆。不論發生任何問題，他都願意傾聽。)
  * come up「發生」

- **He can be a real pain in the neck sometimes, but I try not to let it bother me.**
  (他有時候真的很難搞，不過我都會盡量不讓這問題困擾我。)
  * a pain in the neck「難搞的人」；bother「使煩惱；困擾」

☞ B2

- **We have our personal differences, but we don't let it get in the way of our work.**
  (我們對事情的看法不盡相同，但是我們不會讓這問題妨礙我們的工作。)
  * get in the way of...「妨礙……」

- **There's a strong sense of camaraderie at work. Everyone looks out for each other.**
  (工作上我們有很強烈的同僚情誼。每個人都會彼此照顧。)
  * camaraderie [ˌkɑməˋrɑdərɪ]「同僚間的情誼」；look out for...「注意……；留心……」

- **There's some office politics going on, but I just try to do my job.**
  (辦公室內有些勾心鬥角的情況，不過我就盡量做我的工作。)
  * office politics「辦公室政治；公司內的勾心鬥角」

VOCABULARY 具體描述自己的好用字！

worker morale 員工士氣 / corporate culture 企業文化 / the atmosphere in the office is gloomy / cheerful 辦公室氣氛很陰沉 / 很歡樂 / put a lot of trust in one's employees 非常信賴員工 / get on one's nerves 使某人煩躁 / be hard to please 難以取悅 / be very demanding 要求很嚴格 / department with / lacking unity 有向心力 / 缺乏向心力的部門 / a boss with good / no leadership skills 具備 / 缺乏良好領導能力的上司 / cooperative / uncooperative coworkers 合作的 / 不合作的同事 / incompetent boss / subordinates 無能的上司 / 下屬 / section with good / poor communication 溝通良好的 / 不良的部門

062

When do you feel most fulfilled at work?
你何時最能體會工作上的滿足感？

Dialogue 實戰會話　　　　　　　　　　🎧 Track 63

A: When do you feel most fulfilled at work?
（你何時最能體會工作上的滿足感？）

B1: It's a nice feeling when I come up with a solution that no one else thought of. ☞
（當我想出一個別人都沒想到的解決方案時，那感覺真好。）

A: When do you hate your job?
（你什麼時候會討厭你的工作？）

B2: I hate having to work long hours to make a deadline. ☞
（我最討厭為了趕上最後期限而必須長時間工作。）

* come up with...「想出⋯⋯」；solution「解決方案」

✎ **Exercise** 請寫下自己的答案並試著說出來！

A：When do you feel most fulfilled at work?

B1：

A：When do you hate your job?

B2：

Substitution 更多回應說法！

☞ B1

- **It's a pretty humdrum job, but it's nice when my coworkers tell me I'm doing a good job.**

  （這工作相當單調，但是當同事稱讚我做得很好時，感覺就不錯。）

  ＊ humdrum [ˋhʌmˌdrʌm]「單調的」

- **When I see the finished product, I feel like all the hard work we've put into it was worth it.**

  （當我看見成品，就會覺得我們投入的所有努力都是值得的。）

  ＊ worth...「有……的價值」

- **Nothing is more satisfying than seeing the happy faces of our customers.**

  （沒有什麼比看見顧客開心的表情更令人滿足的了。）

  ＊ nothing is more... than...「沒有什麼比……更……的了」

☞ B2

- **I hate long meetings. They go on and on, and nothing ever gets done.**

  （我討厭冗長的會議。會沒完沒了地一直開下去，卻什麼也決定不了。）

  ＊ go on and on「一直持續下去」

- **I don't like being forced to hang out with coworkers after work.**

  （我不喜歡下班後還被迫要跟同事混在一起。）

  ＊ be forced to...「被迫……」

- **I hate giving presentations. I get nervous when I have to speak to a group of people.**

  （我討厭做簡報。必須在一群人面前發言時，我就會很緊張。）

  ＊ get nervous「緊張不安」

VOCABULARY 具體描述自己的好用字！

a boring job 無聊的工作 / a worthy job 有價值的工作 / a satisfying job 令人滿意的工作 / an fulfilling / unfulfilling job 有滿足感 / 沒滿足感的工作 / do monotonous [məˋnɑtənəs] work 做單調的工作 / do something creative 做些有創意的事 / do the same thing over and over 反覆做相同的事 / a feeling of achievement 成就感 / be able to express oneself 能表達自我 / work is successful 工作成功 / work ends in failure 工作以失敗告終 / hard work is rewarded 辛勤的工作獲得回報 / meeting goes well 會議進行得順利 / presentation is a big success / failure 簡報非常成功 / 嚴重失敗 / fail to get a contract 沒能獲得一紙合約 / sales are good / bad 銷售狀況良好 / 不佳

063

Do you ever feel that your job has helped you grow as a person?
你是否曾覺得你的工作有助於你自我成長？

Dialogue 實戰會話　　　　　　　　　　　　　🅖 Track 64

A: Do you ever feel that your job has helped you grow as a person?
（你是否曾覺得你的工作有助於你自我成長？）

B1: Working in a large company has definitely given me a broader perspective on things. 🔊
（在大公司工作，確實讓我能以更宏觀的角度來看事情。）

A: What's your goal?
（你的目標是什麼？）

B2: I'd like to pass on what I've learned to the younger generation. 🔊
（我想將我所學到的傳給年輕的一代。）

＊ perspective「觀點；看法；角度」；pass on「傳遞」

✎ **Exercise** 請寫下自己的答案並試著說出來！

A： Do you ever feel that your job has helped you grow as a person?

B1：

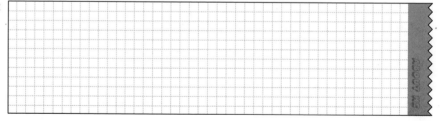

A： What's your goal?

B2：

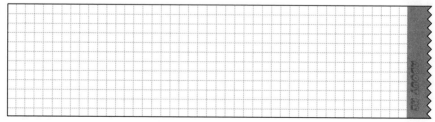

Substitution 更多回應說法！

☞ B1

- **When I look at the new recruits, I feel like I've come a long way.**
  （當我看新進員工的時候，就覺得自己有長足的進步。）
  * come a long way「長足的進步」

- **I cringe when I think about how I acted when I first started working. I was so cocky!**
  （一想起我剛剛開始工作時的樣子，就覺得好慚愧。那時真是太自以為是了！）
  * cringe [krɪndʒ]「感到羞愧；畏縮」；cocky [ˋkɑkɪ]「自以為是的；過度自信的」

- **My coworkers tell me that my English has gotten much better since I started working in sales.**
  （我同事跟我說，自從我開始做業務以來，我的英文變得好多了。）

☞ B2

- **I want to take what I've learned at work and apply it to my own business.**
  （我想將我在工作中學到的，應用在我自己的事業上。）
  * apply「適用；應用」

- **I'm not really interested in climbing the corporate ladder.**
  （我對於在公司體系中升遷並沒有太大興趣。）
  * corporate ladder「公司的升遷體系」

- **Eventually I hope to become head of the department I'm working in.**
  （最終我希望能成為我目前工作之部門的主管。）
  * eventually「最終；終究」；head of the department「部門主管」

VOCABULARY 具體描述自己的好用字！

be more patient with people 對人更有耐心 / be not as self-centered as I used to be 不像我以前那麼以自我為中心 / be better at getting along with different kinds of people 更善於與不同的人相處 / have more realistic expectations 對未來的期望更為務實 / work overseas 在國外工作 / make the most of one's skills 充分運用自己的技能 / make use of one's linguistic skills 運用自己的語言能力 / retire early 提早退休 / work until retirement 一直工作直到退休為止 / achieve as high a position as possible 盡可能高升 / develop better products 研發出更好的產品 / start up a large project of one's own 自行開創大型專案

064

Why did you choose to work at the place you're working now?
你當初為何選擇在現在工作的地方工作？

Dialogue 實戰會話　　　　　　　　　　🔊 Track 65

A: Why did you choose to work at the place you're working now?
（你當初為何選擇在現在工作的地方工作？）

B1: I wanted to work for a big company with lots of opportunities for advancement. ☞
（當時我想在升遷機會較多的大公司工作。）

A: Do you want to keep working there for a long time?
（你想在那裡做很久嗎？）

B2: I can't imagine working anywhere else. ☞
（我無法想像在別的地方工作。）

＊ advancement「升遷」

✎ **Exercise** 請寫下自己的答案並試著說出來！

A： Why did you choose to work at the place you're working now?

B1：

A： Do you want to keep working there for a long time?

B2：

Substitution 更多回應說法！

☞ **B1**

- **Actually, I didn't have much choice. It was the only place that was willing to hire me.**

  （事實上我沒有太多選擇。那是唯一願意雇用我的地方。）

  ＊ be willing to...「有意願……」；hire「雇用」

- **They had the best compensation plan.**

  （他們有最好的報酬制度。）

  ＊ compensation plan「報酬制度；薪資制度」

- **I wanted to work for a company with integrity. I felt like they really want to help people.**

  （我想在一間有誠信的公司工作。我覺得他們真的想幫助人。）

  ＊ integrity「誠信；誠實」

☞ **B2**

- **Eventually, I'd like to move on to a better-paying job.**

  （最終，我希望能換一個薪水比較好的工作。）

- **I haven't thought about it much, but I'm happy where I am for the time being.**

  （我還沒想到那麼多，但是我對現狀相當滿意。）

  ＊ for the time being「目前；當下」

- **When the time comes, I'll look for a better position elsewhere.**

  （待時機來臨時，我會去別處找一個更好的職位。）

𝒱OCABULARY 具體描述自己的好用字！

a stable company 穩定的公司 / a growing company 在成長中的企業 / a company that contributes to society 對社會有貢獻的公司 / a company that takes care of its employees 會照顧員工的公司 / a company that offers good benefits 福利好的公司 / a company with a good maternity [məˋtɛnətɪ] leave plan 具備良好產假制度的公司 / a company whose products I like 產品深受我喜愛的公司 / a trustworthy company 值得信賴的公司 / be in a convenient location 處於便利的位置 / like the atmosphere in the office 喜歡辦公室的氣氛 / a place where I can apply my skills 一個能讓我應用本身技能的地方 / like the corporate culture 喜歡該企業文化 / got the job through one's parent's connection 透過父母的關係找到該份工作 / found a job through a personnel agency 透過人力仲介公司找到一份工作 / was head-hunted by one's current company 被自己現在的公司獵才獵到

065

Where is your office located?
你的辦公室位於何處？

Dialogue 實戰會話　　　　　　　　　　🎧 Track 66

A： **Where is your office located?**
（你的辦公室位於何處？）

B1： **It's in the Sinyi District, which is in the eastern part of Taipei.** ☞
（在信義區，信義區是位在台北市東邊的區域。）

A： **Is that a nice place?**
（那是個好地方嗎？）

B2： **I like it. It's a busy commerical area, and it's also a great place for shopping.** ☞
（我很喜歡。那是個繁忙的商業區，而且是個購物的好地方。）

* commerical area「商業區」

✎ **Exercise** 請寫下自己的答案並試著說出來！

A：**Where is your office located?**

B1：

A：**Is that a nice place?**

B2：

Substitution 更多回應說法！

☞ **B1**

- **It's in downtown Taipei, about five minutes from Taipei Station.**
  （在台北市中心，距離台北車站大約 5 分鐘的地方。）
  ＊ downtown「市中心；鬧區」

- **We're in a part of Taipei called Ximending.**
  （我們公司在台北一個叫「西門町」的區域。）
  ＊ called...「叫做……」

- **I work in Yingge, which is about thirty minutes from Taipei by train.**
  （我在鶯歌工作，鶯歌距離台北大約三十分鐘的火車車程。）

☞ **B2**

- **It's nothing but office buildings. It's a nice place to work, but I wouldn't want to live there.**
  （那裡只有辦公大樓。那個地方很適合工作，但是我不會想住在那裡。）
  ＊ nothing but...「只有……」

- **It used to be a young, funky place but it has gone upscale and arty in recent years.**
  （那地方以前是很年輕、時髦的區域，但是這幾年來已走向高級化和藝術化。）
  ＊ funky「獨特、時髦的」；go upscale「高級化」；go arty「有藝術氣息」

- **It's a quiet place out in the middle of nowhere.**
  （那是個前不著村後不著店的寧靜鄉下。）
  ＊ out in the middle of nowhere「前不著村後不著店的鄉下」

VOCABULARY 具體描述自己的好用字！

general headquarters 總部 / head office 總公司 / main store 總店 / main office 主要辦事處 / annex [ə`nɛks] 擴建的建築物 / branch 分公司 / factory 工廠 / warehouse 倉庫 / subsidiary 子公司 / a bustling and noisy place 繁華喧鬧的地方 / a convenient location 方便的地點 / an inconvenient location 不方便的地點 / close to the station 離車站近 / far from the station 離車站遠 / next to the station 緊鄰車站 / connected to the station 與車站相連 / financial district 金融區 / downtown 市中心 / block of office buildings 辦公大樓區 / commercial area 商業區 / industrial area 工業區 / residential area 住宅區 / in the suburbs 在郊區 / an out-of-the-way location 偏僻的位置 / a city in north Taiwan 位於北台灣的城市 / a city at the southernmost tip of Taiwan 位於台灣最南端的城市 / a city in the middle of Taiwan 位於台灣中部的城市

066

How do you get to work?
你都怎麼去上班？

Dialogue 實戰會話　　　　　　　　　🌐 Track 67

A: **How do you get to work?**
（你都怎麼去上班？）

B1: **I take the train to work. It's about 30 minutes door-to-door.** ☞
（我搭火車上班，從出門到辦公室約需 30 分鐘。）

A: **What do you do during your commute?**
（通勤時你都做些什麼？）

B2: **I check my email and update my blog.** ☞
（檢查我的電子郵件和更新我的部落格。）

* update「更新」

✎ **Exercise** 請寫下自己的答案並試著說出來！

A：How do you get to work?
B1：

A：What do you do during your commute?
B2：

Substitution 更多回應說法！

☞ B1

- **Recently I started commuting by bicycle. When it rains, I take the train.**
  （我最近開始騎腳踏車通勤。下雨時我就搭火車。）
  * commute「通勤」

- **I drive to work. It's about a 30-minute drive.**
  （我開車上班。大約是 30 分鐘的車程。）
  * drive to...「開車去…」；drive「車程」

- **I usually commute by bus and train, but sometimes, when the weather's nice, I walk to the station.**
  （我通常坐公車和火車通勤，但是有時如果天氣好，我會走路去車站。）

☞ B2

- **I listen to music on my iPod.**
  （我都用 iPod 聽音樂。）
  * listen to...「聆聽……」

- **I listen to motivational audiobooks.**
  （我都聽勵志的有聲書。）
  * motivational「勵志的；激發鬥志的」；audiobook「有聲書」

- **I usually read, except when it's too crowded to hold a book.**
  （我通常都會看書，除非擠到沒辦法拿著書。）
  * crowded「擁擠的」

𝒱𝑜𝒸𝒶𝒷𝓊𝓁𝒶𝓇𝓎 具體描述自己的好用字！

doze off 打瞌睡 / **crash out** 很快睡著 / **listen to one's favorite songs on one's MP3 player** 用 MP3 播放器聽個人最愛的歌曲 / **watch videos** 看影片 / **play games on one's cell phone** 用手機玩電動 / **play games on one's Nintendo DS** 玩任天堂 DS 的遊戲 / **read the newspaper** 看報紙 / **read the newspaper on one's iPad / cell phone** 用 iPad／手機看電子報 / **open up one's PC and make documents** 打開電腦處理文件 / **read the news online** 閱讀網路新聞 / **check one's favorite websites** 瀏覽個人最愛的網站 / **browse the Internet** 上網瀏覽 / **do Sudoku puzzles** 玩數獨 / **do crossword puzzles** 玩填字遊戲 / **do brain teasers** 玩益智遊戲；做腦筋急轉彎猜謎 / **write in one's diary** 寫日記 / **plan one's day** 計畫當日行程 / **gaze at the hanging train ads** 盯著火車車廂內的懸掛式廣告

067

What was your major in college?
你大學主修什麼？

Dialogue 實戰會話　　　　　　　　　　　　🔊 Track 68

A: **What was your major in college?**
（你大學主修什麼？）

B1: **Actually, I dropped out of college and went to nursing school.** 📖
（事實上我大學念到一半就輟學去念護校。）

A: **Was that interesting?**
（護校有趣嗎？）

B2: **Yeah, it was great because I got a lot of hands-on experience.** 📖
（很有趣，那裡很棒，因為我獲得很多實務經驗。）

* major「主修」；hands-on「親自動手的；實務的」

✎ Exercise 請寫下自己的答案並試著說出來！

A：**What was your major in college?**

B1:

A：**Was that interesting?**

B2:

Substitution 更多回應說法！

B1

- I majored in English literature, but I never learned how to speak English fluently.

  （我主修英國文學，不過我一直都沒學會說流利的英語。）

  * fluently「流利地」

- I started out as a biology major, but switched to economics in my junior year.

  （我一開始主修生物，但是大三那年轉到經濟系去了。）

  * switch to...「轉換至……」

- I wanted to become a counselor, so I studied psychology.

  （我想成為心理諮商師，所以我學了心理學。）

  * counselor [ˋkaʊnslə]「顧問；諮商師」; psychology「心理學」

B2

- Actually, I spent more time working than I did studying.

  （事實上，我花在工作上的時間比花在念書上要多。）

  * spend more time「花更多時間」

- I hardly ever attended classes. It's a miracle that I graduated.

  （我很少去上課。我能畢業是個奇蹟。）

  * hardly ever...「很少……；幾乎不……」

- Some classes were fun and others weren't. It really depends on the professor.

  （有些課很有趣，有些則不怎麼樣。是要看教授而定。）

Vocabulary 具體描述自己的好用字！

philosophy 哲學 / education 教育 / history 歷史 / art history 藝術史 / literature 文學 / language 語言 / linguistics 語言學 / commerce 商學 / management 管理學 / political science 政治學 / economics 經濟學 / public administration 公共行政 / law 法律 / sports science 運動科學 / health science 健康科學 / anthropology 人類學 / computer science 資訊科學 / engineering 工程學 / sociology 社會學 / physics 物理學 / biochemistry 生物化學 / mathematics 數學 / agricultural science 農業科學 / music school 音樂學校 / dental school 牙醫學院 / veterinary [ˋvɛtərəˌnɛrɪ] school 獸醫學校 / medical school 醫學院

068

Are you in any clubs?
你有沒有參加任何社團？

Dialogue 實戰會話　　　　　　　　　　　　　🔊 Track 69

A： Are you in any clubs?
（你有沒有參加任何社團？）

B1： I'm in the English-speaking society. 👉
（我參加了英語會話社。）

A： Really? What kinds of things do you do?
（真的嗎？那你們都做些什麼呢？）

B2： We get together and talk in English about social issues
and news events. 👉
（我們會聚在一起用英語討論社會問題和新聞事件。）

＊ social issue「社會問題」

✎ **Exercise** 請寫下自己的答案並試著說出來！

A：Are you in any clubs?
B1：

A：Really? What kinds of things do you do?
B2：

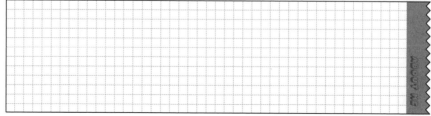

Substitution 更多回應說法！

☞ **B1**

- **I'm in the badminton club.**
  （我參加羽球社。）
  * badminton [ˋbædmɪntən]「羽球」
- **I'm in the tennis club, but I'm thinking of dropping out.**
  （我參加網球社，但是正在考慮要退出。）
  * drop out「退出」
- **I'm in the symphony orchestra.**
  （我參加交響樂團。）
  * symphony orchestra [ˋsɪmfənɪ ˏɔrkɪstrə]「交響樂團」

☞ **B2**

- **It's pretty laid back compared to other clubs. We practice a lot, but we also go drinking a lot.**
  （和其他社團相比，這個社團相當悠閒。我們常常練習，但是也常常出去喝一杯。）
  * compared to...「與……相比」
- **I joined it because I like tennis, but everyone seems to be more interested in partying than playing tennis.**
  （我加入是因為我喜歡網球，但是大家似乎對聚會玩樂比對打網球還有興趣。）
  * party「聚會玩樂」
- **It's pretty grueling. We have to practice six times a week, and perform once every semester.**
  （相當累人。我們每週必須練習 6 次，而且每學期都要表演一次。）
  * grueling [ˋgruəlɪŋ]「很累人的」；semester「學期」

VOCABULARY 具體描述自己的好用字！

tea ceremony club 茶道社 / flower arrangement club 花道社 / judo club 柔道社 / Chinese martial arts club 國術社 / kendo club 劍道社 / track and field club 田徑社 / Folk / Modern / Tap 民族／現代／踢踏舞社 / mountaineering club 登山社 / photo club 攝影社 / softball tennis club 軟式網球社 / cheerleader 啦啦隊 / light music club 輕音樂社 / mixed / boy's / girl's chorus 混聲／男聲／女聲合唱團 / drama society 戲劇社 / cycle club 單車社 / movie club 電影社 / do / participate in an internship 去／參加實習 / compete in a tournament 參加錦標賽 / win a tournament 贏得錦標賽冠軍 / take second place in a tournament 贏得錦標賽第二名

069

What kinds of part-time jobs have you had?
你曾經打過哪些工？

Dialogue 實戰會話　　　　　　　　　　　🎧 Track 70

A: What kinds of part-time jobs have you had?
（你曾經打過哪些工？）

B1: I did various odd jobs in college. I even did some modeling. ☞
（我大學時做過各式各樣的零工。我甚至當過模特兒。）

A: What was the best job?
（哪個工作最好？）

B2: I think I enjoyed working at a coffee shop the most. ☞
（我想我最喜歡在咖啡廳打工。）

* odd job「雜工；零工」

✎ **Exercise** 請寫下自己的答案並試著說出來！

A： What kinds of part-time jobs have you had?
B1:

A： What was the best job?
B2:

Substitution 更多回應說法！

☞ B1

> ● **When I was young, I did anything and everything that came my way.**
> （我年輕的時候，可說是來者不拒，什麼事都做。）
> ＊ come one's way「來到面前的」
>
> ● **I did various odd jobs while I was in college.**
> （我念大學時曾打過各式各樣的零工。）
>
> ● **I did a lot of delivery-type work, like delivering New Year's postcards.**
> （我曾做過不少送貨類的工作，例如送賀年卡。）
> ＊ delivery-type「送貨類的」

☞ B2

> ● **I enjoyed working at a childcare center, since I like being around kids.**
> （我很喜歡在托兒所工作，因為我喜歡和小孩在一起。）
> ＊ childcare center「兒童托育中心；托兒所」
>
> ● **Answering phones was probably the easiest job I ever had.**
> （負責接聽電話大概是我做過最輕鬆的工作。）
> ＊ answering phone「接聽電話」
>
> ● **Being a bike messenger was fun. It was exhausting, but I got to ride all over the city.**
> （做自行車快遞很好玩。雖然非常累人，但是我可以騎遍整個城市。）

✆ＶＯＣＡＢＵＬＡＲＹ 具體描述自己的好用字！

telemarketing 電話行銷 / **nanny** 保姆 / **receptionist** 接待員；櫃台服務人員 / **dog-walker** 負責遛狗的人 / **newspaper delivery** 送報 / **valet** 旅館的代客停車人員；泊車小弟 / **pizza delivery** 比薩外送 / **temping** 做臨時工 / **tutoring** 家教 / **survey interviewer** 市調員 / **waiter**（男）服務生 / **waitress** 女服務生 / **chef at a pub** 酒吧的廚師 / **waiter / waitress at a pub** 酒吧的男 / 女服務生 / **DVD shop clerk** DVD 店的店員 / **cram school teacher** 補習班老師 / **on-the-street flyer / tissue distributor** 在街上發傳單 / 面紙的人 / **supermarket cashier** 超市收銀員 / **mail sorter at the post office** 郵局的分信員 / **gym instructor** 健身房教練

070

What did you work hardest at when you were a student?
你學生時代花最多心力在哪一方面？

Dialogue 實戰會話　　　　　　　　　　　🔊 Track 71

A: **What did you work hardest at when you were a student?**
（你學生時代花最多心力在哪一方面？）

B1: **I was really serious about gymnastics. Our school's team made it to the national tournament.** 👉
（我很認真練體操。我們的校隊成功地進入了全國聯賽。）

A: **Do you ever wish you could go back to those days?**
（你是否曾希望能回到那時候？）

B2: **It was fun, but I think I lead a more fulfilling life now.** 👉
（當時的確很開心，但是我覺得現在的生活更充實。）

* fulfilling life「充實的生活」

✎ **Exercise** 請寫下自己的答案並試著說出來！

A: **What did you work hardest at when you were a student?**

B1:

A: **Do you ever wish you could go back to those days?**

B2:

☞ B1

- **I was too busy thinking about men to devote myself to my studies.**

  （我當時忙著想男人，所以沒能好好念書。）

  * devote oneself to「專心於……」

- **Our club sponsored some events to raise awareness of social issues.**

  （當時我們社團為了提升大家對社會問題的關注，舉辦了一些活動。）

  * sponsor「主辦」

- **Studying abroad was an experience I'll never forget. I really had to study hard to keep up.**

  （出國留學是我永遠都忘不了的經驗。我真的必須很用功才跟得上。）

  * keep up「跟上」

☞ B2

- **No, but I wish I had studied harder. If I had studied harder, I could've gotten a better job.**

  （不，但是我很希望當時能更用功些。如果我再用功點，或許就能找到更好的工作。）

  * get a better job「找到更好的工作」

- **No, I don't like to dwell on the past.**

  （不，我不喜歡沉湎於過去。）

  * dwell on「沉湎於；老是想著」

- **Yeah, sometimes I think that was the happiest time of my life.**

  （是啊，有時我覺得那是我人生中最快樂的一段時光。）

ⓋⓄⒸⒶⒷⓊⓁⒶⓇⓎ 具體描述自己的好用字！

I have / don't have fond memories of school life. 我擁有／沒有美好的學生時代回憶。/ Those were the (good old) days. 那些日子真美好。/ devoted oneself to one's club activities 致力於社團活動 / focused on classes / studies 專注於課業／學業 / applied oneself to one's part-time job 努力打工 / worked hard at drinking 拚命喝酒 / threw oneself into job-hunting 全心投入求職 / worked hard to raise one's TOEIC score 努力提高多益測驗成績 / got a CPA certification 拿到合格會計師證照 (CPA = Certified Public Accountant) / attended college and technical school at the same time 同時念大學和技術學校 / got working experience through a company internship 透過企業實習獲得工作經驗

071

Is there something you would like to try studying in the future?
未來你有沒有想要進修什麼？

Dialogue 實戰會話　　　　　　　　　　　🎧 Track 72

A: Is there something you would like to try studying in the future?
（未來你有沒有想要進修什麼？）

B1: I'm thinking of trying to get an accounting certification. ☞
（我在想要去取得會計師資格。）

A: Really? Why?
（真的嗎？為什麼？）

B2: If I can do accounting, I'll never have to worry about finding work. ☞
（如果能做會計，我就不用煩惱找工作的問題了。）

✎ **Exercise** 請寫下自己的答案並試著說出來！

A：Is there something you would like to try studying in the future?

B1:

A：Really? Why?

B2:

☞ B1

- **I want to learn how to make my own website.**
  （我想學習怎麼做自己的網站。）
- **If I can save up enough money, I'd like to go abroad to study English.**
  （如果能存到足夠的錢，我想出國去學英文。）
  * save up「存錢」
- **If I have time, I want to go to cooking school.**
  （如果有時間，我想進烹飪學校。）

☞ B2

- **I want to make a website so that I have a medium to present my poetry and fiction to the public.**
  （我想做個網站，這樣我就有個媒介能對外發表我的詩詞和小說作品了。）
  * medium「媒介；媒體」；present「發表」
- **I can learn English and also learn how to be more independent at the same time.**
  （我可以學習英文，同時也能學會如何更獨立自主。）
- **I've always had a complex about not being able to cook.**
  （我對於自己不會做菜這件事一直有種自卑情結。）
  * complex「情結」

VOCABULARY 具體描述自己的好用字！

get 900 on the TOEIC 拿到多益測驗 900 分 / pass middle-level on the GEPT 通過全民英檢中級檢定 / get a nursing license 取得護理執照 / get a real estate license 取得不動產證照 / learn how to play an instrument 學習彈奏一種樂器 / get a license to be a psychiatric [ˌsaɪkɪˈætrɪk] social worker 取得精神醫學社工執照 / go back to school and study English again 回學校重新學英文 / take on high school mathematics again 再次挑戰高中數學 / study Taiwanese history more deeply 更深入研究台灣史 / prepar for one's employment exam 準備就業考試 / study for the mass media entrance exam 為考進傳播媒體而念書 / study Excel macros 研習 Excel 巨集 / study about care for the elderly 研習老人看護

liberal arts ▸ 通識課程	**job hunting** ▸ 求職
major course ▸ 主修課程	**job fair** ▸ 就業博覽會
selective course ▸ 選修課	**new graduate** ▸（剛畢業的）社會新鮮人
required course ▸ 必修課	**mid-career recruit** ▸ 招募轉職者
required credit ▸ 必修學分	**resignation notice** ▸ 離職通知；辭呈
transcript ▸ 成績單	**foreign company** ▸ 外商公司
excused absence ▸ 請假	**subsidiary** ▸ 分公司
school tuition fee ▸ 學費	**affiliate** ▸ 關係企業
tuition waiver ▸ 學費減免	**paid vacation** ▸ 有薪休假
undergraduate student ▸ 大學生	**housing allowance** ▸ 住宅津貼
graduate student ▸ 研究生	**probation period** ▸ 試用期
bachelor's degree ▸ 學士學位	**beginning salary** ▸ 起薪
master's degree ▸ 碩士學位	**annual income** ▸ 年收入
Ph.D. ▸ 博士學位	**annual salary system** ▸ 年薪制
teaching credential ▸ 教師證書	**payday** ▸ 發薪日

對話回應好用句 ⑤：猶豫・反對

「我不同意」

● **I'm not too sure about that.**（那部分我不是很確定。）

　▸ 心有疑慮時會這樣說。not too sure 直譯為中文就是「不太確定」。

● **That I'm not sure.**（那部分我不確定。）

　▸ 這句話特別強調「那部分」。

● **I wouldn't bet on it.**（我看不一定。）

　▸ bet on... 是「下注在……上」的意思。這句話直譯成中文就是「我不會下注在這件事上」。

● **I wouldn't go that far.**（我不會那麼篤定。）

　▸ 也就是「我無法那麼確定」之意。go that far 直譯為中文是「到那麼遠的程度」。

Unit 6

生活・健康・美容
Life, Health and Beauty

這些都是不可或缺的日常生活主題。
如果能事先將一些推薦個人喜好的句型準備妥當，
會話一定能更加愉快。

Do you cook?
What food do you like?
Are you health-conscious?
Do you go to the gym?
What do you do to relieve stress?
...

appearance

name

Taiwan culture

friends

work

dreams

interest

families

religion

experience

Do you cook?

你做菜嗎？

Dialogue 實戰會話　　　　　　　　　　🎧 Track 73

> **A: Do you cook?**
> （你做菜嗎？）
>
> **B1：I cook on the weekends, but I'm usually too busy to cook during the week.** 📖
> （我週末會做，但是平日通常忙得沒空做菜。）
>
> **A: What are you good at cooking?**
> （你擅長做什麼菜？）
>
> **B2：I wouldn't call myself a great cook, but my family likes my mapo tofu.** 📖
> （我不算是什麼厲害的大廚，但是我們家的人都很喜歡我做的麻婆豆腐。）

✎ **Exercise** 請寫下自己的答案並試著說出來！

A：Do you cook?

B1：

A：What are you good at cooking?

B2：

Substitution 更多回應說法！

☞ B1

- **I'm lazy, so I tend to cook a lot of fried dishes.**
  （我很懶，所以總是做很多熱炒類的菜餚。）
  * fried dish「熱炒料理」

- **I don't cook as much as I should. It's no fun cooking for one person.**
  （我應該要更常做菜，但是我並沒有。做一人份的菜實在很沒意思。）
  * not... as much as one should「沒有達到應……的程度」

- **I try to cook as much as possible. Eating out is so expensive.**
  （我盡量常做菜。外食很貴。）
  * expensive「昂貴的」

☞ B2

- **I like making pot dishes called "hot pot." Let's have a hot pot party sometime!**
  （我喜歡做「火鍋」類的大鍋菜。哪天我們來辦個火鍋派對吧！）
  * pot dish「鍋類料理」；hot pot「火鍋」

- **Actually, I'm better at making Italian dishes than Taiwanese dishes. My lasagna is always a big hit at parties.**
  （事實上，比起台灣菜，我更擅長做義大利菜。我的千層麵在派對中總是大受歡迎。）

- **I'm not very good at cooking, but I can make a decent "beef stew."**
  （我不是很擅長做菜，不過我做的「燉牛肉」還挺像樣的。）
  * decent「像樣的」；stew「燉肉」

𝒱𝒪𝒞𝒜ℬ𝒰ℒ𝒜ℛ𝒴 具體描述自己的好用字！

like cooking for people 喜歡為人做菜 / **one's girlfriend cooks for him** 某人的女朋友為他做菜 / **boiled food** 水煮料理 / **simmered fish** 燜魚 / **deep-fried food** 油炸料理 / **pork fillet cutlet** 日式里肌豬排 / **fried food** 熱炒食物 / **stir-fried meat and vegetables** 青菜炒肉絲 / **stir-fried spinach and bacon** 培根炒菠菜 / **steamed food** 清蒸料理 / **steamed egg custard** 蒸蛋 / **steamed vegetables** 清蒸蔬菜 / **giblet hot pot** 下水鍋；內臟火鍋 / **boiled tofu** 日式湯豆腐 / **grilled dishes** 燒烤料理 / **grilled chicken on skewers** 串烤雞肉

TIPS 介紹家鄉菜時，最好能先直接說出中文名稱，再接著補充說明，這樣對方會比較容易理解。很多菜餚像麻婆豆腐、宮保雞丁等料理，其中文發音和英文是一模一樣的。

073

What Taiwanese food do you recommend I try?

你推薦哪些台灣菜？

Dialogue 實戰會話　　　　　　　　　　　　　🎧 Track 74

A: What Taiwanese dish do you recommend I try?
（你推薦哪些台灣菜？）

B1: I think you should try oyster vermicelli, since it's hard to find outside of Taiwan. 📖
（我覺得你應該試試蚵仔麵線，因為很難在台灣以外的地方找到。）

A: Really? What place do you recommend?
（真的嗎？你推薦哪間店？）

B2: I know a good place in Gongyuan Road. The service is not that great, but the food is incredible. 📖
（我知道公園路上有一家店很不錯。那裡的服務沒有很好，但是東西真是美味得不可思議。）

* incredible「不可思議的；驚人的」

✎ **Exercise** 請寫下自己的答案並試著說出來！

A： What Taiwanese food do you recommend I try?

B1：

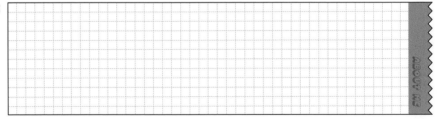

A： Really? What place do you recommend?

B2：

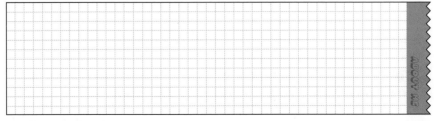

☞ **B1**

- **You'd probably like "spicy hot pot," a type of hot pot made with different kinds of chilis and spices.**
  （你可能會喜歡「麻辣火鍋」，一種用各式辣椒和香料煮成的火鍋。）
  * spicy hot pot「麻辣火鍋」；a type of...「一種……」

- **It's not exactly Taiwanese food, but I think you'd like steamed dumplings.**
  （雖然不算是真正的台灣菜，但是我想你會喜歡蒸餃。）
  * steamed dumplings「蒸餃」

- **While you're in Tainan, you should definitely have danzai noodles.**
  （在台南時，你肯定該吃吃擔仔麵。）
  * definitely「肯定地」

☞ **B2**

- **I heard there's a good place in a building called "Bestro 18," but I've never been there myself.**
  （我聽說在一棟叫 Bistro 18 的大樓裡有一家店很不錯，不過我自己還沒去過。）

- **It's actually a chain, but Din Tai Fung is pretty good. You can find them all over Taipei.**
  （那事實上是一間連鎖店，不過「鼎泰豐」真的相當好吃。你在台北各處都找得到。）
  * all over...「……各處；……各地」

- **I know a great place near Chihkan Tower. There's always a long line, but it's worth the wait.**
  （我知道在赤崁樓附近有一間店，總是大排長龍，但是值得等待。）
  * worth the wait「值得等待」

VOCABULARY 具體描述自己的好用字！

a little-known place 一個少有人知的地方（店）/ an out-of-the-way place 一個偏僻隱密的地方（店）/ a place famous for its sliced noodles 一個以刀削麵聞名的地方（店）/ the best beef noodles in town 城裡最棒的牛肉麵店 / shabu-shabu (beef / pork hot pot) 涮涮鍋（牛肉／豬肉火鍋）/ Hakka food 客家菜 / dim sum restaurant 港式飲茶餐廳 / Sichuanese food 四川菜 / Cantonese food 廣東菜 / street food 路邊攤 / barbequed corn 烤玉米 / stinky tofu 臭豆腐 / oyster omelet 蚵仔煎 / fried rice noodles 炒米粉 / fried potsticker 煎餃；鍋貼 / pearl milk tea 珍珠奶茶 / tofu pudding 豆花

074

What food do you like?

你喜歡什麼食物？

Dialogue 實戰會話 🔊 Track 75

A： **What food do you like?**
(你喜歡什麼食物？)

B1： **I like most kinds of food. I'm not picky.** ☞
(大部分食物我都喜歡。我不挑食。)

A： **What food do you dislike, then?**
(那，你不喜歡什麼食物？)

B2： **I don't see how people can eat natto. I find it disgusting.** ☞
(我不懂怎麼有人敢吃納豆。我覺得超噁心的。)

＊ picky「挑剔的」；disgusting「噁心的」

✎ **Exercise** 請寫下自己的答案並試著說出來！

A：**What food do you like?**

B1：

A：**What food do you dislike, then?**

B2：

Substitution 更多回應說法！

☞ **B1**

- **I like most countries' food, but nothing beats Chinese food.**
  （大部分國家的菜我都喜歡，但是沒有哪國料理能贏過中國菜。）
  * beat「勝過；打敗」

- **I'm really into Southeast Asian food. I particularly like Thai food.**
  （我真的很愛東南亞的食物，尤其喜歡泰國菜。）
  * be into...「熱衷於……；對……極有興趣」

- **I suppose my favorite is Italian food. I could live on pasta.**
  （我想我最愛的是義大利菜。我可以只靠義大利麵過活。）
  * suppose「猜想」

☞ **B2**

- **I'm not a big fan of fast food, like hamburgers and fried chicken.**
  （我不愛漢堡、炸雞之類的速食。）
  * fast food「速食」

- **I've never understood the appeal of Japanese eel.**
  （我一直都不懂鰻魚的魅力何在。）
  * appeal「魅力」；eel [il]「鰻魚」

- **Oily foods don't agree with me.**
  （油膩食物不合我的胃口。）
  * ... don't agree with someone「……不適合某人」

- - - - - - **VOCABULARY** 具體描述自己的好用字！ - - - - - -

healthy food 健康的食物 / **high-calorie food** 高熱量的食物 / **low-calorie food** 低熱量的食物 / **rich-tasting food** 重口味的食物 / **light-tasting food** 清淡的食物 / **organic food** 有機食品 / **instant food** 即食食品 / **frozen food** 冷凍食品 / **salty** 很鹹的 / **spicy** 富有香料味的；辣的 / **hot and spicy** 又香又辣 / **sweet** 甜的 / **sour** 酸的 / **sweet and sour** 酸酸甜甜的 / **bland** 沒味道的 / **bad-tasting** 難吃的 / **Mediterranean food** 地中海料理 / **Mexican food** 墨西哥菜 / **Turkish food** 土耳其菜 / **Thai food** 泰國菜 / **French food** 法國菜 / **Tex-Mex food** 德州風墨西哥菜

075

Do you drink much?

你酒喝得多嗎？

Dialogue 實戰會話　　　　　　　　　　　🔊 Track 76

> **A：Do you drink much?**
> （你酒喝得多嗎？）
>
> **B1：I wouldn't call myself a heavy drinker, but I drink fairly regularly.** ☞
> （我酒喝得不算多，但是還滿常喝的。）
>
> **A：Really? What do you usually order when you go drinking?**
> （真的嗎？出去喝酒的時候你通常都點什麼？）
>
> **B2：I usually start off with a beer, and then order shochu.** ☞
> （我多半從啤酒開始喝起，接著點日本燒酒。）
>
> ＊ start off with... 「從⋯⋯開始」

✎ **Exercise** 請寫下自己的答案並試著說出來！

A：Do you drink much?

B1：

A：Really? What do you usually order when you go drinking?

B2：

Substitution 更多回應說法！

☞ B1

- **No, I'm not much of a drinker. I only go drinking around once a month.**
  （不，我不是那麼愛喝酒的人。我一個月大約只去喝一次。）
  * be not much of a... 「不是那麼……」

- **Actually, my body can't take alcohol. I don't mind going to drinking parties once in a while, though.**
  （事實上，我的身體無法接受酒精。不過我也不介意偶爾參加飲酒聚會就是了。）
  * can't take 「（身體）無法接受」

- **I don't drink that often, but once I get going, I can drink quite a lot.**
  （我不是很常喝酒，不過一旦喝開，就能喝很多。）
  * get going 「展開」

☞ B2

- **It depends on the occasion. When I'm out with friends, I like to drink cocktails.**
  （這要看場合。如果是跟朋友出去，我就喜歡喝雞尾酒。）
  * occasion 「場合；時機」；cocktail 「雞尾酒」

- **I'm a beer person. I tend to stay away from spirits.**
  （我是啤酒愛好者。我通常不碰烈酒。）
  * stay away from... 「遠離……」；spirit 「蒸餾酒；烈酒」（如威士忌、白蘭地等）

- **I usually order a Coke or ginger ale. I enjoy the atmosphere, so I don't really feel like I'm missing anything.**
  （我通常都點可樂或薑汁汽水。我享受的是氣氛，所以並不覺得少了什麼東西。）
  * ginger ale [el] 「薑汁汽水」；atmosphere 「氣氛」

VOCABULARY 具體描述自己的好用字！

plum wine 梅酒 / red / white wine 紅 / 白酒 / rosé 粉紅酒 / highball 威士忌加可樂或蘇打的調酒 / whisky 威士忌 / brandy 白蘭地 / vodka 伏特加 / tequila 龍舌蘭酒 / rum 蘭姆酒 / cognac（法國）干邑白蘭地 / straight 純的 / on the rocks 加冰塊 / whisky on the rocks 威士忌加冰塊 / whisky and water 威士忌對水 / whisky with soda 威士忌加蘇打 / whisky with hot water 威士忌加熱水 / be pretty tolerant 酒量很好 / have no tolerance 酒量很差 / get drunk 喝醉 / get blind drunk 喝得爛醉 / get a hangover 宿醉 / get sick 想吐

076

What kind of place do you live in?
你住在什麼樣的地方？

Dialogue 實戰會話　　　　　　　　　　🎧 Track 77

A: What kind of place do you live in?
(你住在什麼樣的地方？)

B1: I live in an apartment on the top floor of a 4-story building. ☞
(我住在一棟 4 層公寓的頂樓。)

A: How do you like it?
(你喜歡那裡嗎？)

B2: I like it because I have a great view of the city. The rent is a little high, though. ☞
(我很喜歡，因為有美麗的城市街景可看。不過租金有點貴。)

＊ rent「租金」

✏️ **Exercise** 請寫下自己的答案並試著說出來！

A：What kind of place do you live in?
B1：

A：How do you like it?
B2：

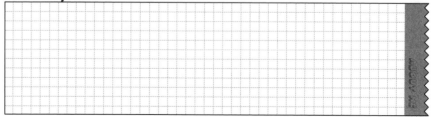

Substitution 更多回應說法！

☞ B1

- **I live in a one-bedroom apartment in a quiet, rural area.**
  （我住在幽靜鄉下的一間公寓套房裡。）
  - * one-bedroom apartment「只有一個房間的公寓；套房」；rural「鄉下的；田園的」
  - **TIPS** 在英語中，通常都以房間數表示家的大小。
- **I have a small condominium in Taipei.**
  （我在台北有一間小的大樓住宅。）
  - * condominium [ˌkɑndə`mɪnɪəm]「大樓住宅；有獨立產權的公寓」（簡稱 condo）
- **I live with my parents in a 3-bedroom house in a suburb of Taipei.**
  （我和父母住在台北郊區一個 3 房的屋子裡。）
  - * in a suburb of...「在……的郊區」

☞ B2

- **I really like the area, but I want to move to a bigger place.**
  （我真的很喜歡這個區域，但是我想搬到大一點的地方。）
- **It's quite cramped, but the location is convenient.**
  （那房子相當狹小，不過位置很方便。）
  - * cramped「狹窄的」；location「位置」
- **It's great. I'm lucky to have a nice place that's close to my office.**
  （很棒啊。我很幸運能住在離公司這麼近的地方。）
  - * close to...「離……很近」

ᏉᎾᏟᎪᏴᏌᏞᎪᎡᎩ 具體描述自己的好用字！

two / three-bedroom apartment / house 2／3 房的公寓／屋子 / studio apartment 小套房 / one's own house 自己的房子 / apartment 公寓 / public apartment house 國宅 / town house（2 到 3 層樓的）市區住宅 / stand-alone house 獨棟洋房；透天厝 / spacious 寬敞的 / roof with solar panels 裝有太陽能板的屋頂 / Japanese tile roof 日式瓦片屋頂 / bright entrance area 明亮的玄關 / dining room with a table for 6 有張 6 人坐餐桌的飯廳 / living room with a large sofa 有張大沙發的客廳 / verandah [vəˋrændə] that gets plenty of sunshine 有充足陽光的陽台 / with a yard 有個庭院 / lawn 草坪 / prefabricated [ˌpriˋfæbrɪketɪd] bath 組裝浴室 / integrated kitchen system 整合式廚房 / floor heating 地板型暖氣 / pets not allowed 禁止飼養寵物 / neighbor 鄰居

077

What kind of clothes do you like?
你喜歡哪種服裝？

Dialogue 實戰會話 　　　　　　　　　　　　　　　🎧 Track 78

A: **What kind of clothes do you like?**
（你喜歡哪種服裝？）

B1: **I like sporty clothes that are easy to move around in.** ☞
（我喜歡方便活動的運動類服飾。）

A: **Where do you buy your clothes?**
（你都去哪裡買衣服？）

B2: **I like to shop at outdoor brand shops.** ☞
（我喜歡到戶外用品的品牌店去買。）

✎ Exercise 請寫下自己的答案並試著說出來！

A：What kind of clothes do you like?

B1:

A：Where do you buy your clothes?

B2:

Substitution 更多回應說法！

B1

- **I like clothes that are stylish but functional.**
  （我喜歡時髦但是又實用的衣服。）
  * stylish「時髦的」；functional「有機能的；實用的」

- **I'm not that into fashion. I just wear whatever I feel like.**
  （我對時尚沒那麼有興趣。我總是想穿什麼就穿什麼。）
  * whatever one feel like「想穿什麼就穿什麼」

- **I like clothes that are feminine, but not too cutesy.**
  （我喜歡女性化的衣服，但是不能太裝可愛。）
  * feminine [ˈfɛmənɪn]「女性的；女性化的」；cutesy「故作討人喜愛的」

B2

- **I buy most of my underwear at places like UNIQLO, but for outerwear I shop at department stores.**
  （我大部分的內衣褲都去優衣庫之類的地方買，不過外衣就會去百貨公司買。）
  * undererwear「內衣」；outerwear「外衣」

- **I often go shopping at secondhand clothing stores.**
  （我經常去二手服飾店購物。）
  * secondhand clothing store「二手服飾店」

- **Those days I do most of my shopping online.**
  （最近我幾乎都在網路上購物。）
  * online「在網路上」

VOCABULARY 具體描述自己的好用字！

be in style 流行的；時尚的 / go out of style 跟不上流行 / be on the cutting edge 最先進的；走在時代尖端的 / follow the latest trends 跟隨最新趨勢 / wear what other people are wearing 別人穿什麼就跟著穿什麼 / be particular about... 對……特別講究 / standard design 標準設計 / unusual design 特殊設計 / casual 休閒的 / formal 正式的 / chic 時髦的 / flashy 俗豔的 / subdued 柔和的 / bright-colored 色彩鮮豔的 / dark-colored 深色的 / cold- colored 冷色系的 / warm-colored 暖色系的 / with a floral pattern / vertical stripes / horizontal stripes / a paisley pattern 有花朵圖樣的 / 直條紋的 / 橫條紋的 / 佩斯利渦旋圖樣的 / handmade clothes 手工製作的服裝 / hand-sewn clothes 手工縫製的服裝 / hand-knit sweater / gloves 手工編織的毛衣 / 手套 / tailored dress shirt 訂做的西裝襯衫 / made-to-order suit 訂做西裝 / ready-made suit 成衣西裝 / designer-brand dress 設計師品牌的連身裙

078

Is there any aspect of your appearance that you are particularly careful about?
在自己的外觀上，是否有哪方面是你特別注意的？

Dialogue 實戰會話　　　　　　　　　　　🔊 Track 79

A: Is there any aspect of your appearance that you are particularly careful about?
（在自己的外觀上，是否有哪方面是你特別注意的？）

B1: I try to pay attention to the way I carry myself. I think good posture is very important. ☞
（我會盡量注意自己的舉止，我認為良好的姿勢非常重要。）

A: What do you wish people of the opposite sex paid more attention to?
（你希望異性能多注意哪個方面？）

B2: I wish men paid more attention to how they dress. ☞
（我希望男人能多注意他們的穿著。）

＊ aspect「方面」；pay attention to「注意」；Carry oneself「舉止」；posture「姿勢」

✎ **Exercise** 請寫下自己的答案並試著說出來！

A：Is there any aspect of your appearance that you are particularly careful about?

B1:

A：What do you wish people of the opposite sex paid more attention to?

B2:

☞ **B1**

- **As I get older, I worry more about my skin.**
  （隨著年齡增加，我越來越擔心我的皮膚。）
- **I think people pay a lot of attention to the eyes, so I'm careful about how I do my eyes.**
  （我覺得大家都很注意眼睛，所以我會仔細地畫眼妝。）
  * do one's eyes「畫眼妝」
- **I think your shoes say a lot about who you are.**
  （我認為一個人的鞋子就代表了他的人。）
  * who you are「你是怎樣的人」

☞ **B2**

- **I always look at a man's hands to make sure he is well-manicured.**
  （我總會觀察一個男人的手，確認他指甲修剪得很好。）
  * well-manicured「指甲修剪得很好的」
- **I wish men had better taste in fashion. There aren't enough well-dressed men around.**
  （我希望男人的時尚品味能更好些。穿著體面的男人實在不夠多。）
  * well-dressed「穿著體面的」
- **Being well-dressed is not a bad thing, but worrying too much about it is a turn-off.**
  （衣著體面並不是件壞事，但是太在意穿著可是會令人反感的。）
  * turn-off「令人反感的人或事物」

VOCABULARY 具體描述自己的好用字！

pay attention to one's clothes / hairstyle / skin / makeup / shoes / under-wear / cleanliness 注意某人的服裝 / 髮型 / 皮膚 / 化妝 / 鞋子 / 內衣褲 / 清潔 / **proper clothes / appearance / hairstyle** / 適當的服裝 / 外觀 / 髮型 / slovenly [ˈslʌvənlɪ] / shabby [ˈʃæbɪ] clothes 邋遢的 / 窮酸 的服裝 / **don't worry much about how I look** 不是很在意我的外表 / **looks are not important** 外 貌不重要 / **always worry about how I come off to the opposite sex** 總是很在意異性對我的觀感 / **have a complex about one's nose** 對自己的鼻子有一種複雜的情結 / **I wish I had fairer / darker skin.** 我希望我的皮膚更白 / 黑些。 / **I wish I had naturally curly hair.** 我希望我有自然捲。

079

Are you health-conscious?

你注重健康嗎？

Dialogue 實戰會話　　　　　　　　　　　🔊 Track 80

A: **Are you health-conscious?**
（你注重健康嗎？）

B1: **I try to watch my diet, but I don't exercise as much as I should.** ☞
（我會注意飲食，但是我的運動量不夠。）

A: **I think staying healthy is so important.**
（我覺得保持健康非常重要。）

B2: **Yeah, you don't appreciate your health until you get sick.** ☞
（是啊，人總是病了之後才了解到健康的重要。）

＊ appreciate「體會；領會（事物的真正價值）」

✎ **Exercise** 請寫下自己的答案並試著說出來！

A：**Are you health-conscious?**

B1：

A：**I think staying healthy is so important.**

B2：
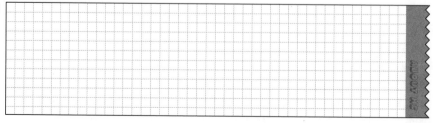

Substitution 更多回應說法！

☞ B1

● **I would say so. I take vitamins every day, and I work out two or three times a week.**
（我想是吧。我每天都吃維他命，而且每週運動二或三次。）
＊ take「服用（藥物）」；work out「運動」

● **I think I lead a pretty healthy lifestyle, except for the occasional chocolate binge.**
（除了偶爾會狂吃巧克力外，我覺得我的生活方式相當健康。）
＊ binge [bɪndʒ]「狂吃狂喝」

● **Since my doctor told me my cholesterol level is high, I've started becoming more health-conscious.**
（自從醫生跟我說我的膽固醇過高後，我就開始更注意健康了。）
＊ cholesterol [kəˋlɛstəˏrol]「膽固醇」

☞ B2

● **I agree. I wish I had taken better care of my health when I was younger.**
（我同意。真希望我年輕時有更妥善照顧自己的健康。）
＊ take care of...「照顧……」

● **I can't argue with that. What's your secret to staying healthy?**
（這點我無可爭議。你維持健康的秘訣是什麼？）

● **That's true, but I think it's also important to enjoy life while you are healthy.**
（沒錯，但是我覺得趁身體還健康時趕快享受人生也是很重要的。）
＊ enjoy life「享受人生」

𝒱ocabulary 具體描述自己的好用字！

watch one's calorie / sodium [ˋsodɪəm] intake 注意個人的熱量／鈉的攝取 / watch one's diet 注意個人的飲食 / avoid fatty foods 避免油膩食物 / pay attention to one's blood pressure 注意個人的血壓 / choose low calorie foods 選擇低熱量食物 / eat foods that are good for the body 吃對身體有益的食物 / take care not to drink too much alcohol 小心不要喝太多酒 / cut down on cigarettes 少抽菸 / quit smoking 戒菸 / continue exercising 持續運動 / burn calories through exercise 靠運動燃燒熱量 / cut down on eating and drinking to excess 減少暴飲暴食 / change one's eating habits 改變個人飲食的習慣 / try various diets 嘗試各種飲食 / make a habit of taking waist-deep baths 養成泡半身浴的習慣

Do you go to the gym?

你上健身房嗎？

Dialogue 實戰會話   🅖 Track 81

A: Do you go to the gym?
（你上健身房嗎？）

B1: I just joined last month. I try to go at least twice a week. 📖
（我上個月才加入。我盡量一週至少去兩次。）

A: What do you do? Do you swim?
（你都做些什麼？你游泳嗎？）

B2: No, I mainly work out on the machines and do a little running. 📖
（不游，我主要利用運動器材運動，並稍微跑個步。）

✎ **Exercise** 請寫下自己的答案並試著說出來！

A： Do you go to the gym?

B1：

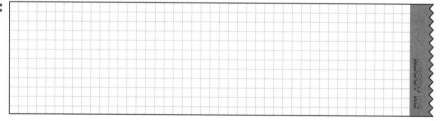

A： What do you do? Do you swim?

B2：

Substitution 更多回應說法！

☞ **B1**

- I used to go two or three times a week, but recently I've been slacking off.
  （我以前一週去個兩、三次，但是最近懈怠了。）
  * slack off「鬆懈；懈怠」
- Yeah, my friend forces me to go with her every week.
  （去啊，我朋友強迫我每週都跟她一起去。）
  * force someone to...「強迫（某人）做……」
- Yeah, it's one of the perks of my job. I often stop by after work.
  （去啊，這是我們公司的福利之一。我下班後通常會順便過去一趟。）
  * one of the perks of one's job「某人工作（公司）的福利之一」

☞ **B2**

- No, I'm not a very good swimmer. I usually lift weights.
  （不游，我不是很會游泳。我通常都練舉重。）
  * lift weights「舉重」
- No, I usually just go to the aerobics and yoga classes.
  （不游，我通常只去上有氧舞蹈課和瑜珈課。）
  * aerobics「有氧舞蹈」
- Yeah, I try to swim at least 20 laps.
  （游，我會試著游至少 20 趟。）
  * lap「（游泳池的泳道）一個來回」

······ 𝒱ᴏᴄᴀʙᴜʟᴀʀʏ 具體描述自己的好用字！

join a gym 加入健身房（成為健身房會員）/ become a weekday / holiday / night member 成為平日 / 假日 / 夜間會員 / have someone make a personal training menu 請某人幫忙設計個人訓練清單 / have a personal trainer 有私人教練 / be on a special program 在進行特別的計畫 / do stretches 伸展運動 / do the Stairmaster 用模擬爬樓梯的機器做運動 / do bench presses 做臥舉訓練運動 / do push-ups 做伏地挺身 / do sit-ups 做仰臥起坐 / do pull-ups 做引體向上 / take t'ai chi / aerobics / yoga / dance classes 上太極拳 / 有氧舞蹈 / 瑜珈 / 舞蹈課程 / change into a swimsuit 換上泳衣 / put on goggles 戴上護目鏡 / take a shower 沖澡；淋浴 / get in the Jacuzzi [dʒəˋkuzɪ] 進入按摩浴池 / go in the sauna [ˋsɑunə] 進三溫暖浴室 / get a massage 讓人按摩

What do you do to relieve stress?

你都做些什麼來紓解壓力？

Dialogue 實戰會話　　　　　　　　　　　　🔊 Track 82

A：**What do you do to relieve stress?**
（你都做些什麼來紓解壓力？）

B1：**I've found that lists are helpful.** 🔊
（我發現列清單很有用。）

A：**Hmmm, maybe I should try that. What exactly do you do?**
（嗯，也許我也該試試。那你到底做些什麼？）

B2：**For example, if I'm stressed about a project, I write down the specific things I need to do.** 🔊
（舉例來說，當我因為某個案子覺得壓力大的時候，我就把必須做的具體事項寫下來。）

＊ specific「特定的；明確的；具體的」

✎ **Exercise** 請寫下自己的答案並試著說出來！

A：What do you do to relieve stress?

B1：

A：Hmmm, maybe I should try that. What exactly do you do?

B2：

☞ **B1**

- **Massage works really well for me.**
  （對我來說按摩真的很有效。）
  * work「有效」

- **When I get stressed out, I go for a drive.**
  （當我覺得壓力太大的時候，就去開車兜風。）
  * get stressed out「壓力過大」

- **I set aside a few minutes every evening for meditation.**
  （我每天傍晚會撥出幾分鐘進行冥想。）
  * set aside「撥出時間」；meditation「冥想」

☞ **B2**

- **I go to a professional reflexologist. I can give you her number, if you like.**
  （我都去找一個專業的腳底按摩師。如果你也想試試，我可以把她的電話號碼給你。）
  * reflexologist「腳底按摩師」

- **Well, I turn the music up loud and sing along while I'm driving on the highway.**
  （嗯，我會在開車奔馳於高速公路上的時候，把音樂聲轉大並跟著唱。）
  * sing along「跟著唱」

- **Actually, I have a CD. I just do what the teacher says.**
  （事實上我有一張 CD。我只是跟著老師說的做而已。）

╌╌╌ **VOCABULARY** 具體描述自己的好用字！

manage one's time 管理個人的時間 / clean one's room 打掃個人的房間 / look at one's aquarium fish 看著水族箱裡的魚 / take a bath 泡個澡 / go to karaoke 去唱卡拉 OK / do some exercise 做些運動 / get out of the house 出門去 / go for a walk 去散步 / take deep breaths 深呼吸 / smoke (cigarettes) 抽菸 / drink hot coffee 喝熱咖啡 / have a silly talk with a friend 和朋友聊些五四三 / go drinking with a coworker 和同事去喝一杯 / stuff oneself (to ease stress) 大吃一頓（來紓壓）/ waste money 亂花錢 / go to a place with lots of greenery 去充滿綠意的地方 / take it easy at the park 在公園放鬆一下 / go traveling 去旅行 / do boxercise 做健身拳擊 / talk to a friend 與朋友聊聊 / read self-help books 閱讀自我啟發書籍 / play the piano 彈鋼琴 / go on a shopping binge 瘋狂購物 / take it out on other people 拿別人出氣

How often do you exercise?
你多久運動一次？

Dialogue 實戰會話　　　　　　　　　　　🔊 Track 83

A: **How often do you exercise?**
（你多久運動一次？）

B1: **I do yoga every morning, right after I get up.** 📖
（我每天早上起床後，都會馬上做瑜珈。）

A: **Do you ever find it difficult to keep it up?**
（你是否曾覺得要持續下去很不容易？）

B2: **It was difficult at first, but now it's just part of my daily**
routine. 📖
（一開始很難，但是現在這已經成為我日常作息的一部分了。）

* keep up「持續；保持」；routine「日常作息；固定要做的工作」

✎ **Exercise** 請寫下自己的答案並試著說出來！

A：**How often do you exercise?**

B1:

A：**Do you ever find it difficult to keep it up?**

B2:
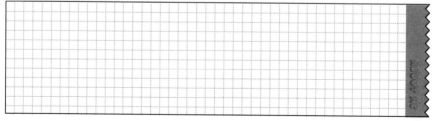

Substitution 更多回應說法！

☞ B1

- **Since I commute by bicycle, I manage to get some aerobic exercise every day.**
  （因為我騎自行車通勤，所以每天都能做到一點有氧運動。）
  * manage to... 「設法做到……」
- **I take classes at the health club nearly every day.**
  （我幾乎每天都去健身俱樂部上課。）
  * health club 「健身俱樂部」
- **I go jogging in my neighborhood almost every other day.**
  （我幾乎每隔一天就去附近慢跑一次。）
  * every other day 「每隔一天」

☞ B2

- **I'm often tempted to take the train when the weather's bad, but I usually stick to my regimen.**
  （天氣不好的時候，我常常會忍不住想坐火車，但是我通常都還是堅守我的養身方法。）
  * stick to... 「堅持……；堅守……」；regimen [ˋrɛdʒmɛn] 「養生法」
- **I actually enjoy it, so I have no trouble making myself do it.**
  （我事實上樂在其中，所以強迫自己那麼做並不難。）
  * have no trouble Ving 「做……並不困難」
- **When I'm busy it's tough, but I try to go at least two days a week.**
  （忙的時候就很辛苦，但是我都盡可能一週至少去兩次。）
  * at least 「至少」

VOCABULARY 具體描述自己的好用字！

every night 每晚 / once a week 一週一次 / three times a week 每週三次 / once every two weeks 每兩週一次 / exercise that's easy to continue doing 容易持續的運動 / can do in one's spare time 可在閒暇時做 / be difficult to continue doing 很難持續做 / while watching a DVD 在看 DVD 的同時 / in the bath 在泡澡時 / exercise for increasing stamina [ˋstæmənə] 增強體力的運動 / for increasing flexibility 為了增加柔軟度 / for building muscles 為了鍛鍊肌肉 / for losing weight 為了減重 / to get rid of the fat on one's upper arms / waist / hips / thighs 消除上臂 / 腰部 / 臀部 / 大腿的贅肉 / to stay young 保持年輕 / to stay healthy 維持健康 / to increase one's metabolism [mɛˋtæbḷˌɪzm] 提升代謝率 / aerobic exercise 有氧運動 / rigorous / moderate / leisurely exercise 激烈的 / 適度的 / 悠閒輕鬆的運動

083

What do you recommend as a way to stay healthy?
你會推薦用什麼方式來維持健康？

Dialogue 實戰會話　　　　　🔊 Track 84

A: What do you recommend as a way to stay healthy?
（你會推薦用什麼方式來維持健康？）

B1: I recommend walking. I make a point of walking at least three thousand steps a day. ☞
（我推薦走路。我每天必定至少走三千步。）

A: That sounds good. You look great. What's your beauty secret?
（聽起來真不錯。你看來氣色很好。你美麗的祕訣是什麼？）

B2: I go to a beauty treatment salon once a week. ☞
（我每週去一次美容沙龍。）

　* make a point of... 「必定做……；把……視為必要」；beauty treatment salon「美容沙龍」

✎ **Exercise** 請寫下自己的答案並試著說出來！

A: What do you recommend as a way to stay healthy?
B1:

A: That sounds good. You look great. What's your beauty secret?
B2:

☞ **B1**

● **I try as much as possible to go to bed and get up early.**
（我盡量早睡早起。）
 ＊ as much as possible「盡量」

● **I feel much better since I started doing aerobics.**
（自從我開始做有氧運動，就覺得身體狀況好多了。）
 ＊ feel better「覺得（身體狀況）更好了」

● **I think it's important to eat right and get plenty of exercise.**
（我認為正確的飲食和大量運動是很重要的。）
 ＊ eat right「正確地飲食」；plenty of...「大量的……」

☞ **B2**

● **I avoid eating rich, fatty foods. Junk food makes my skin break out.**
（我會避免吃高脂、高熱量的食物。垃圾食物會讓我的皮膚長疹子。）
 ＊ avoid「避免」；rich, fatty foods「高脂、高熱量的食物」；break out「長滿（疹子、痘子等）」

● **Actually, I do 50 sit-ups every day in order to maintain my figure.**
（事實上，為了維持體態，我每天都做 50 個仰臥起坐。）
 ＊ sit-ups「仰臥起坐」；maintain「維持」；figure「體型」

● **I don't do anything special, but I try to get plenty of beauty sleep.**
（我沒做什麼特別的，不過我會設法睡足美容覺。）
 ＊ beauty sleep「美容覺（為了美容而保持充足睡眠）」

⋯⋯ 𝒱ᴏᴄᴀʙᴜʟᴀʀʏ 具體描述自己的好用字！

eat foods that are low in cholesterol 吃低膽固醇的食物 / eat plenty of vegetables 多吃蔬菜 / eat a wide variety of foods 吃各式各樣不同的食物 / cut down on red meat 減少紅肉的攝取量 / avoid getting stressed out 避免壓力過大 / drink in moderation 飲酒適量 / do stretches on breaks from work 在工作的休息時間做伸展運動 / get plenty of rest on the weekend 在週末充分休息 / keep a smile on one's face 時時保持笑臉 / drink green tea 喝綠茶 / drink hyaluronic [ˌhaɪljuˈrɑnɪk] acid 喝玻尿酸 / get lots of fiber 多攝取纖維質 / never go without one's oil massages 精油按摩（油壓）絕不可少 / apply plenty of moisturizing cream 擦很多保濕乳液

084

Do you have an inferiority complex?

你有自卑感嗎？

Dialogue 實戰會話　　　　　　　　　　　　　　🔊 Track 85

A: Do you have an inferiority complex?
（你有自卑感嗎？）

B1: I've always been self-conscious about my legs. ☞
（我總是對自己的腿感到不自在。）

A: No way! Why?
（不會吧！為什麼？）

B2: They're too short. I wish I had long legs like you. ☞
（我的腿太短了。我真希望能像你一樣擁有一雙修長的腿。）

* be self-conscious about... 「在意……；對……感到不自在」

✎ **Exercise** 請寫下自己的答案並試著說出來！

A： Do you have an inferiority complex?

B1:

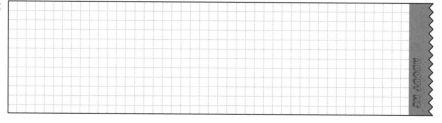

A： No way! Why?

B2:

Substitution 更多回應說法！

☞ **B1**

- **Sometimes I wish I weren't so tall.**
  （有時我會希望自己沒這麼高。）

- **Yeah, I've always suffered from feelings of inferiority.**
  （有啊，我一直為自卑感所苦。）
  * feelings of inferiority [ɪnfɪrɪˋɑrətɪ]「自卑感」

- **I wouldn't go so far as to call it a complex, but I don't like my eyes.**
  （我還不至於稱它為自卑情結，但是我確實不喜歡我的眼睛。）
  * wouldn't go as far as to...「不至於……」

☞ **B2**

- **For one thing, I can't wear high heels. Also, I get tired of people asking me how tall I am.**
  （一則是我不會穿高跟鞋。再者，我對於大家總是問我多高感到非常厭煩。）
  * for one thing「一則是；首先是」

- **I don't like my figure. My butt is too big and my bust is too small.**
  （我不喜歡自己的體態。我的屁股太大，胸部又太小。）
  * figure「體態」

- **I have single eyelids. I wish I had double eyelids like Westerners.**
  （我是單眼皮。我希望能擁有像西方人那樣的雙眼皮。）
  * single / double eyelids「單 / 雙眼皮」

𝒱ᴏᴄᴀʙᴜʟᴀʀʏ 具體描述自己的好用字！

have confidence 有自信 / be lacking in confidence 缺乏自信 / suffer from low self-esteem 為自卑所苦 / my face is big 我的臉很大 / have lots of wrinkles / flab on one's face 臉部有很多皺紋 / 鬆弛的肥肉 / have lots of spots / freckles / pimples 有很多斑點 / 雀斑 / 痘子 / have bags under one's eyes 有眼袋 / have lots of unwanted hair 有很多雜毛 / thin / drooping / slanted / bulging eyes 很小 / 下垂 / 斜 / 凸眼睛 / have high canines / buck teeth / a bad bite 有虎牙 / 暴牙 / 牙齒咬合不良 / one's nose is big / small / hooked / bulbous 鼻子大 / 鼻子小 / 鷹勾鼻 / 蒜頭鼻 / thick / thin lips 厚 / 薄嘴唇 / large / small ears / mouth 大 / 小耳朵 / 嘴巴 / bowlegged O型腿 / pigeon-toed 內八字（腳）/ fingers / arms / upper arms / hips / waist / thighs / calves / ankles are / is fat 手指 / 手臂 / 上臂 / 臀部 / 腰部 / 大腿 / 小腿 / 腳踝很粗

085

Do you have any chronic health problems?
你有慢性的健康問題嗎？

Dialogue 實戰會話　　　　　　　　　🔊 Track 86

A： Do you have any chronic health problems?
（你有慢性的健康問題嗎？）

B1： I've had asthma ever since I was little. ☞
（我從小就有氣喘的毛病。）

A： That's too bad. How do you deal with it?
（真糟糕。你都怎麼應付這問題？）

B2： As long as I stay away from certain plants, I'm OK. ☞
（只要遠離某些植物就行了。）

* chronic [`krɑnɪk]「慢性的」；asthma [`æzmə]「氣喘」；stay away from...「遠離……」

✎ **Exercise** 請寫下自己的答案並試著說出來！

A： Do you have any chronic health problems?
B1：

A： That's too bad. How do you deal with it?
B2：

☞ **B1**

- **I suffer from hay fever every year in early spring.**
  （我每年初春都苦於花粉熱。）
  ＊ suffer from... 「患有；苦於（疾病）」；hay fever 「花粉熱」

- **I suffer from lower back pain.**
  （我為腰痛所苦。）
  ＊ lower back pain 「腰痛」

- **I'm very sensitive to the cold.**
  （我很怕冷。）

  ＊ sensitive to... 「對……敏感」

  TIPS 想談「手腳冰冷」之類的話題時，就要像這樣講。另外也可說成 I tend to get cold hands and feet.（我很容易手腳冰冷。）

☞ **B2**

- **I take medication, but it doesn't help much.**
  （我有吃藥，但是幫助不大。）
  ＊ take medication 「服藥」

- **I see an acupuncturist once a month.**
  （我每個月會去針灸一次。）
  ＊ acupuncturist [ˌækjʊˋpʌŋktʃərɪst] 「針灸師」；once a month 「每月一次」

- **Nothing in particular. I just try to keep warm at all times.**
  （我沒特別做什麼。我就是時時注意保暖。）
  ＊ in particular 「特別地」

⌒⌒⌒ **Ⓥⓞⓒⓐⓑⓤⓛⓐⓡⓨ** 具體描述自己的好用字！ ⌒⌒⌒

be allergic to cats / mold / house dust 對貓 / 黴菌 / 室內灰塵過敏 / **rhinitis** [raɪˋnaɪtɪs] 鼻炎 / **have anemia** [əˋnimɪə] 有貧血 / **be very sensitive to chemicals / fragrances** 對化學物質 / 香味很敏感 / **have eczema** [ˋɛksɪmə] 有濕疹 / **have high / low blood pressure** 血壓高 / 低 / **have kidney** [ˋkɪdnɪ] **disease** 有腎臟病 / **have heart disease** 有心臟病 / **have diabetes** [ˌdaɪəˋbitiz] 有糖尿病 / **have rheumatism** [ˋrumə,tɪzəm] 有風濕症 / **have a weak stomach** 腸胃不好 / **have migraines** [ˋmaɪgren] 有偏頭痛 / **have a hernia** [ˋhɜnɪə] 有疝氣 / **be susceptible** [səˋsɛptəbl] **to dislocation** 容易脫臼

086

Have you ever had a serious injury / illness?
你是否曾受過嚴重的傷 / 生過大病？

Dialogue 實戰會話　　　　　　　　　　　🎧 Track 87

> **A：** **Have you ever had a serious injury?**
> （你是否曾受過嚴重的傷？）
> ＊ serious「嚴重的；重大的」
>
> **B1：** **I once got hit by a car when I was riding my bike. I was in the hospital for 3 weeks.** 📖
> （我曾經在騎自行車時被汽車撞到。當時在醫院住了 3 個禮拜。）
> ＊ get hit「被撞」
>
> **A：** **Nothing beats being in good health.**
> （健康比什麼都重要。）
>
> **B2：** **You can say that again. I wish I were as healthy and fit as you.** 📖
> （確實如此。我真希望自己能像你一樣健康。）
> ＊ healthy and fit「健康的」

✎ **Exercise** 請寫下自己的答案並試著說出來！

A：Have you ever had a serious injury?

B1：

A：Nothing beats being in good health.

B2：

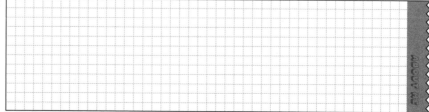

☞ **B1**

- **I once broke my collarbone in a car accident.**
  （我曾經在一次車禍中撞斷了鎖骨。）
  * collarbone [ˋkɑlɚˌbon]「鎖骨」；accident「意外事故」

- **I suffer from diabetes, but I'm fine as long as I take my medication.**
  （我為糖尿病所苦，但是只要好好吃藥就沒問題。）
  * diabetes「糖尿病」

- **I've never had a serious injury, but I was once hospitalized for pneumonia.**
  （我從沒受過嚴重的傷，不過曾經因為肺炎而住院。）
  * be hospitalized for...「因……住院」；pneumonia [njuˋmonɪə]「肺炎」

☞ **B2**

- **That is so true. It's easy to take your health for granted.**
  （的確是這樣。人很容易就把健康視為理所當然。）
  * take... for granted「把……視為理所當然」

- **The older I get, the more I appreciate my health.**
  （活得越老，我就越懂得珍惜健康的價值。）
  * appreciate「理解；體會真正的價值」

- **It sounds like you've had some health problems of your own.**
  （聽起來，你本身似乎有一些健康問題。）
  * sound like...「聽起來像……」

VOCABULARY 具體描述自己的好用字！

stay healthy 保持健康 / have a complete physical (examination) 接受完整的健康檢查 / get sick 生病 / have surgery 接受手術 / have a tumor removed 切除腫瘤 / get (radiation) treatment 做（放射線）治療 / undergo rehabilitation 進行復健 / recover 恢復 / leave the hospital 出院 / have the flu 感染流行性感冒 / food poisoning 食物中毒 / get cancer 罹癌 / be burned badly 嚴重燒傷 / break one's arm 手臂骨折 / get in a car accident 遭遇車禍 / fall down the stairs 摔下樓梯

have a headache ▸ 頭痛	wisdom tooth ▸ 智齒
have a backache ▸ 背痛；腰痛	dentures ▸ 假牙
have a stomachache ▸ 胃痛	eyesight ▸ 視力
have a runny nose ▸ 流鼻水	nearsighted ▸ 近視的
head cold ▸ 傷風	farsighted ▸ 遠視的
catch a cold ▸ 得了感冒	canker sore ▸ 口瘡；口內潰瘍
get constipated ▸ 便祕	stiff shoulders / neck ▸ 肩 / 頸僵硬
have diarrhea ▸ 拉肚子	disc herniation ▸ 椎間盤突出
sneeze ▸ 打噴嚏	sprain ▸ 扭傷
have a sore throat ▸ 喉嚨痛	period ▸ 生理期
vomit / throw up ▸ 嘔吐	have cramps ▸ 生理痛
get dehydrated ▸ 脫水	get pregnant ▸ 懷孕
get food poisoning ▸ 食物中毒	have a miscarriage ▸ 流產
feel nauseous ▸ 覺得噁心	feel weak ▸ 覺得虛弱
cavity ▸ 蛀牙	get depressed ▸ 感到沮喪

對話回應好用句 ⑥：反對

「我不同意」

● **I don't agree with you.**（我不贊同你的看法。）
▸ 也就是「我認為你的看法不對」之意。

● **I don't agree with you at all.**（我一點都不贊同你的看法。）
▸ not... at all 就是「一點也不………」。本句用來表達完全不認同對方的意見。

● **I don't think so at all.**（我一點兒也不這麼認為。）
▸ 用於表達「完全不以為然」的反對態度。

● **I disagree.**（我不同意。）
▸ 表示「我不覺得是這樣；我反對」等強烈否定之意。

● **I totally disagree.**（我完全不認同。）
▸ totally 就是「全然地；完全地」。

● **I disagree with you completely.**（我完全不認同你的意見。）
▸ completely 就是「完全地；徹底地」。

● **I can't disagree with you more.**（我非常不認同你的意見。）
▸ 這是非常強烈的說法，直譯成中文就是「我不能再更不認同你了」。

Unit 7

台灣二三事
About Taiwan

明明是與自己國家有關的話題卻「一問三不知」，如何能聊得盡興？
在介紹自己家鄉的二三事時，最好也能表達自己的意見，
才能讓對方留下深刻的印象。

Where should I go while I'm in Taiwan?
What is the Lunar New Year like in Taiwan?
What is Taiwan most well known for
internationally?
...

appearance

name

Taiwan
culture

friends

work

dreams

interest

families

religion

experience

087

Where should I go while I'm in Taiwan?
在台灣的時候我該去哪些地方好？

Dialogue 實戰會話　　　　　　　　　　　🔊 Track 88

A: **Where should I go while I'm in Taiwan?**
（在台灣的時候我該去哪些地方？）

B1: **You should definitely visit Tainan.** ☞
（你一定要到台南看看。）

A: **What do they have there?**
（那兒有些什麼？）

B2: **They have a lot of old temples and forts. Chihkan Tower is a must-see.** ☞
（那裡有很多古老的廟宇和堡壘。赤崁樓絕不能錯過。）

＊ fort「堡壘」；must-see「必看之物」

✎ **Exercise** 請寫下自己的答案並試著說出來！

A：**Where should I go while I'm in Taiwan?**

B1：

A：**What do they have there?**

B2：

Substitution 更多回應說法！

☞ B1

- **If you're in Taipei, I suggest that you visit the National Palace Museum.**
  （如果你人在台北，我會建議你去參觀國立故宮博物院。）
- **If you want to enjoy the nightlife, you should go to the Eastern District.**
  （如果你想享受一下夜生活，就該去東區。）
- **Maokong is a good place to visit. It's popular among college students.**
  （貓空是個值得一去的好地方。那裡很受大學生歡迎。）

☞ B2

- **It has the finest collection of Chinese art in the world.**
  （那裡有世界上最棒的中國藝術品收藏。）
- **It has lots of dance clubs, KTVs, and bars.**
  （那裡有很多舞廳、KTV 和酒吧。）
- **You can enjoy nice views of the Taipei skyline, and there are lots of restaurants and teahouses there.**
  （你可以欣賞到台北美麗的天際線，而且那裡還有許多餐廳和茶館。）

  * skyline「天際線」；tea house「茶館」

VOCABULARY 具體描述自己的好用字！

Longshan Temple 龍山寺 / Asia's tallest building, Taipei 101 亞洲最高大樓，台北 101 / the famous Beitou hot springs 著名的北投溫泉 / Yangmingshan National Park 陽明山國家公園 / the picturesque [ˌpɪtʃəˈrɛsk] villages of Jiufen and Jinguashi 風景如畫的九份與金瓜石小鎮 / Keelung's famous Miaokou night market 基隆有名的廟口夜市 / the Suao cold spring 蘇澳冷泉 / Taroko Gorge [gɔrdʒ] 太魯閣峽谷 / whitewater rafting in Rueisuei 瑞穗激流泛舟 / the orange daylilies of Taimali 太麻里的橘色金針花 / the world's largest collection of Taiwanese art at Taichung's National Museum of Fine Art 台中國立美術館藏世界最多的台灣藝術品收藏 / Taiwan's largest and most scenic lake, Sun Moon Lake 台灣最大且風景最秀麗的湖，日月潭 / the ancient temples of Lukang 鹿港的古老寺廟 / watching the sunrise from the top of Alishan 在阿里山山頂看日出 / the beautiful beaches of Kenting 墾丁的美麗海灘

088

Is it true that all students in Taiwan go to cram school?
台灣所有的學生都會去補習是真的嗎？

Dialogue 實戰會話　　　　　　　　　🔊 Track 89

A: Is it true that all students in Taiwan go to cram school?
（台灣所有的學生都會去補習是真的嗎？）

* cram school「補習班」

B1: No, that's not true. I didn't go myself, and I still got into a good college. ☞
（不，那不是真的。我自己就沒有補習，也還是進了一所好大學。）

A: What do you think about cram schools?
（你對補習班有何看法？）

B2: I feel sorry for kids who have to go to school until 8 or 9 p.m. ☞
（我對於必須去補習班上課上到 8、9 點的小孩感到十分同情。）

✎ **Exercise** 請寫下自己的答案並試著說出來！

A： Is it true that all students in Taiwan go to cram school?

B1:

A： What do you think about cram schools?

B2:

196

Substitution 更多回應說法！

☞ B1

- **Not everyone goes, but I hear it's becoming more and more common.**
  （並不是每個人都去，但是我聽說補習變得越來越普遍。）
  * common「常見的；一般的」
- **That's not entirely true, but I think most students living in urban areas go to cram school nowadays.**
  （那並不完全屬實，但是我想現在住在都市的學生大部分都有補習。）
  * urban area「市區」
- **Yeah, if you don't go to cram school, it's really hard to keep up with your studies.**
  （是啊，如果你不補習，功課就很難跟上。）
  * keep up with...「跟上……」

☞ B2

- **I think it's fine, as long as parents don't force their children to go.**
  （我覺得沒什麼，只要父母不強迫小孩去就行了。）
  * force someone to...「強迫某人做……」
- **I didn't like it much at the time, but I'm glad I went. I learned a lot at cram school.**
  （當時我不太喜歡補習班，但是我很高興我有去補。我在補習班學到了很多。）
- **Nowadays, you need to go to cram school to get into a good college.**
  （現今，你必須去補習才能考上好大學。）

········ **VOCABULARY** 具體描述自己的好用字！ ········

public school 公立學校（美式說法，英式說法為 **state school**） / **private school** 私立學校 / **compulsory education** 義務教育 / **early childhood education** 幼兒教育 / **special education** 特殊教育 / **boarding school** 寄宿學校 / **preschool** 托兒所（美式說法，英式說法為 **nursery school**） / **elementary school** 小學 / **junior high** 國中 / **high school** 高中 / **college entrance exam** 大學聯考；大學入學考 / **vocational school** 職業學校 / **community college** 社區大學 / **technical college** 技術學院 / **public university** 公立大學 / **private university** 私立大學 / **graduate school** 研究所

089

Taiwanese people have a strong sense of their own culture, don't they?
台灣人對自己文化的意識很強烈，是嗎？

Dialogue 實戰會話　　　　　　　　　　　　🔊 Track 90

> **A:** Taiwanese people have a strong sense of their own culture, don't they?
> （台灣人對自己文化的意識很強烈，是嗎？）
>
> **B1:** I never thought of it that way. I suppose it's just a part of being Taiwanese. ☞
> （我從沒那樣想過。我想那就是台灣人的部分特質吧。）
>
> **A:** What should I do if I want to learn more about Taiwanese culture?
> （如果我想更了解台灣文化，該怎麼做？）
>
> **B2:** You should watch talk shows on TV and definitely visit some temples. ☞
> （你應該看看電視上的談話節目，而且一定要去參觀一些寺廟。）
>
> * talk show「談話性節目」

✎ **Exercise** 請寫下自己的答案並試著說出來！

A： Taiwanese people have a strong sense of their own culture, don't they?

B1：

A： What should I do if I want to learn more about Taiwanese culture?

B2：

198

Substitution 更多回應說法！

☞ B1

- **Taiwanese people love to complain about Taiwan, but actually we are very proud of our culture.**
  （台灣人很愛抱怨台灣，但是事實上我們對自己的文化感到非常自豪。）

- **Some people certainly do, but I think young people are also influenced by Japanese and Korean culture.**
  （有些人的確如此，但是我想年輕人也受到了日本和韓國文化的影響。）

- **Yes, even though the local Taiwanese culture was suppressed for decades, it's now stronger than ever.**
  （是的，即使台灣本土文化曾經被打壓了幾十年，現在卻比以往任何時候都還強大。）

  ＊ suppress「壓制；壓抑」

☞ B2

- **The best way to learn the culture is to learn the language.**
  （了解這個文化的最佳途徑，就是學習它的語言。）

- **Speaking even a few words of Taiwanese will make a very positive impression.**
  （即使只會說一點點台灣話，都能給人非常正面的印象。）

- **You should try as much as possible to hang out with Taiwanese people while you're in Taiwan.**
  （在台灣的時候，你應該盡量多和台灣人相處。）

  ＊ hang out with someone「和某人相處；和某人一起消磨時間」

VOCABULARY 具體描述自己的好用字！

the lunar calendar 農曆；陰曆 / religious festivals 宗教慶典 / local handicrafts such as oil paper umbrellas and wood carvings 如油紙傘和木雕等本土工藝 / traditional Taiwanese puppets 布袋戲 / Taiwanese opera 歌仔戲 / Taike 台客 / betel [ˋbit]] nut beauties 檳榔西施 / Mid-Autumn Festival street-side barbeque 中秋節路旁烤肉 / Cloud Gate Dance Theater 雲門舞集 / Taiwanese pop music 台灣的流行音樂 / The films of Ang Lee, Hou Hsiao-hsian, Edward Yang, and Tsai Ming-liang 李安、侯孝賢、楊德昌、蔡明亮的電影 / Taiwanese TV dramas 台灣的電視劇 / night markets 夜市 / hot springs 溫泉 / Taiwanese online games 台灣的線上遊戲

090

What's a traditional Taiwanese wedding ceremony like?
台灣傳統的結婚儀式是怎樣的？

Dialogue 實戰會話　　　　　　　　　　　　　🔊 Track 91

A: **What's a traditional Taiwanese wedding ceremony like?**
（台灣傳統的結婚儀式是怎樣的？）

B1: **The traditional Taiwanese wedding is basically a big banquet with a few speeches.** 👈
（台灣傳統的結婚儀式基本上就是一個盛大的宴會加上幾段發言。）

A: **What kind of wedding ceremony did you have?**
（那你的結婚儀式是怎樣的？）

B2: **We had a Christian-style wedding. It was my dream to walk down the aisle like in the movies.** 👈
（我們採取基督教式的婚禮。像電影裡那樣步上紅毯是我的夢想。）

* banquet [ˋbæŋkwɪt]「宴會；盛宴」；walk down the aisle「結婚；步上紅毯」

✎ **Exercise** 請寫下自己的答案並試著說出來！

A: **What's a traditional Taiwanese wedding ceremony like?**
B1:

A: **What kind of wedding ceremony did you have?**
B2:

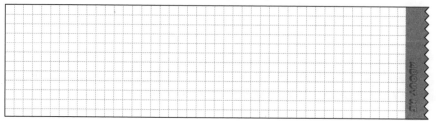

Substitution 更多回應說法！

☞ B1

● **Many weddings these days are held at hotels or special wedding centers.**
（近來許多婚禮都在飯店或專門的婚宴中心舉辦。）

● **Guests usually don't buy the couple gifts. Instead, they give them a red envelope filled with cash.**
（賓客們通常不送禮，而是直接給新人裝了現金的紅包。）

● **It's common for the bride to change her dress two or three times.**
（新娘換個兩到三次禮服是很常見的。）
* change one's dress「換裝」

☞ B2

● **We had a church wedding. I wore a white wedding dress instead of a traditional Chinese dress.**
（我們在教堂舉辦婚禮。我穿的是白色的婚紗，而不是傳統的中式禮服。）
* church wedding「教堂婚禮」

● **I'm not married yet, but if possible, I'd prefer to have a simple secular ceremony at a restaurant.**
（我還沒結婚，但是如果可能的話，我比較想在餐廳辦一場簡單的非宗教婚禮。）
* secular [ˈsɛkjələ]「非宗教的；世俗的」

● **We had a short Buddhist ceremony at my parents' home, followed by a banquet with our family and friends.**
（我們在我父母家進行了簡短的佛教儀式，接著宴請親朋好友。）
* followed by...「接著……」

Ⓥ🄾🄲🄰🄱🅄🄻🄰🅁🅈 具體描述自己的好用字！

arranged marriage 相親結婚 / **Buddhist wedding** 佛教婚禮 / **Christian wedding** 基督教婚禮 / **overseas wedding** 海外婚禮 / **take their vows** 宣誓 / **exchange wedding vows** 交換結婚誓詞 / **exchange rings** 交換戒指 / **cake cutting** 切蛋糕 / **emcee** [ˈɛmˋsi] 司儀 / **wedding entertainment** 婚禮的餘興節目 / **see a slideshow of the bride and groom's background** 觀賞新娘與新郎成長過程的幻燈片播放 / **best man** 伴郎 / **bridesmaid** 伴娘 / **give a congratulatory speech** 發表祝賀之詞 / **make a toast** 舉杯祝賀；敬酒 / **offer congratulations to the couple** 祝福新人 / **catch the bouquet** [buˋke] 接到捧花

What is the Lunar New Year like in Taiwan?
台灣的農曆新年是什麼樣子？

Dialogue 實戰會話　　　　　　　　　　　🔊 Track 92

A: What is the Lunar New Year like in Taiwan?
（台灣的農曆新年是什麼樣子？）

B1: A lot of stores and restaurants close and people tend to stay home. 👈
（很多商店和餐廳都關門，而大家往往都待在家裡。）

A: So, what do people usually do during the New Year holiday?
（那，新年假期期間大家通常都做些什麼？）

B2: In my family, we always get together with our relatives and eat a lot of special dishes. 👈
（在我家，我們總是和親戚聚在一起享用許多特別的菜餚。）

✏️ **Exercise** 請寫下自己的答案並試著說出來！

A： What is the Lunar New Year like in Taiwan?

B1：

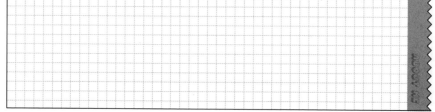

A： So, what do people usually do during the New Year holiday?

B2：

Substitution 更多回應說法！

☞ B1

- **It's basically a time to relax and hang out with your family.**
  (基本上，這個時候是要放鬆並和家人共度。)
  * basically「基本上」；hang out「共度」

- **Before, most people would go back to their parents' homes, but now a lot of people go traveling.**
  (以往，大部分人都會回到父母親家，但是現在很多人都去旅遊。)

- **Most people have about a week-long holiday, but because the dates change, every year is a little different.**
  (大部分人會有大約一星期的假，但是由於日期會變，所以每年都稍有差異。)

☞ B2

- **New Year's is a quiet time. Most people stay home and watch TV or play mahjongg.**
  (過年期間是很寧靜的。大部分人都待在家裡看電視或打麻將。)
  * mahjongg「麻將」

- **Some people go to temples to pray for good health and good luck in the coming year.**
  (有些人會去廟裡祈求新的一年身體健康、運勢亨通。)
  * pray for...「祈求……」；coming「即將來到的；下一個的」

- **Adult children will give red envelopes filled with money to their parents, and young children will receive red envelopes from their older relatives.**
  (成年的子女會包紅包給父母，而年紀小的小孩則會收到親戚長輩給的紅包。)
  * red envelopes「紅包」

𝒱ℴ𝒸𝒶𝒷𝓊𝓁𝒶𝓇𝓎 具體描述自己的好用字！

traditional markets 傳統市場 / traditional New Year's dishes 傳統年菜 / uncut noodles 整根不切斷的麵條（長壽麵）/ boiled dumplings 水餃 / glutinous [ˋglutənəs] rice cake 米糕 / turnip cake 蘿蔔糕 / cleaning the house 大掃除 / New Year's greetings 祝賀新年 / new clothes 新衣 / upside-down fu 上下顛倒的福字（代表「福氣到」）/ the writing of couplets, or duilian 春聯或對聯 / fireworks 煙火；爆竹 / lion dance 舞獅表演 / Lantern Festival 元宵節 / glutinous rice balls 湯圓

092

People in Taiwan work quite hard, don't they?

台灣民眾工作相當勤奮，是嗎？

Dialogue 實戰會話　　　　　　　　　　🔊 Track 93

A： People in Taiwan work quite hard, don't they?
（台灣民眾工作相當勤奮，是嗎？）

B1： Yeah, they do. It's perfectly normal for workers to come home well after dinnertime. 📖
（是啊，他們確實很勤奮。遠超過晚飯時間才回到家是極為正常的事。）

A： Do you work a lot of overtime?
（你經常加班嗎？）

B2： In my company, we're not encouraged to work overtime. It's kind of unusual in Taiwan. 📖
（我們公司不鼓勵加班。這在台灣算是很少見的。）

* work overtime「加班」

✎ **Exercise** 請寫下自己的答案並試著說出來！

A： People in Taiwan work quite hard, don't they?

B1：

A： Do you work a lot of overtime?

B2：

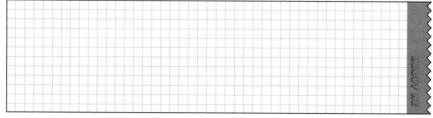

Substitution 更多回應說法！

☞ B1

- **Yeah, Taiwanese people have a strong work ethic.**
  （是啊，台灣民眾具有強烈的工作熱忱。）
  * work ethic「（以勤奮工作為美德的）職業道德」

- **That's true, but people in Taiwan are also pretty good at relaxing.**
  （這是真的，但是台灣民眾也很懂得放鬆自己。）

- **I suppose. In Taiwan, being a diligent worker is seen as a virtue.**
  （我想是的。在台灣，勤奮工作者被視為是一種美德。）
  * diligent「勤奮的」；virtue「美德」

☞ B2

- **I put in about twenty hours of overtime a month.**
  （我每個月大約會加班 20 個小時。）
  * put in「花費；投入（時間）」

- **Since I don't get paid for it, I avoid working overtime as much as possible.**
  （由於沒有加班費，所以我都盡量避免加班。）
  * get paid「獲得報酬」；avoid「避免」；as much as possible「盡量」

- **Well, if I don't work overtime, I can't make enough to support my family.**
  （嗯，如果我不加班，就不夠錢養家。）
  * support「支持；扶養」

VOCABULARY 具體描述自己的好用字！

workaholic 工作狂 / unpaid overtime 無薪加班 / paid vacation 有薪假 / unpaid leave 無薪假 / public holiday 國定假日 / long working hours 長工時 / salaried employee 支薪員工 / hourly employee 計時人員 / full-time employee 全職員工 / part-time employee 兼職員工 / contract worker 約聘人員 / temp worker 臨時雇員 / intern 實習生 / lay off workers 裁員 / annual bonus 年終獎金 / performance bonus 業績獎金

093

What kinds of social issues are people talking about in Taiwan now?
現在在台灣大家都討論些什麼樣的社會問題？

Dialogue 實戰會話　　　　　　　　　　　　🔊 Track 94

A: What kinds of social issues are people talking about in Taiwan now?
（現在在台灣大家都討論些什麼樣的社會問題？）

B1: The aging population is a big problem now. ☞
（現在人口老化是個大問題。）

A: What do you think about it?
（你對這問題有何看法？）

B2: I think the government has to do more to raise the birth rate. ☞
（我覺得政府必須在提高生育率方面做更多努力。）

　＊ birth rate「生育率」

✎ **Exercise** 請寫下自己的答案並試著說出來！

A：What kinds of social issues are people talking about in Taiwan now?

B1：

A：What do you think about it?

B2：

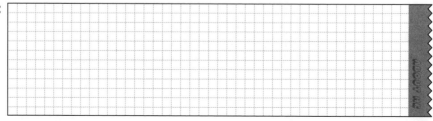

Substitution 更多回應說法！

- **The birth rate in Taiwan is the lowest in the world.**
  （台灣的生育率是全世界最低的。）
- **There's not enough support for working families.**
  （對於雙薪家庭的資助不夠。）
- **Childcare and schooling are very expensive.**
  （幼兒托育和就學的費用很昂貴。）
  * childcare「幼兒托育」

☞ B2

- **I think part of the problem is that Taiwanese parents don't raise their kids to be independent.**
  （我覺得有部分問題出在台灣父母並不培養小孩獨立自主的能力。）
  * independent「獨立的」
- **In my opinion, the government needs to attract more foreigners into the country.**
  （我認為，政府必須吸引更多外國人進入國內。）
- **The problem is that many people expect women to work full time while also raising a family.**
  （這問題就在於，很多人都期待女性能全職工作同時又能養育家庭。）

VOCABULARY 具體描述自己的好用字！

low birth rate 低生育率 / child abuse 虐待兒童 / bullying at school 校園霸凌 / political corruption 政治腐敗 / organized crime 組織型犯罪 / high unemployment 高失業率 / sluggish economy 經濟不景氣 / real estate bubble 房地產泡沫化 / unpaid leave 無薪假 / growing inequality 不平等現象日益加劇 / food safety 食品安全 / water pollution 水源汙染 / the aging of Taiwan's farmers 台灣農民的高齡化 / Taiwan's political status 台灣的政治情勢 / discrimination against aboriginal peoples 對原住民的歧視 / access to healthcare 醫療保健的取得

What is the weather like in Taiwan?
台灣的天氣如何？

Dialogue 實戰會話   🔊 Track 95

A: What is the weather like in Taiwan?
（台灣的天氣如何？）

B1: In Taipei, it's hot and humid in the summer and cold
and wet in the winter. 📖
（在台北，夏天又濕又熱，而冬天則又濕又冷。）

A: What's your favorite season?
（你最喜歡哪個季節？）

B2: I like the spring. It's not too hot or too cold, and it
doesn't rain as much. 📖
（我喜歡春天。春天不會太熱也不會太冷，而且雨下得沒那麼多。）

✎ **Exercise** 請寫下自己的答案並試著說出來！

A：What is the weather like in Taiwan?

B1:

A：What's your favorite season?

B2:

Substitution 更多回應說法！

☞ **B1**

- **Keelung is famous for being rainy all the time.**
  （基隆以長年下雨的天氣而聞名。）
  * be famous for... 「以……而聞名」
- **Taichung probably has the best weather in Taiwan.**
  （台中的天氣大概是全台灣最好的。）
- **It can get very hot in southern Taiwan.**
  （南臺灣熱起來可是非常地酷熱。）

☞ **B2**

- **Summer is my favorite season. I love to swim and hang out at the beach.**
  （夏天是我最愛的季節。我喜歡游泳並在沙灘上消磨時間。）
- **I really like the cool, rainy weather in Taipei in the fall.**
  （我真的很喜歡台北秋天時那種涼爽、多雨的天氣。）
- **I love to drive up to the mountains to see the snow in winter.**
  （我喜歡在冬天時開車上山去看雪。）

🔤 **VOCABULARY** 具體描述自己的好用字！

comfortable spring mornings 舒適的春天早晨 / **hot, humid summer days** 濕熱的夏天 / **cold, wet winter nights** 濕冷的冬日夜晚 / **windy fall afternoons** 多風的秋日午後 / **spring / autumnal / fall equinox** [ˈikwəˌnɑks] 春 / 秋分 / **summer / winter solstice** [ˈsɑlstɪs] 夏 / 冬至 / **occasional snow in the high mountains** 高山上偶爾下的雪 / **average temperature** 平均氣溫 / **high / low temperature** 高 / 低溫 / **afternoon rains** 午後雷陣雨 / **typhoon season** 颱風季節 / **monsoon** [mɑnˈsun] 雨季 / **overcast** 陰暗的；多雲的 / **foggy** 霧濛濛的 / **climate change** 氣候變遷 / **global warming** 全球暖化

095

What do you think is the most interesting aspect of Taiwanese culture?
你覺得台灣文化最有趣的一面是什麼？

Dialogue 實戰會話　　　　　　　　　　　　　🔊 Track 96

A: What do you think is the most interesting aspect of Taiwanese culture?
（你覺得台灣文化最有趣的一面是什麼？）

B1: To me, there's nothing more Taiwanese than drinking gongfu tea. ☞
（對我來說，沒有什麼比喝功夫茶更具台灣味的了。）

A: Why is that?
（為什麼？）

B2: I love the idea of enjoying good tea with good friends and just talking about whatever. ☞
（我很喜歡和好友分享好茶並談天說地的想法。）

✎ **Exercise** 請寫下自己的答案並試著說出來！

A： What do you think is the most interesting aspect of Taiwanese culture?

B1：

A： Why is that?

B2：

Substitution 更多回應說法！

☞ B1

- **I love the way family members in Taiwan help each other out.**
  （我很喜歡台灣家庭成員彼此相互扶持的方式。）
- **The more you know about Taiwanese popular culture, the more interesting it is.**
  （越是了解台灣的流行文化，你就會覺得越有意思。）
- **I think the entrepreneurial culture here is completely unique.**
  （我覺得這裡的創業文化非常獨特。）
  * entrepreneurial [ˌɑntrəprəˋnjʊrɪəl]「創業者的」

☞ B2

- **People talk and play cards or other games as they drink.**
  （大家會一邊喝酒一邊聊天打牌，或玩別的遊戲。）
  * play card「玩牌」
- **It's a lot of fun to go up into the mountains to have tea.**
  （上山喝茶是很有趣的。）
- **The way gongfu tea is served can be very elaborate.**
  （功夫茶的喝法可以是相當講究的。）
  * elaborate [ɪˋlæbərɪt]「講究的」

VOCABULARY 具體描述自己的好用字！

the Maokong gondola [ˋɡɑndələ] 貓空纜車 / **oolong tea** 烏龍茶 / **Oriental Beauty Tea** 東方美人茶 / **boil the water** 把水燒開 / **warm the pot and cups** 溫壺溫杯 / **discard the first pot** 第一壺不喝 / **wash the cups** 洗杯 / **pour the tea** 倒茶 / **scent cups** 聞香杯 / **green tea** 綠茶 / **bubble tea** 泡沫紅茶 / **syrup** 糖漿 / **pearl milk tea** 珍珠奶茶 / **tapioca** [ˌtæpɪˋokə] **balls** 粉圓 / **half sugar** 半糖 / **no ice** 不加冰 / **big straw** 大（粗）吸管

096

What is Taiwan most well known for internationally?
台灣在國際上最知名的是什麼？

Dialogue 實戰會話   🔊 Track 97

A: What is Taiwan most well known for internationally?
(台灣在國際上最知名的是什麼？)

B1: Probably Taiwan's computer and electronics industries. ☞
(可能是台灣的電腦與電子工業吧。)

A: Do you use any Taiwanese electronics?
(你有沒有用任何台灣的電子產品？)

B2: Of course. You probably do too! ☞
(當然有。你都可能也有！)

✎ **Exercise** 請寫下自己的答案並試著說出來！

A：What is Taiwan most well known for internationally?

B1：
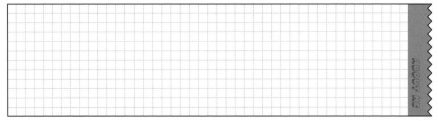

A：Do you use any Taiwanese electronics?

B2：
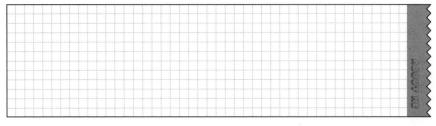

Substitution 更多回應說法！

☞ B1

- **I think the food in Taiwan makes it a popular travel destination.**
  （我認為台灣的美食使台灣成為熱門的旅遊景點。）
  * destination「地點；目的地」
- **I guess it's probably the unsettled political situation with China.**
  （我想大概是台灣和中國之間不穩定的政治情況吧。）
  * unsettled「不穩定的；動盪的」
- **I'm not sure, but I think Taiwan's stunning natural scenery should be more well-known.**
  （我不確定，但是我想台灣令人驚嘆的自然風光應該是比較知名的。）
  * stunning「令人震驚的」；well-known「出名的；眾所周知的」

☞ B2

- **Yes. More and more local manufacturers are branding and selling their own products now.**
  （有啊。現在有越來越多的本土廠商，都開始建立品牌並銷售自己的產品了。）
- **Sure. There's a good chance that a Taiwanese company made at least some of the parts of your computer or smart phone.**
  （當然，你的電腦或智慧型手機中，很可能至少有部分零件就是由台灣公司製造的。）
- **Of course. Many people here go out of their way to buy locally made products.**
  （當然有。這裡有很多人都竭盡所能地購買本土製造的產品。）

Vocabulary 具體描述自己的好用字！

export-oriented economy 以出口為導向的經濟型態 / small and medium-sized enterprises (SMEs) 中小企業 / original equipment manufacturer (OEM) 原始設備製造商；專業代工生產 / original design manufacturer (ODM) 原始設計製造商；專業代工設計製造 / science park 科學園區 / government incentive 政府獎勵 / tax break 賦稅減免 / information technology industry 資訊科技產業 / semiconductor industry 半導體產業 / LED panels LED 面板 / local brands like Acer, Asus, and HTC 如宏碁、華碩和宏達電等本土品牌 / research and development (R&D) 研究與開發（研發）/ supply chain 供應鏈 / offshore production to China 生產外移至中國 / rapid production 快速生產 / low margins 低利潤

097

Are you interested in politics?
你關心政治嗎？

Dialogue 實戰會話　　　　　　　　　　　　　　　🔊 Track 98

> **A:** Are you interested in politics?
> （你關心政治嗎？）
>
> **B1:** I follow it, but I don't normally talk about it with friends. ☞
> （我會留意政治動態，但是通常不會和朋友談論政治。）
>
> **A:** Why is that?
> （為什麼？）
>
> **B2:** I think it's because people in Taiwan have such strong feelings about politics. ☞
> （我想是因為台灣民眾對政治的感受是非常地強烈。）

✎ **Exercise** 請寫下自己的答案並試著說出來！

A：Are you interested in politics?

B1：

A：Why is that?

B2：

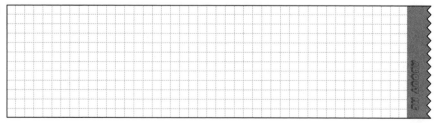

Substitution 更多回應說法！

☞ B1

● **I try as much as possible to keep up with what's going on in politics.**
（我會試圖盡力掌握目前政治上發生的事情。）

● **No, I'm not. I usually don't even bother to vote.**
（不，我不關心。我通常連票都懶得投。）
 * bother to...「費心地做……」

● **I'm interested in politics, but it's easy to get frustrated with politics in Taiwan.**
（我很關心政治，但是台灣的政治很容易令人覺得沮喪。）
 * get frustrated「感到挫折；覺得沮喪」

☞ B2

● **If we don't pay attention, the politicians will take advantage of us.**
（如果我們不留意，政客就會利用我們。）
 * take advantage of someone「利用某人；占某人便宜」

● **It seems like it doesn't matter who's in power. They're all the same.**
（不管誰掌權似乎都不重要。都是一個樣。）
 * be in power「掌權」

● **The politicians are more concerned with their own careers than they are with the welfare of the people.**
（比起人民福祉，政治人物更關心的是他們自己的事業。）
 * be concerned with...「關切……」；welfare「福祉」

───────────────────────────

𝒱𝒪𝒞𝒜ℬ𝒰ℒ𝒜ℛ𝒴 具體描述自己的好用字！

multiparty democracy 多黨民主政治 / **Kuomintang (KMT, or Chinese Nationalist Party)** 國民黨（中國國民黨）/ **Pan-Blue coalition** [ˌkoɑˋlɪʃən] 泛藍陣營 / **Democratic Progressive Party (DPP)** 民主進步黨（民進黨）/ **Pan-Green coalition** 泛綠陣營 / **the five branches of government, or yuan** 中央政府五院 / **the president serves a four-year term** 總統任期為四年 / **the Executive Yuan is headed by the premier** 行政院由行政院長領導 / **laws are passed by the Legislative Yuan** 法律由立法院通過 / **the Judicial Yuan** 司法院 / **the Examination Yuan** 考試院 / **the Control Yuan** 監察院 / **the civil service system** 公務員體系 / **Taiwan's political status** 台灣的政治情勢 / **Taiwan independence** 台灣獨立 / **unification** [ˌjunəfəˋkeʃən] **with China** 與中國的統一

098

What do you think about the status of women in Taiwanese society?
你認為台灣女性的社會地位如何？

Dialogue 實戰會話　　　　　　　　　　　🎧 Track 99

A: What do you think about the status of women in Taiwanese society?
（你認為台灣女性的社會地位如何？）

B1: Well, it's better than it was, but we still have a long way to go. ☞
（嗯，比以前好多了，但是我們還有很長的路要走。）

A: Are there any women in Taiwan who you particularly admire?
（你是否有特別欣賞的台灣女性？）

B2: I've always been impressed by Cher Wang, one of Taiwan's leading businesswomen. ☞
（我對王雪紅的印象一直都很好，她是台灣傑出的女企業家之一。）

✎ **Exercise** 請寫下自己的答案並試著說出來！

A: What do you think about the status of women in Taiwanese society?

B1:

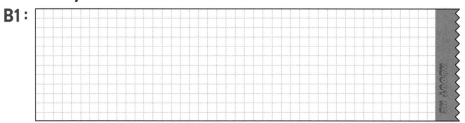

A: Are there any women in Taiwan who you particularly admire?

B2:

Substitution 更多回應說法！

☞ **B1**

- **I think women are still underrepresented in the business world in Taiwan.**
  （我認為在台灣的商業世界裡，女性的比例仍偏低。）
  ＊ underrepresented「代表不足的；低於適當比例的」

- **Too many women are forced to make a difficult choice between family and career.**
  （有太多女性被迫在家庭與事業之間做出困難的抉擇。）
  ＊ make a choice between A and B「在 A 和 B 之間做選擇」

- **Women are often discouraged from pursuing careers in science and technology.**
  （女性不被鼓勵從事科技方面的職業。）

☞ **B2**

- **Cheng Yen, the founder of one of Taiwan's largest Buddhist organizations, is a very impressive woman.**
  （證嚴法師，台灣最大佛教團體之一的創辦人，就是一位非常令人欽佩的女性。）

- **Chen Shu-chu, an ordinary vegetable seller, became quite well-known when she donated NT$ 10 million to charity.**
  （陳樹菊，一位平凡的菜販，在她捐出一千萬台幣給慈善機構後便聲名大噪。）

- **There have been a number of high-profile female politicians like Annette Lu and Tsai Ying-wen.**
  （有一些備受矚目的女政治家，如呂秀蓮和蔡英文等。）
  ＊ high-profile「備受矚目的」

VOCABULARY 具體描述自己的好用字！

women's rights 婦女的權利 / female executive 女性主管 / maternity [mə`tɜnətɪ] leave 產假 / gender discrimination 性別歧視 / pay disparity [dɪs`pærətɪ] between men and women 男女間的薪資差異 / disparity in employment opportunities 就業機會的差異 / glass ceiling（指女性在職場遇到的）無形升遷障礙 / work-life balance 工作與生活的平衡 / managing work and childcare 安排工作和育兒 / underrepresentation in many business fields 在許多商業領域的任職比例偏低 / unequal access to education 教育機會不平等 / unequal representation in politics 在政治代表性上的不平等 / sexual harassment 性騷擾 / violence against women 針對女性的暴力 / feminist movement 女權運動 / empowerment 賦予權力

099

Are Taiwanese people very religious?
台灣人篤信宗教嗎？

Dialogue 實戰會話　　　　　　　　　🔊 Track 100

A: **Are Taiwanese people very religious?**
（台灣人篤信宗教嗎？）

B1: **You could say that, though many people don't strictly follow a single religion.** ☞
（可以這麼說，不過很多人並不嚴格信仰單一宗教就是了。）

A: **What about you?**
（那你呢？）

B2: **My family is the same. We visit both Buddhist and Taoist temples. And we had a Christian wedding!** ☞
（我們家也一樣。我們去佛教寺廟也去道教寺廟，而且還辦過一場基督教婚禮！）

✎ **Exercise** 請寫下自己的答案並試著說出來！

A：Are Taiwanese people very religious?

B1：

A：What about you?

B2：

Substitution 更多回應說法！

☞ **B1**

- I think so. Many people have small altars in their homes that they use to pay respects to their ancestors.

  （我想是的。許多人家裡都有小型供桌，用以祭拜他們的祖先。）

  * altar「供桌；聖壇」；ancestor「祖先」

- I suppose that's true, though many people wouldn't be able to tell you exactly what they believe in.

  （我想這是真的，雖然很多人都說不清楚他們到底信奉什麼。）

  * believe in...「信奉⋯⋯；相信⋯⋯」

- Most people follow some combination of Buddhism and Taoism.

  （大部分人都信仰某種佛教與道教的綜合體。）

☞ **B2**

- I'm not religious myself, but I like to visit temples anyway.

  （我自己並不篤信宗教，不過我還是喜歡參觀廟宇。）

- I'm a Christian. I started studying the Bible in college.

  （我是個基督徒。我從大學時開始研讀聖經。）

- I consider myself a Buddhist because I believe in the teachings of the Buddha.

  （我自認是個佛教徒，因為我相信佛陀的教誨。）

  * teaching「教誨；教義」

- - - - - - - - **VOCABULARY** 具體描述自己的好用字！ - - - - - - - -

Buddhism 佛教 / **Taoism** 道教 / **Confucianism** 孔子學說；儒學 / **Christianity** 基督教 / **Islam** 伊斯蘭教 / **Hinduism** 印度教 / **folk religions** 民間宗教 / **ancestor worship** 祖先崇拜 / **Tudi Gong** 土地公 / **monotheism** [ˋmɑnəθiˌɪzəm] 一神論 / **polytheism** [ˋpɑləθiˌɪzəm] 多神論 / **syncretism** [ˋsɪŋkrəˌtɪzm] 宗教綜攝；融合主義 / **atheism** [ˋeθiˌɪzəm] 無神論 / **Taoist rituals** 道教儀式 / **food offerings** 供品 / **incense** [ˋɪnsɛns] 香（也可作動詞，為「向⋯⋯敬香」）

What do the animal symbols for each year mean?
代表各年的象徵動物有何意義？

Dialogue 實戰會話   🔊 Track 101

> **A:** **What do the animal symbols for each year mean?**
> （代表各年的象徵動物有何意義？）
>
> **B1:** **They're the twelve signs of the Chinese zodiac.** ☞
> （他們是中國黃道帶的十二個生肖代表。）
>
> **A:** **What sign are you?**
> （你生肖屬什麼？）
>
> **B2:** **I'm a Rooster. That means I'm a deep thinker.** ☞
> （我屬雞。這意味我是個深思熟慮的思想家。）

✎ **Exercise** 請寫下自己的答案並試著說出來！

A：What do the animal symbols for each year mean?

B1：

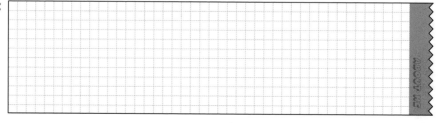

A：What sign are you?

B2：

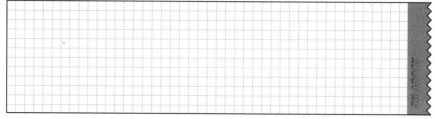

☞ **B1**

- **It's the same as the signs of the zodiac, except it goes in a twelve-year cycle instead of a one-year cycle.**
  （那和黃道十二宮是一樣的，只不過它是以十二年為週期，而不是以一年為週期。）
  ＊ except...「除了……」

- **I don't know exactly what each animal means, but everyone knows the animal of the year they were born.**
  （我不知道各個動物到底代表什麼意義，不過每個人都知道自己所屬的生肖。）
  ＊ exactly「正確地」；be born「出生」

- **The twelve animals of the Chinese zodiac are associated with different personality traits.**
  （中國十二生肖的十二種動物分別與不同的個性特徵相關聯。）
  ＊ associated with...「與……相關聯」；trait [tret]「特點；特徵」

☞ **B2**

- **I was born in the Year of the Sheep. In Chinese, we say yang nian.**
  （我是羊年生的。中文說成「羊年」。）

- **I'm a dragon. That's why I'm brave and energetic!**
  （我屬龍。這正是為什麼我既勇敢又精力旺盛！）
  ＊ brave「勇敢的」；energetic「精力旺盛的」

- **I was born in the Year of the Monkey. What year were you born in?**
  （我是猴年生的。你是什麼年生的？）

𝒱𝑜𝒸𝒶𝐵𝓊𝐿𝒶𝓇𝓎 具體描述自己的好用字！

Year of the Rat 鼠年 / **Ox** 牛 / **Tiger** 虎 / **Rabbit** 兔 / **Dragon** 龍 / **Snake** 蛇 / **Horse** 馬 / **Sheep** 羊 / **Monkey** 猴 / **Rooster** 雞 / **Dog** 狗 / **Boar** [bor] 豬 / **zodiac** 黃道帶 / **horoscope** 星座 / **fortune-telling** 算命 / **have one's fortune told** 去算命

Bonus

研究所・求職面試
Graduate Studies and Job Interview

想必各位已針對本書彙整的 100 個自我介紹常見話題,用自己的話將關於自己的所有事統整歸納成筆記了吧!在最後我們要再練習一些參加「研究所或求職面試」時,經常會出現的提問及其應對方式。你會發現有些問題可能與本書前面練習過的部分重複了,但請留意在進行正式的英語面談或面試時,由於場合不同,如何適切地表達、如何展現出自己的專長和優勢,這些都必須經過事先整理準備,才能在面談時博得好感,脫穎而出!

Can you tell us something about your family background?
能不能跟我們聊聊你的家庭背景？

Dialogue 實戰會話   🔊 Track 102

A: Can you tell us something about your family background?
（能不能跟我們聊聊你的家庭背景？）

B: My name is ① <u>Jerry</u>, and I'm from ② <u>Taoyuan City</u>, in Taiwan, and I'm ③ <u>23</u> years old. I'm the ④ <u>middle</u> son/daughter in my family.
（我叫 Jerry，來自台灣的桃園市，23 歲。我是家裡的次男／女。）

A: What do your parents do?
（你的父母從事什麼工作？）

B: My father is a ⑤ <u>businessman</u> and my mother is a ⑥ <u>office worker</u>.
（家父是生意人，家母是上班族。）

📥 Suggested answers 答題建議＆好用字句補充！

① 使用英文名。
② 報上家鄉名稱。
③ 報上自己的年紀。
④ 長幼次序的說法：oldest（排行）最大的／ youngest（排行）最小的／ middle（排行）中間的／ only 唯一的、獨生的
⑤ ⑥ 常見的職業類型：teacher 老師／ doctor 醫生／ lawyer 律師／ businessman 商人／ office worker 上班族／ farmer 農民／ homemaker 家庭主婦

✏️ Exercise 請寫下自己的答案並試著說出來！

A: Can you tell us something about your family background?

B: _____

A: What do your parents do?

B: _____

Where did you study?
你之前在哪裡就讀？

Dialogue 實戰會話　　　　　　　　　　　　　　　🎧 Track 103

A: **Where did you study?**
（你之前在哪裡就讀？）

B: I was educated at ① <u>Wu-Ling</u> senior high school, and went to ② <u>Tamkang</u> University in ③ <u>Tamsui</u>.
（我讀武陵高中，後來上位於淡水的淡江大學。）

A: **What was your major in college?**
（你在大學主修什麼？）

B: My major was ④ <u>computer science</u>, and I graduated in ⑤ <u>2016</u>.
（我主修電腦科學，畢業於 2016 年。）

📥 **Suggested answers** 答題建議＆好用字句補充！

① 報上高中校名。
② 報上大學校名。
③ 報上大學所在的城鎮。
④ 常見的學科名稱：accounting 會計／ business administration 企管／ chemistry 化學／ civil engineering 土木工程／ computer science 電腦科學／ design 設計／ education 教育／ electronics 電子學／ engineering 工程（學）／ IT 資訊科技／ media studies 媒體研究／ philosophy 哲學／ physics 物理／ psychology 心理學／ sociology 社會學
⑤ 報上畢業年份。

✏️ **Exercise** 請寫下自己的答案並試著說出來！

A: **Where did you study?**

B: _____

A: **What was your major in college?**

B: _____

What are you studying?
你念的是什麼？

　　　　　　　　　　　　　　　🔊 Track 104

A: **What are you studying?**
（你念的是什麼？）

B: **My major is ① Computer Science and Information Engineering, and I will graduate in ② 2020.**
（我主修電腦科學和資訊工程，並將於 2020 年畢業。）

A: **What's your special focus?**
（你特別著重的是哪方面？）

B: **I'm really interested in ③ Computer Programming, so I'm focusing on that.**
（我對電腦程式設計十分感興趣，所以著重的是那方面。）

📥 **Suggested answers 答題建議 & 好用字句補充！**

① 常見的學科名稱：accounting 會計／ business administration 企管／ chemistry 化學／ civil engineering 土木工程／ computer science 電腦科學／ design 設計／ education 教育／ electronics 電子學／ engineering 工程（學）／ IT 資訊科技／ media studies 媒體研究／ philosophy 哲學／ physics 物理／ psychology 心理學／ sociology 社會學
② 報上將在哪一年畢業。
③ 報上特別感興趣的領域。

✎ **Exercise 請寫下自己的答案並試著說出來！**

A: **What are you studying?**

B: _____

A: **What's your special focus?**

B: _____

What are you currently working on?
你現在做的是什麼工作？

Dialogue 實戰會話　　　　　　　　　　　　　　🎧 Track 105

A: **What are you currently working on?**
（你現在做的是什麼工作？）

B: **At the moment I'm ① leading ② an R&D team.**
（我目前帶領一個研發團隊。）

A: **What does that involve?**
（那是在做什麼的？）

B: **It mostly involves ③ doing research and developing new products.**
（主要是在做研究和開發新產品。）

📥 Suggested answers 答題建議＆好用字句補充！

① looking after 照顧；顧好／ managing 管理／ leading 領導；帶領／ handling 處理
② 聊聊你現在的工作性質或正在進行的案子。
③ collecting information 蒐集資訊／ managing a team 管理團隊／ doing research 進行研究／ redesigning a system 重新設計系統／ helping my customers 協助顧客

✎ Exercise 請寫下自己的答案並試著說出來！

A: What are you currently working on?

B: _____

A: What does that involve?

B: _____

What does your current job involve?
你現在的工作是在做什麼？

Dialogue 實戰會話　　　　　　　　　　　　　🎧 Track 106

A: **What does your current job involve?**
（你現在的工作是在做什麼？）

B: **My current job involves a lot of responsibility. ① I receive ② phone calls from customers and deal with all kinds of their problems.**
（我現在的工作責任很多。我必須接聽顧客的來電並因應他們的各種問題。）

A: **Do you have any leadership role in your current job?**
（你在現在的工作中有沒有擔任什麼領導角色？）

B: **Yes, ③ I manage a team.**
（有，我管理一個團隊。）

📥 Suggested answers 答題建議&好用字句補充！

① I have to handle … 我必須處理……／I look after … 我得顧好……
② 聊聊你的職責和任務。
③ I manage … 我管理……／I lead … 我帶領……

✏️ Exercise 請寫下自己的答案並試著說出來！

A: What does your current job involve?

B: _____

A: Do you have any leadership role in your current job?

B: _____

What are your plans for your future studies?
你未來的進修計畫是什麼？

A: What are your plans for your future studies?
（你未來的進修計畫是什麼？）

B: For the future I'm planning to take a masters degree in ① engineering.
（未來我計畫攻讀工程的碩士學位。）

A: Why is that?
（為什麼是那科？）

B: The reason for this is that ② it's the best choice for a career in my future.
（原因在於它是我未來就業上的最佳選擇。）

📥 Suggested answers 答題建議＆好用字句補充！

① 常見的學科名稱：accounting 會計／ business administration 企管／ chemistry 化學／ civil engineering 土木工程／ computer science 電腦科學／ design 設計／ education 教育／ electronics 電子學／ engineering 工程（學）／ IT 資訊科技／ media studies 媒體研究／ philosophy 哲學／ physics 物理／ psychology 心理學／ sociology 社會學

② I'm interested in 我對……感興趣／ I want to learn more about 我想了解更多關於……／ I want to get a job in 我想做……方面的工作／ it's the best choice for a career 它是就業上的最佳選擇

✎ Exercise 請寫下自己的答案並試著說出來！

A: What are your plans for your future studies?

B: _____

A: Why is that?

B: _____

228

Can you tell us a bit more about your research proposal?
你能不能多聊一點你的研究提案？

Dialogue 實戰會話　　　　　　　　　　　　🔊 Track 108

A: Can you tell us a bit more about your research proposal?
（你能不能多聊一點你的研究提案？）

B: My special area of interest in this field is ① **X**. I want to ② **address the issue of** ③ **Y**.
（我對這個領域特別感興趣的是 X。我要探討的問題是 Y。）

A: How will you do that?
（這點你要怎麼做到？）

B: I'm going to ④ **do field research into Z**.
（我會針對 Z 進行田野調查。）

⬇ Suggested answers 答題建議＆好用字句補充！

① 報上你特別感興趣的研究領域。

② address the issue of 探討……的問題／ attempt to 力圖；嘗試／ solve the problem of 解決……的問題／ evaluate the effect of A on B 評估 A 對 B 的作用／ look at the relationship between A and B 討論 A 和 B 之間的關係

③ 針對你特別感興趣的研究課題來舉例。

④ carry out a study on 對於……加以研究／ do field research into 針對……做田野調查／ do a statistical evaluation of 對……做統計評估／ build a model of 建構……的模型

✎ Exercise 請寫下自己的答案並試著說出來！

A: Can you tell us a bit more about your research proposal?

B: _____

A: How will you do that?

B: _____

How would you describe yourself?
你會怎麼形容自己？

Dialogue 實戰會話　　　　　　　　　　　　🔾 Track 109

A: How would you describe yourself?
（你會怎麼形容自己？）

B: I believe I have the skills and determination necessary to achieve my goal. I am ① **creative** and ② **energetic.**
（我相信我有達成目標的必備技能和決心。我具創造力而且精力充沛。）

A: What are your personal strengths?
（你的個人優點是什麼？）

B: I am ③ **productive** and ④ **responsible**, and I think I'm pretty ⑤ **trustworthy.** I've also been told that I'm ⑥ **considerate.**
（我做事有成效又認真負責，而且我想我還滿值得信賴的。也有人跟我說過，我很體貼。）

⬇ **Suggested answers 答題建議＆好用字句補充！**

① creative 有創造力／ dedicated 專注的；用心的／ devoted 專心致志的；獻身的／ dynamic 充滿活力的 ② energetic 精力充沛的；積極的／ enthusiastic 熱心的／ experienced 有經驗的／ inventive 有創意的；善於創造的 ③ dependable 可靠的／ knowledgeable 有見識的／ mature 成熟的／ productive 多產的；富有成效的 ④ resourceful 機智的；有策略的／ responsible 認真負責的；有責任感的／ skilled 熟練的；有技能的 ⑤ stable 穩定的／ steady 穩固的；穩定的／ trustworthy 值得信賴的；可靠的／ meticulous 一絲不苟的 ⑥ caring 有愛心的／ committed 忠誠的／ compassionate 有同情心的／ considerate 體貼的；考慮周到的

✎ **Exercise 請寫下自己的答案並試著說出來！**

A: How would you describe yourself?

B: _____

A: What are your personal strengths?

B: _____

Can you give us an example of a success?
你能不能舉個你成功的例子？

Dialogue 實戰會話 Track 110

A: Can you give us an example of a success?
（你能不能舉個你成功的例子？）

B: For example, in my ① <u>previous job</u>, I ② <u>had overall responsibility for</u> ③ <u>training our new recruits</u>. It was a very valuable experience.
（例如，在我在做前一份工作時，曾全面負責訓練新進員工。那是非常寶貴的經驗。）

A: And what was your greatest achievement?
（那你的最大成就是什麼？）

B: During that time, I ④ <u>established</u> ⑤ <u>a system of employee training</u>.
（在那期間，我建立了一套員工培訓制度。）

⬇ Suggested answers 答題建議＆好用字句補充！

① 1ˢᵗ/2ⁿᵈ/3ʳᵈ/4ᵗʰ year in college 大一／二／三／四／ previous job 前一份工作
② assisted 協助／ had overall responsibility for 全面負責／ was the president of 擔任……會長／ scored very highly 拿到非常高分／ travelled to 前往
③ 舉出成功的例子。
④ raised money 募款／ researched 研究／ chaired 擔任主席／ coached 擔任教練／ established 建立
⑤ 舉出成就的例子。

✎ Exercise 請寫下自己的答案並試著說出來！

A: Can you give us an example of a success?

B: _____

A: And what was your greatest achievement?

B: _____

Can you give us an example of a failure?

你能不能舉個你失敗的例子？

A: Can you give us an example of a failure?

（你能不能舉個你失敗的例子？）

B: For example, in my ① <u>previous job</u>, I ② <u>could have done better at a project</u>, but ③ <u>I ignored customers' opinions and designed something that failed to satisfy my customers' needs</u>. It was one of my least successful experiences.

（例如，在我在做前一份工作時，原本有一個案子可以做得更好，但是我忽略了客戶的意見，因而設計出不符顧客需求的東西。那是我最不成功的經驗之一。）

A: What did you learn from this failure?

（你從那次的失敗中學到了什麼？）

B: ④ <u>I learned that a good product R&D person should design products based on customers' real demands.</u>

（我學到了一個優秀的產品研發人員應該根據客戶的實際需求來設計產品。）

📥 Suggested answers 答題建議＆好用字句補充！

① 1st /2nd/3rd/4th year in college 大一／二／三／四／ previous job 前一份工作

② could have done better 原本可以做得更好 / didn't manage to 沒有做到

③ 舉出失敗的例子。

④ I learned that 我學到了

✎ **Exercise** 請寫下自己的答案並試著說出來！

A: Can you give us an example of a failure?

B: _____

A: What did you learn from this failure?

B: _____

What do you dislike about your current job?

對於你現在的工作你有什麼不喜歡的地方？

Dialogue 實戰會話　　　　　　　　　　　　　🔊 Track 112

A: What do you dislike about your current job?
（對於你現在的工作你有什麼不喜歡的地方？）

B: The ① <u>employee training program</u> could be better. Also, the ② <u>system of reporting to management</u> could be more clear.
（員工培訓計畫可以更好。另外，向管理階層呈報的制度可以更明確。）

A: Can you say more?
（你能多說一點嗎？）

B: ③ <u>There doesn't seem to be enough support for the staff to take some training course.</u>
（對於讓員工去參加一些教育訓練課程似乎沒有足夠的支持。）

📥 Suggested answers 答題建議＆好用字句補充！

① ② 舉出對目前工作或公司不滿意的具體實例。

③ 針對前面自己提到的不滿意部分做進一步說明。例如：There doesn't seem to be enough support 支持似乎不足夠／Sometimes things are not as … as they should be. 有時候事情沒有應該的那麼……

✏ Exercise 請寫下自己的答案並試著說出來！

A: What do you dislike about your current job?

B: _____

A: Can you say more?

B: _____

Why should we choose you?
我們為什麼該選擇你？

Dialogue 實戰會話   🔊 Track 113

A： Why should we choose you?
（我們為什麼該選擇你？）

B1： I have a strong interest in the field, and I believe I have what it takes to be an excellent ① <u>graduate student</u>.
（我對這個領域有強烈的興趣，而且我相信我具備了成為傑出研究生的各項條件。）

A： What would convince us to hire you?
（有什麼理由足以說服我們錄取你？）

B2： I will always try to ② <u>perform at my optimum level</u>. I sincerely hope that you will give me a chance to prove this to you.
（我會一直努力表現出我的最佳水準。我誠摯希望能有機會可以向各位證明這點。）

📥 Suggested answers 答題建議＆好用字句補充！

① graduate student 研究生／ employee 員工／ team player 團隊成員／ staff member 職員

② do my best 全力以赴／ give my all 全心付出／ perform at my optimum level 表現出最佳水準／ deliver the goods 不負眾望

✏️ Exercise 請寫下自己的答案並試著說出來！

A: Why should we choose you?

B1: _____

A: What would convince us to hire you?

B2: _____

Are there any questions you would like to ask us?
你有沒有什麼問題想要問我們？

Dialogue 實戰會話　　　　　　　　　　　Track 114

A: Are there any questions you would like to ask us?
（你有沒有什麼問題想要問我們？）

B1: Yes. ① <u>I'd like to know more about</u> the scope of the job.
（有。我想多了解一點這個工作的範疇。）

A: Any other questions you would like to ask?
（你還有什麼想要問的問題嗎？）

B2: ② <u>I'm interested in</u> ③ <u>the management style of your company</u>. Can you tell me more about this?
（我對貴公司的管理風格很感興趣。能不能在這方面多告訴我一點？）

📥 Suggested answers 答題建議＆好用字句補充！

① ② I'd like to know more about 我想多了解一點／ I'm interested in X 我對 X 有興趣
③ 提出你對應徵的公司或職務想了解更多的問題。

✎ Exercise 請寫下自己的答案並試著說出來！

A: Are there any questions you would like to ask us?

B1: _____

A: Any other questions you would like to ask?

B2: _____

國家圖書館出版品預行編目（CIP）資料

About Me我怎麼介紹我? / 長尾和夫, Ted Richards 作.
—— 二版. —— 臺北市：波斯納，2019. 08
　　面：　公分

　　ISBN: 978-986-97684-2-9（平裝）

　　1. 英語　　2. 會話

805.188　　　　　　　　　　　　　　　108007987

About Me 我怎麼介紹我?【增篇加值版】

作　　者 / 長尾和夫、Ted Richards
執行編輯 / 莊碧娟、朱曉瑩

出　　版 / 波斯納出版有限公司
地　　址 / 台北市 100 館前路 26 號 6 樓
電　　話 / (02) 2314-2525
傳　　真 / (02) 2312-3535
客服專線 / (02) 2314-3535
客服信箱 / btservice@betamedia.com.tw
郵撥帳號 / 19493777
帳戶名稱 / 波斯納出版有限公司

總 經 銷 / 時報文化出版企業股份有限公司
地　　址 / 桃園市龜山區萬壽路二段 351 號
電　　話 / (02) 2306-6842

出版日期 / 2019 年 8 月二版一刷
定　　價 / 280 元
I S B N / 978-986-97684-2-9

貝塔網址：www.betamedia.com.tw

唤醒你的英文語感！

Get a Feel for English !